T0356390

AND THE LAKE WILL TAKE THEM

LINDA NORLANDER

SEVERN RIVER

PUBLISHING

Severn River Publishing
www.SevernRiverBooks.com

ISBN: 978-1-64875-618-4 (Paperback)

ALSO BY LINDA NORLANDER

Sheriff Red Mysteries

And the Lake Will Take Them

The Pines Were Watching

To find out more about Linda Norlander and her books, visit

severnriverbooks.com

For Jerry

PROLOGUE
NOT ME

Pearsal County 2003

Not Me is thirteen when Jubal comes to stay. He wears a white collar like a priest, but he is not a priest. Mother welcomes him, hugging him, kissing him, weeping over him. Not Me stands back. Jubal's slate eyes search over Mother's shoulder. He smiles at Not Me, and he has a gap between his front teeth. The room is cold and hot at the same time.

He gives Mother a rosary and tells her it is a gift from the Virgin Mary. She fingers it with tears in her eyes. Not Me shudders.

Adam, Abraham, Jacob hunted, Jubal tells Not Me. I will teach you.

Mother says, Go with Jubal, he is a man of God.

When they are in the woods, Jubal pulls his hands down the shaft of the long metal rifle. See, it's an instrument. And then he touches Not Me. Beads of cold sweat cling to Not Me's hair beneath the orange hunting cap.

Not me! Not me!

But no one is listening.

Mother loves Jubal. Trusts him. He's a good man, she says before she leaves for three days. Jubal locks Not Me in the dank, cold cellar. Stay there with the spiders and the rats until you can love me.

Jubal is going to be with us for the winter, Mother's voice sings. He needs a break from his duties. Not Me turns away. The house is filled with the smoke of his cigarettes. It sticks to clothes and skin and makes Not Me's throat ache. Not Me breathes it in and plans.

They are back in the woods. The November air smells of decaying underbrush and coming snow. A cold, damp mist glistens on Not Me's skin. Jubal walks ahead, deeper into the forest of jack pine and birch. He is humming.

Not Me stands back, waiting.

Jubal turns, his slate eyes fogged and his face slack with lust.

Not Me lifts the rifle and squeezes. *Bang!* A hole forms between Jubal's eyes, and the lust drains from them. Not Me feels a rush of fear and disgust and relief—and euphoria.

I didn't do it. Not me. Someone else. Not me.

Not Me covers Jubal with underbrush and leaves him for the animals who will drag his bones into the woods, where they will molder under the rotting compost of the forest.

Not Me sleeps the years away, awakening for the man who challenges and then once again for the girl who steals. Not Me has killed and plans to kill again.

1

MISSY
THE PLAN

Missy took the tightly rolled money from her bottom drawer and stuffed it in her blue backpack. It felt greasy and tainted in her hand. So much heartache wrapped in those tens and twenties. Still, she had her bargaining chip—the truth for the money. Jared would have to help her. She added her schoolbooks, a woolen stocking cap, and two granola bars to the pack.

Grampa Jack called to her. "Hey, kid, hurry or you'll miss your bus." The last thing Missy wanted to do was miss the bus. Today was an important day—a day of setting things straight. After she talked with Jared and he agreed, she'd go to that woman sheriff. It would be over, and people would know who killed her dad.

She slipped the phone with the grainy dark video on it into her back pocket. More evidence of the evil that cast a shadow on her life.

When she opened the door, she was hit with a blast of the cold Minnesota winter air. It stung her cheeks and caused her eyes to tear up. Maybe the tears were from the cold, but maybe they were because she was leaving her warm home where she lived with Grampa Jack to go on a dangerous mission. For a moment, she wondered if her dad had felt the same way those years back when he went hunting for the truth.

She called back to Grampa Jack in the kitchen, "Remember, I'm spending the night with Tiffy and Sara. They'll drive me home tomorrow—okay?"

Grampa Jack waved at her. He looked tired, and she hoped what she knew would help erase the dark circles under his eyes.

Jared was waiting for her at school. His unwashed dark hair fell over his eyes. His skin, once so clear, was marked with pimples, and his cheeks looked hollowed. He grabbed her arm as soon as she stepped off the bus. "We gotta find that money, Missy, or something bad will happen."

She pulled away. "Don't yank on me like that! We'll work it out." Little did he know the money was festering in her pack.

"But they want it now!"

The *Followers*, she thought. The enforcers—bad people.

"Remember, we have a plan. Up to the old shack today, away from everyone, where we can talk. We'll figure it out."

Jared swore under his breath as they entered the school. Missy punched him lightly in the arm. "It'll be okay. Meet me after fourth period. Can you get the snowmobile?"

"Whatever." Shoulders hunched, he walked away from her to his locker. He looked like a sulky little boy. His jeans bagged because he'd lost weight in the last couple of weeks. When she'd started seeing him in the fall, he seemed so confident, so arrogant. Now he looked diminished and scared.

She sat through first period, her fingers clamped in a fist to keep them still. The hour dragged as the teacher talked about taking the PSATs. She hardly cared about college at this point. Maybe when all was revealed and the *Followers* were taken care of—maybe then it would be important.

The teacher droned on, and she thought more about Jared. Would he agree with her? Would he help her? Could she trust him? He liked the drugs and he used the drugs, and it made him high and happy, but it also brought out a mean streak in him. Maybe this wasn't the best plan—to show him the money and insist they tell the truth.

By the end of second period, her stomach roiled as the doubts built up. Grampa Jack always told her it was a good idea to have a plan but to also have a "plan B" just in case. As the worry grew, she realized she needed a plan B. If her dad had thought it through and come up with another plan, maybe he wouldn't be buried in the cemetery.

Just before the bell rang for third period, Missy hurried to her locker, grabbed her pink jacket and backpack, and ran out the door. When the cold hit her face, she hardly noticed it. She had a new plan. The money would be safe.

2

SHERIFF RED
THE UNSOLVED CASES

The courthouse creaked and settled in the January cold. A general winter dreariness blanketed the town of Lykkins Lake. Residents peered at the steel-gray clouds, wondering if it meant snow. Everyone knew that a snowfall would layer the town in pristine whiteness and turn the roads into ice rinks. And sunshine would bring an icy sharpness to the air and sub-zero temperatures.

Sheriff Red Hammergren sat at her desk, staring at the files in front of her. She would rather be outside on cross-country skis in the quiet where the only sound would be the rustle of the wind through the pines.

Instead, she studied the old files as the aging courthouse radiator clanked and spit out dry heat. A five-by-seven photo of Red and Will standing together in Pearsal County sheriff's uniforms sat on the desk as if overseeing her work. The ravages of the cancer that took Will were evident on his gaunt face, but his eyes still sparkled with amusement.

She glanced at the photo. "For you, my love."

Once a year, she brought them out—a New Year's rite. Rollie Hammergren, her father-in-law, had started the ritual years ago when he was sheriff. His son Will had continued it.

And now Red, Will's widow, fingered the stack. Four files, four unsolved deaths in Pearsal County dating back to the early twentieth century. Once a year, each sheriff in their time had reviewed them, searching for new clues and new meanings.

The two on top were from Will's time as sheriff, before the years of smoking ruined his lungs and the cancer killed him. Now, they had been passed on to Red, the first female sheriff in Pearsal County.

Unidentified human skull. The skull had been discovered by a landowner as he cleared brush in his remote woods near Hammer Lake. The file was dated 2004. Nothing other than the skull had been found at the site. The file included several faded color photos of it and the surroundings. No one had come forward to report a missing person.

Red scrutinized the photos. The teeth in the skull were still intact with an obvious gap between the front uppers. Who was this gapped-tooth person?

Something in the background of one of the photos caught her attention. A slight metallic glint partially hidden under a leaf. She took out a magnifying glass and studied it more. Perhaps a bullet? It was too fuzzy to tell, and nothing else in the file indicated that a bullet had been found. Was this evidence of a shoddy investigation, or was the glint simply a reflection of light in the photo? She scribbled "bullet or something else?" on a Post-it note and put it on the front of the file before closing it.

She opened the second file. *John "Junior" Klein.* The body had been found by Junior's father, Jack, four years ago near a hunting shack off Hammer Lake. Red had been a deputy at the time and filling in for Will because of his health. She remembered interviewing Junior's widow, a woman so skinny and twitchy that Red wondered if she was on drugs. And she remembered Junior's daughter, Missy, dark like her mother with eyes that were round and filled with confusion.

"Who would shoot Daddy?" she'd asked over and over.

Red had turned the investigation over to the neighboring county because she was too busy trying to hold the department together and care for Will.

She flipped through the pages of the file and shook her head. "I should have done the investigation. I would have been more thorough."

Before she set the file aside, she reread the autopsy report. Something in the report caused her to frown. The notes indicated that the gunshot had been at fairly close range. Yet the investigator had labeled the death a probable hunting accident. Junior had been in the wrong place at the wrong time. No one had stepped forward to claim responsibility. That was what bothered Red the most.

Pearsal County might be a gun-supporting Minnesota backwoods, but people were honest and responsible here. If a hunter had been in the area and heard about the death, he or she would have stepped forward. The hunter would have said, "I fired a shot in that direction."

She set the two files down. It bothered her that both of the bodies had been found near Hammer Lake, yet she couldn't see a connection.

Of the other two files, one was a hit-and-run death of a teenager in 1956. His body had been found in a ditch off Highway 63. The other was simply labeled *Child, 1921, probably female.* The little girl had been buried in a shallow grave just outside the old Norwegian cemetery. She'd been wrapped in a pink woolen blanket. No name, no identification, and no one stepping forward to claim her. The sketchy file contained brief notes about the location of the grave and the condition of the body. By the size of the skeleton and the length of the femur, the coroner estimated the little girl to be about three years old. A little pink ribbon with a tuft of blond hair was also found in the grave.

Red flipped the file shut. No DNA or sophisticated forensics in those days. She expected this would remain an open case forever.

Outside the courthouse, a snowmobile buzzed in the distance on Lykkins Lake. The low, almost imperceptible hum gave Red a headache. Her headaches were the kind that could predict weather. Another snowy front was coming in. She knew it without looking up weather.com. She knew it by the way her jaw ached.

After finishing with the files, she reached her arms up and stretched with a sense of relief. The annual review had been completed. It was similar to the relief she felt every April when she finally filed her taxes.

No new information. No new insights. The files would go back into the bottom of her filing cabinet and await next year's review. This year, though, as she slid them into the hanging folder marked "Unsolved Deaths 1920 to ___," she didn't feel as much relief. Perhaps it was the grayness of the day. Perhaps the headache. Or perhaps it was the autopsy note on Junior Klein.

If he had been shot at close enough range, the shooter would have known he'd shot someone. She had that gut tightening feeling that his death was no accident.

Red turned back to the filing cabinet, pulled out the Klein file, and opened it again. She remembered the scene, the clearing in the woods near Hammer Lake. She remembered the look on Jack Klein's weathered face as she talked with him. He'd grimaced, fighting back tears as he said to her, "How can I tell Missy that her dad is dead?"

She recalled hearing something about Junior's wife, Missy's mother, dying recently in the Twin Cities. What a loss for the girl, who would be a teenager now. Red dropped the file into her "in" basket. Maybe tomorrow, when her head didn't pound so much, she'd look at it again. Something didn't feel right about this case.

3

SHERIFF RED

TO PROJECT AND SERVE

Red's eyes drooped shut in the warmth of the overheated office, and she dozed off. The skull with the gap tooth floated just inside her consciousness, and it was trying to tell her something. Laughter from the front office pulled her out of her stupor. Jason, Red's deputy, and Billie, the second-shift dispatcher, tittered. The laughter grew until Jason came lumbering to the door.

Without knocking, he said, "Sheriff? I think you'd better see this."

"I hope it's something that will cheer me up." She squeezed her eyes shut to blink away the grogginess and the image of the skull.

Jason grinned. "I doubt it. The new website is up. Take a look."

She switched on her desktop computer, tapping in the web address for the new Pearsal County Sheriff's Department page. It took time to load because internet connectivity in Pearsal County, like other rural areas, was behind the times. Her proposal for federal grant money to upgrade the county's internet still sat with the commissioners because several of them were opposed to getting involved with federal funds. "You don't want them feds breathing down our necks."

The radiator clanked and then quieted as Red stared in disbelief when the home page opened. "Oh, my God!"

A banner at the top of the page announced, "Pearsal Country Sheriff's Department." A grinning cartoon woman wearing a buckskin skirt and a large white cowboy hat with a badge that said "Sheriff" on it danced in the upper right-hand corner. Bold letters announced, "**Our Mission Statement: To Project and To Serve.**" Instead of bullet points, icons of a Colt .45 pointed to phone numbers for the sheriff's office, including Red's private cell.

Red rubbed her temples. "Please tell me this is a beta site."

Jason pulled up a chair and sat beside her. At twenty-five, he was already growing a paunch from a steady diet of hamburgers and French fries. At this rate, in ten years he'd be on the road to his first heart attack. Meanwhile, he was a good deputy, and he knew the internet world better than Red.

A smile tugged at his lips. "Sheriff doesn't look a lot like you."

"Thanks. My buckskin skirt is at the cleaners. Now please tell me we are the only people who can see this."

Jason took a cell phone out from his pocket and tapped it. In a few moments, he had the website up. "Looks like it's out there for the whole world to admire."

Red made a hissing sound as she gritted her teeth. Last summer, when she'd gone to the commissioners with a proposal to develop the website, she'd run into skepticism from the senior members. Why, they asked, would the citizens of Pearsal County need a separate website for the sheriff's office? The county site already had the sheriff's phone number. If it wasn't an emergency, couldn't they look it up? And besides, many of the taxpayers didn't even have access to the internet. It would be a waste of dollars.

After Red pointed out that a website might lessen the number of 911 calls, the commissioners reluctantly agreed to put out a request for proposals for the design. Unfortunately, when the bids came in, the commissioners decided they were too expensive. Instead, they awarded the design to the nephew of one of the commissioners. The kid promised the site would be so unique that it could go viral. The commissioners had no idea what he was talking about, but they liked his three-figure price.

"We have to get this thing down before everyone knows that in Pearsal

Country, we *project*...and serve." She pictured the irate calls that would start coming in. And most of them would come to her cell phone.

The designer did not answer his phone, and his voicemail was full. "I ought to send you out to arrest the dope."

"Text him."

Red grabbed her cell phone and typed in, *Take website down now!*

Jason shook his head. "How many people are going to look up the Pearsal County Sheriff's Department?"

"You'd be surprised."

Her phone beeped as a text came back. *Sorry, skiing. Can't.* He included an emoji of a skier.

Red tapped so hard on her phone that she almost dropped it. *Now!! Or you're under arrest for your stash.*

Jason was surprised. "You know he has a stash?"

"He's nineteen years old, for God's sake. Of course he does."

After closing the web page, she took a couple of ibuprofens. Outside, car tires crunched on the sanded parking lot as county employees drifted home for the weekend.

It took an hour before the site read, "Under Construction." No dancing sheriffs and no pistol bullet points. Red was amazed at what could be done with a smartphone.

She waited for her cell phone to ring, for someone to ask why the Pearsal *Country* sheriff *projected*, but her phone remained silent until her friend Georgia called.

"Just reminding you that we have a meeting tonight of the Florence Nightingale Memorial Poker Club. Supper at six, followed by your opportunity to win lots of money."

"Thanks." Red stared down at her budget spreadsheet. "I need to win some money so I can balance the budget." Or find a secret cache of money. She didn't say this to Georgia. Georgia knew the vagaries of public service, having once been the state Commissioner of Health.

Even though the file on Junior Klein called to her as it sat in her inbox on her desk, she knew she had to look at the budget. It was the middle of the month, and she was already over because of her dispatcher's unexpected medical leave. Both Billie and Cal were putting in overtime to cover.

She stretched as the figures floated in her head. As Will once told her, being county sheriff was more about business management than law enforcement. He never warned her, however, about other things like the internet and websites. Pearsal *Country*, for God's sake.

Outside, the city plow dropped a mixture of sand and salt. The winter deep freeze had dried the pavement to a frosty white powder, but beneath it were patches of black ice formed by the exhaust of the cars. Twice today she'd already seen cars sliding through the intersection in front of the courthouse. Both vehicles were SUVs.

She pushed her hand through her thick, curly bangs before returning to the spreadsheet. Among other things, she needed a haircut. Soon her eyes drifted shut again as she stared at the figures that wouldn't add up. What if she took the afternoon off and headed to her snow-covered acres to cross-country ski? She and Will had spent quiet time skiing and hiking through some of the last privately owned virgin forest in the state. Now when she went alone, she still felt his presence. It was a place where she could talk with him. She wanted to tell him about Junior Klein and about the web page and about this overall feeling that something was not right in Pearsal County.

Outside, Ed, the janitor, scraped the drifting snow off the main steps to the courthouse. The metallic sound of the shovel against the concrete stopped as he shouted to someone in the parking lot, "Cold enough for you?" She didn't hear the reply.

Her office phone rang while she was still thinking about the conversation she would have in the woods.

"Sheriff? This is Wendy Farnsworth. Sorry to bother you, but Dad has gone missing again."

So much for a quiet day in the office. It was time to go out and *project* and serve in Pearsal *Country*. She stood up, wondering what her five-foot-ten frame would look like in a buckskin skirt.

4

SHERIFF RED

THE MISSING UNDERTAKER

Wendy's father, Albert Larsen, had been the Lykkins Lake funeral director until ten years ago when he'd mixed up George Sanders and Evelyn Goodenough. He embalmed Evelyn and fixed her up with a new permanent, manicure, and red lipstick. George, he sent to the cities to be cremated. Unfortunately, Evelyn was supposed to be cremated and George prepared for the reviewal. Red was a new deputy at the time and had to keep George's son from punching the old undertaker out. A lawsuit was settled out of court, and Albert retired. He lived with his daughter now and her problematic son, Trevor.

Red looked at the thermometer outside her window. It registered ten above zero. If Albert was out in this, he might not last long. Old people and babies were the most susceptible to hypothermia.

"When did he leave?"

Wendy paused. "Um, Trevor was supposed to watch him, but, you know, he got caught up in a video game and..." Her voice trailed off.

"It's okay." Red kept her voice sympathetic.

Wendy's son had been suspended from high school due to drugs. The poor woman was sandwiched between the two of them with little to help her out since her husband was an over-the-road trucker and gone for days at a time. Albert had "escaped" his daughter's house once before. They found him walking down Main Street barefoot. He was on his way to work, he said. Fortunately, that escape happened in the summer.

"Can you tell if he dressed for the cold?"

"His coat is in the closet." Wendy's voice cracked.

Jason was sitting in the outer office, talking with the file clerk from across the hall.

"Bundle up, Jason." She described the situation and asked him to go to the house and talk with Wendy and her son. Meanwhile, Red slipped into her down jacket, pulled on a heavy woolen cap, and headed for the car.

"I'll scout out some possible haunts. Let's hope he didn't head into the woods. And let's hope he has shoes on this time."

Main Street was Friday-afternoon quiet. A woman emerged from the post office clutching a package. She had her head down as she hurried to her car. No one else was on the street, not even a confused old undertaker.

Back when Red was young, downtown Lykkins Lake had been a hub of activity even on the coldest days. Now the Super Value on the corner and the Ben Franklin were empty buildings. The major businesses had moved out to the highway. Still, the two banks, the hardware store, the bakery, and the Town Talk Café kept the street alive.

Where would a retired undertaker with dementia go? In her experience, they tended to go back to someplace familiar. Dementia was such a perplexing condition. Red thought about how her own mother refused to leave the house in her early stages of the disease. She couldn't handle anything new, and slowly she forgot things—glasses in the refrigerator, mismatched socks, and eventually her daughter.

Red headed for the highway and the Larsen-Nord Funeral Home. She suspected Albert was headed back to work.

The parking lot of the funeral home was carefully plowed, sanded, and salted. It was empty. Most funerals were either in the morning or early afternoon in Pearsal County. Morning funerals always included a potluck funeral lunch—usually a hamburger hot dish with tater tots on top, rolls, and fancy Jell-O.

Red sat in the parking lot for a minute, remembering Junior Klein's funeral here. Red had attended it both as a courtesy to the family and because she wondered if the person who fired the gun that killed him might show up. She witnessed nothing out of the ordinary except an odd interaction between Junior's widow, Mayme, and Bobbi Norgren, an old high school classmate. When Bobbi reached her in the receiving line, Mayme had stomped her foot and cried out, "You!" Then she'd resumed a glassy-eyed stare into the distance. At the time, Red thought it was either a grief reaction or that Mayme was on drugs.

Before she stepped out of the car, she thought about Will's funeral two years ago. It had been a chilly late-October day. The oak trees on the edge of the parking lot stood barren, and the fallen leaves swirled in little eddies across the pavement of the parking lot. Inside the funeral home, a grizzled old man grumbled when he found there would be no reviewal for Will. Instead of a casket, a plain brown clay urn sat on a table at the front of the room.

The old guy had said loud enough for the others in the room to hear, "When Rollie Hammergren died, they displayed him real nice—like he was sleeping. He even had his sheriff's badge with him. What's this jar thing? Don't tell me they burnt him up."

Red had fought back both tears and a smile. Pearsal County didn't know her secret, and she hoped they never would.

Stepping out of the car, Red was greeted with a blast of cold air. Could Albert survive long enough to walk here from his daughter's?

Ryan Nord sat at his desk in the office just off the main chapel, working a crossword puzzle. His mop of blond hair was beginning to show streaks of gray. Red used to babysit Ryan when she was a teenager and he was a gawky eight-year-old. It was hard to reconcile this serious-looking man in a pressed white shirt, red necktie, and pullover sweater with the kid whose socks never matched. She had occasional dealings with him because he was a mandated reporter of any suspected abuse. Sometimes bodies came to him with suspicious injuries. Other times he would call her with a heads-up about drug deaths in the surrounding counties. Red knew drugs were coming into Pearsal County, but fortunately no one had overdosed and died—yet.

"Hey." He grinned. "Are you 'projecting' or 'serving' today?"

Red shook her head. "Don't you have enough to do without surfing the web?"

He shrugged. "Word got out. One of the commissioners who shall not be named told everyone at the Town Talk that his nephew had, in his words, 'constructed a fine website that would probably go like an infection.'"

"Clearly he wasn't smart enough to look at it before he started bragging."

"Who says it isn't fine?"

Red pulled off her cap and pressed her lips into a tight line to keep from smiling. "I'm not up to *projecting* right now."

Ryan nodded, setting the pencil down. "So, what brings you here today?"

"Albert Larsen walked out of the house earlier today. We're trying to find him. I thought he might come here."

Ryan shook his head. "I haven't seen him. It's only me and Mrs. Nelson. We could ask her, but she's dead, of course."

Red smiled. "I guess it would be a waste of time, then, to interview her."

"We can check the back, if you'd like. I'm sure she won't mind."

They walked to the back through a display room with all the coffins. She remembered walking through this room with Will. By then, he was down to 140 pounds on his six-foot-five-inch frame. He had to stop every few feet to catch his breath because he refused to use the portable oxygen tank in public. Ryan had shown them a variety of caskets, but Will was very specific. "I want a plain pine box. No silk, no satin—just a box."

Albert was not in the back. Nor had he slipped into the hearse that was parked in a carport next to the building.

"Call me if he shows up," Red said as they hurried back inside the building.

Ryan pulled the service entry door shut with the same thoughtful look he used to get as a kid when Red played cards with him.

"You know, I built this place after Albert retired. Remember, the Larsen Funeral Home was over by St. Peter's Lutheran Church on Oak Street. Maybe he went there."

Damn, Red thought. Of course. The old funeral home housed a daycare and preschool now.

She pulled out her cell phone and called the dispatcher. "Can you put me through to the St. Peter's day care?"

"Yup."

The phone rang eight times before it was picked up. A harried voice said, "Hello?"

Red explained the situation and asked the aide to look around and see if Albert had come in.

A few minutes later, she came back. "Sorry, no one has seen him."

In the background, Red heard the noises of children playing. It sounded like they were throwing toys at each other. She hoped not.

If Albert wasn't at the day care and no one else had seen him, her next option was the cemetery. Lykkins Lake had two. A small, little-used cemetery stood in the back of the deconsecrated Norwegian Lutheran Church that was now the Pearsal County Family Planning Center. It was on the edge of town, at least a mile from Wendy's house. The municipal cemetery was located out on Highway 63 but closer to where Albert lived. Red decided to try the highway.

She turned up the heater fan to high and pulled out onto the highway. Snow danced across the dry pavement and into the ditch. The road was quiet for a Friday. Often in the summer, cars were backed up for several blocks because of the one traffic light in Lykkins Lake. City folks heading to the Northwoods for a little respite. Other than the ice fishermen and the snowmobilers, winter was a slow season for the tourists.

A quarter of a mile outside of town, Red decided to turn around. The old guy couldn't possibly get this far without someone noticing. As she pulled into a plowed driveway to make her U-turn, her radio crackled to life.

"Sheriff, the day care called. Said some of the kids saw Santa Claus at the window. Might be Albert."

When she reached the day care, Jason's patrol car was already in the parking lot. Inside, the children were chanting, "Santa! Santa!" and pointing to a window on the side of the building. Between the paper snowflakes taped to the glass, she caught a glimpse of a red stocking cap.

Red found Jason tugging at the old man. "Come on, Mr. Larsen. You need to come with me."

It would have been comical if it hadn't been so damn cold. Albert had on a red stocking cap, red woolen stockings over his hands, an orange hunting jacket, and gray woolen socks over his feet. His flannel pajama bottoms were tucked into the socks. Red hoped he had shoes on under the socks, but she couldn't be sure.

Albert batted at Jason. "Get away from me! I'll call the sheriff. He's a good friend of mine."

Red stepped forward and signaled Jason to let go. "Hi, Albert. Remember me? I'm Sheriff Hammergren."

He looked at her with a bright gleam in his eyes. "Hammergren? Are you Rollie's girl?"

She moved in a little closer but far enough away that he couldn't hit her. "I'm Will's wife—Red."

Albert squinted at her, studying her face with a growing suspicion. "Rollie didn't have a girl. He only had that nice boy who played basketball and that other one that they had to put away. Such a sad story." He backed up, nearly falling. Oatmeal from his breakfast was dried in his wild white beard.

Red moved in and gently took his arm to steady him. "It's cold out here. Let's get you someplace warm."

He jerked away. "Oh, no you don't. I have work to do. I don't want to be late." He turned to the back of the building.

Inside the building, little voices continued to chant, "Santa! Santa!"

"It wouldn't be good for the funeral director to be late for the funeral. Would it?"

Albert shook his head. "Not good for business at all."

"Let me give you a lift, then. Which funeral is it?"

Jason looked at her as if she were crazy. She whispered to him, "Play along. We need to get him out of the cold."

"It's old Washburn. His wife will be very upset if I don't get there."

Red took his arm and pointed to Jason. "Jason is strong. He can help you get that casket into the church."

Albert looked Jason up and down and nodded. "You look like a nice strong boy."

They guided Albert to Red's car. "Jason will come behind us with the hearse. Is that okay?"

"Always nice to have a hand." He squinted at her. "Say, aren't you that lady who helped me the other day when that woman wanted me to open the coffin after it was all closed up? She wanted her mother's rosary."

Red had no idea what he was talking about. "Oh?"

"All the fuss over those Catholic beads. I guess you never know."

With dementia, it was hard to tell if this was a true story or a mashup of old experiences. Red turned up the heat to keep Albert warm. "You don't want to catch cold before the service, do you?"

Albert nodded. "You're a nice girl."

As they drove down the street, Albert suddenly turned to Red with his eyes narrowed. "Where are you taking me? I can't be late for the funeral."

Red kept her voice calm. "No, we don't want you to be late. What church are we going to?"

Albert relaxed and said, "Faith." Faith Lutheran was the deconsecrated church that was now a family planning clinic. It hadn't held a service in twenty years.

"Okay, we just have to make a stop at the hospital to pick up Mr. Washburn."

By the time she reached the emergency entrance to the little hospital, Albert was asleep, his head dropped down and a little spittle spilling from his mouth. It was time for him to go to a locked memory-care unit. She was saddened that a man who had served the community for so long now needed to be locked in, but the Alberts of the county took up a lot of her staff's time.

After she had him safely settled into the emergency room, she walked back to her car, thinking about the conversation with him. She wondered about the story behind the rosary in the coffin. Someday, if she remembered, she'd ask Georgia.

5

SHERIFF RED
MISSING MISSY

It was nearly three in the afternoon by the time she got back to her office. The day was graying out, and she had the beginnings of another headache. Fortunately, tonight was poker night. She could play cards with her friends and forget the dancing sheriff and the sense that something bad was happening somewhere in her county.

For good measure, she checked the website again. It still said, "Under Construction." Good, she wouldn't have to arrest the teenage designer and nephew of one of her commissioners. At least not yet.

Outside, the trees cast long shadows across the snow as weak sunlight poked through the western cloud bank. Red thoroughly disliked the low sun and the short winter days. She made note in December of the date of the winter solstice to remind herself that the days would indeed get longer. Since Will died, it seemed the world had gotten darker and less bright even in the summer.

When she said something about it to Georgia, she'd responded, "It's grief, girl. It takes time."

Red had raised her eyebrow with a short laugh. "What a relief. I thought it might be climate change."

The courthouse was closing for the weekend. As footsteps from the two clerks in the registrar's office faded down the hallway, Ed the janitor called out to them, "Cold enough for you?"

Red smiled as she wondered if Ed had more than two phrases in him: "cold enough for you" and "hot enough for you." She bit into a stale peanut-butter-and-jelly sandwich that she had stashed in her drawer and signed the report on Albert Larsen. They were keeping Albert in the hospital overnight for observation. Perhaps they could convince Wendy to place him in a nursing home this time.

Red peered out the window, thinking about this past year, and shook her head. With Will's illness and death, plus all the work in the sheriff's office, plus an election campaign, she'd gotten run down to the point where she'd woken up last summer with a mean case of shingles. At least now that she didn't have to think about a campaign for sheriff again for another couple of years, she could concentrate on the needs of the county and the mess of paperwork she had at home trying to settle Will's estate.

She groaned as she stretched. The last thing she wanted was to go home and try to deal with finalizing the estate. Specifically, she needed to figure out how to get the 160 acres that had been in the Hammergren family for generations into her name.

The wooden floorboards of the old building creaked in a rhythm of footsteps as someone walked down the hall toward her office. Her door was closed, but she heard voices from the dispatching office and then a knock on her door.

"Beldon Rafferty here." He opened the door and swept in before she could say anything. Beldon wore a red puffy North Face jacket and black creased trousers. Red had no doubt that beneath the jacket was a pressed white shirt and a conservative tie. His cologne wafted into the room. Probably a fragrance from Nordstrom at the Mall of America, not the drugstore in town. A curl of silver-gray hair fell boyishly over his forehead.

"Beldon." She acknowledged him and pointed at a chair in front of her desk. He was the Lykkins Lake city manager and a major headache for Red.

He sat down, crossed his legs, and leaned back in the chair. "I've had another complaint about your people and the slow responses to calls."

Red said nothing. She knew Beldon was working up his case to create a city police force and hire his son, Mitch, to run it. This was yet another ploy.

He would present it to the county board as, "I register complaints, and nothing is ever done."

"You know that I and the chamber of commerce are trying to build up the community—attract new folks to the town. We need to be able to say we have good protection."

Red was about to mention the crime rate in Lykkins Lake was lower than that of most towns with a population under five thousand, but she knew it would be like arguing gun control with the NRA. Instead, she said, "Can you tell me more? What calls? When did they occur? Who called?"

Beldon cleared his throat and sat up a little straighter. "Well, I don't have the details with me."

Red smiled sympathetically. "Sometimes details trip us up. Don't they?" She reached into her desk and pulled out a form.

"Why don't you fill this out so I can investigate." She leaned closer to him. "As city manager, you know how much it helps to have complaints like this in writing."

He looked at the form with a scowl.

"Is there something else I can do for you?" She raised her voice.

He folded his arms and glanced up at the ceiling. "I'm hearing from folks in town that we've got a drug problem here. They're wondering what you're doing about it. Mitch says the kids in the high school say you can buy just about anything."

Beldon's son Mitch helped coach the wrestling team. "Maybe Mitch needs to come in and talk with me." She leaned across her desk. "He can give me more specifics so I can investigate."

Beldon let out a quick disgusted snort. "You mean fill out a form?"

Unsmiling, Red kept a steady gaze on him, not rising to the bait. "If that helps, yes."

Beldon looked away as she stared at him. "Ah, well...I'll give him the word."

It wasn't news to her that there were drugs available at the high school. Trevor Farnsworth was a perfect example.

She sat back with a tight smile. "I'd love to hear more before we have a drug-overdose death on our hands. I'm sure Mitch feels the same way." She paused. "By the way, how's the cleanup coming on Pine Acres? I hope the state pollution people were helpful."

Beldon flinched. After moving to Lykkins Lake, his wife had purchased Pine Acres, the trailer court that sat within the city limits. It had been a sore spot for the sheriff's office for years and didn't improve after the purchase. Last fall, when she and Jason investigated a loud party, they found the remains of a meth lab. Half the residents had to be evacuated while they cleaned up the site.

When Beldon left, he held the complaint form as if he'd picked up a dirty piece of toilet paper.

She watched him walk out and sighed. One of the reasons Beldon wanted a city police force was to have control over the law and the dealings with Pine Acres. She wondered how people like Beldon ever got the jobs they did.

And then there was his son Mitch. At the urging of a couple of the county commissioners, Will had hired him as a deputy.

"I don't like him," Will had said to her. "But I can't use that as an excuse not to hire him. After all, I'm not exactly overwhelmed with applicants, and he does have policing experience."

Mitch resigned abruptly when Red was named as the acting sheriff. His campaign against her for sheriff this fall turned ugly when he accused her of carrying on Will's "inept" practices. Apparently, that was too much for the citizens of the county, who had a long history of loving the Hammergrens. Her victory was overwhelming.

Red pulled out the budget spreadsheet and stared at it with the sense that she was drowning. Maybe the county should take up Beldon's proposal, and Mitch could figure out how to pay for the police force. The ringing phone pulled her from her ruminations.

"Sheriff Hammergren."

Scotty, a member of the poker club, sounded like she was talking through a wind tunnel. "Lou and I are at the Church. We'd like you to come and talk with a couple of the girls."

"You're supposed to be at Georgia's Antiques warming up the cards. Why are you still at the Church?"

"It's a semi-crisis. We need our sheriff. We have two girls here who are worried about their friend Missy. I think you can help sort it out."

"Missy?"

"Missy Klein. You know, Jack's granddaughter."

"How worried are they?"

"Just come." The call ended abruptly.

With a quick glance at the Junior Klein file in her inbox, Red threw on her coat and hurried out the door.

6

SHERIFF RED

THE CHURCH

The Church stood on a lonely tract of ground on the edge of town. A cemetery of snow-shrouded, sagging headstones covered the back part of the lot. *Child, 1921* had been found just outside the border of the cemetery.

Beyond the cemetery fence, the land sloped to the marshy lowlands of Lykkins Lake. The lake had once been a popular fishing spot. Development and runoff from the fields had turned it into a weedy swamp. In the summer, as soon as the weather warmed, the water turned green with scum. In the winter, the reeds poked through the ice like sprouts of unruly whiskers. Efforts to revive the lake died when federal restoration money dried up during the recession.

Three cars were pulled up close to the entrance: Scotty's, Lou's, and a bright red SUV. A dim light over the double doors in front cast a sickly glow on the entrance.

The old church building had become the home of the Pearsal County Family Planning Center two years ago. Red's nurse friends and fellow poker players Scotty, Lou, and Georgia had cobbled together grant money to start the clinic after the county commissioners in their infinite wisdom had voted to close the county-funded clinic.

"They thought family planning promoted fornication, lewd living, and abortion," Scotty once told Red. "When I suggested to the commissioners that if that was the case, they all could use a little family planning, I quickly became the ex–public health nursing director."

The rate of teen pregnancy in the county had dropped by half since the little clinic opened. Lou had cleverly rented the empty church because of its isolated location and because the clients could honestly tell their parents they were going to church if they asked. Most parents didn't ask.

Scotty waited just inside the entrance of the building. She was fiftyish with long, straight Earth-mother hair pulled back into a single braid. She wore dark-rimmed round glasses. People teased her about being a Harry Potter wannabe. She waved them away, saying, "Works well for relating to the kids."

"We've got a couple of worried young women," she said to Red in a low voice.

Red rubbed her hands together to warm them up as she waited to hear about the "worry."

"Tiffy Norgren and Sara Weick are up in our classroom with Lou. They're pretty upset."

Red knew that Georgia, Lou, and Scotty worked very hard to solve client problems without involving the sheriff. The last thing they wanted was a rumor that the Church had called the law—for any reason.

Red waited patiently for Scotty to continue.

"I'll let the girls tell you. But I have a bad feeling about this." She tugged at the salt-and-pepper braid resting over her right shoulder.

Her tone surprised Red. Normally Scotty was upbeat to the point of coming across as ditzy. After losing her job as the county public health nursing director, she bought the only café in town, the Town Talk. It was her mission to provide Lykkins Lake with nutritious food. She ground carrots and broccoli into the meatloaf, served burgers that were more veggie than meat, and made the worst banana oatmeal bran muffins in the state. During the week, the place was always packed. Red never could figure out why.

Red glanced up at the classroom. It was the old altar area of the church. They'd cleared the choir space and brought in posters and a whiteboard. Lou sat in her white lab coat with the two girls. The three were talking intently. Red watched Lou interact with the teenagers. Lou, in her mid-thirties, was a hometown girl who became a nurse practitioner and came back to serve her community. She was short and wiry with a disarming calmness.

"Will they talk with me?" Red asked.

Scotty nodded solemnly. "I told them they had to. This is too serious."

The oaken pews so piously placed by the Norwegian Lutherans back in the 1920s still filled the main part of the small sanctuary. Instead of hymnals, though, pamphlets and magazines were strategically placed in the slots in the backs of the pews. One lay open as Red walked by. It had a full-color graphic illustration of genital herpes. Red could almost hear lilting moans from the old Scandinavians as they rolled over in their graves behind the church. She suppressed an urge to smile.

Benches in the choir area had been replaced with second-hand folding chairs facing a portable whiteboard. A poster of a female figure showed ovaries, fallopian tubes, and the vagina.

"We call it 'preaching to the choir,'" Scotty whispered.

Red sat down next to Tiffy. Lou looked at her with a slight smile. "I think we need your help," she said quietly.

Red smiled at Tiffy and Sara with an "aw shucks" shrug to her shoulders. "I'm here to help."

The girls both had that northern Minnesota teenage wholesomeness to their faces—clear blue eyes and rosy complexions. Both had multiple ear piercings, but neither wore any makeup.

"What can I do for you?" Red kept her tone neutral. She knew that if she handled this interview poorly, the Church could be in trouble. Both Tiffy and Sara were leaders among their high school peers.

"Go ahead," Lou urged.

"You won't tell my folks I was here?" Sara's brow wrinkled with a worried expression.

Red shook her head. "If anyone asks, I ran into you at the hardware store. Okay?" Sara worked for Ace Hardware after school and on weekends.

"Me, too?" Tiffy looked scared. Her father coached wrestling at the high school. He was known for keeping his teams and his daughter on a short leash.

"Weren't you in Ace helping Sara?"

Tiffy nodded as relief swept her face. Red was sure none of the parents knew their daughters volunteered for the Church.

Red leaned a little closer to the girls and said, "Okay, we've established the rules. Now, what can I do for you?"

Outside, several blocks away, a snowmobile buzzed across Lykkins Lake. Otherwise, the Church was suddenly very quiet.

"Tiffy?" Red looked at the girl.

Tiffy took a deep breath and started, "Well, it's like. It's like..." She looked at Sara for help.

Sara stared at a spot beyond Red's head. Red waited patiently. The furnace in the basement of the old building kicked in with a wheezy cough, spitting out tepid air from a heating vent in the floorboard close to Red.

Finally, Sara blurted a finish to the sentence. "Our friend Missy Klein is missing, and we think something has happened."

"She's gotten into a bad crowd," Tiffy added. "You know Trevor Farnsworth—well, maybe not Trevor right now, since he got kicked out of school. But that Jared Peterson is a creep."

Red kept her eyes fixed on the girls, nodding. "Go on." She felt a tightening in her chest as she pictured the Junior Klein file. The photo of his bloodied body from the file on her desk flashed back to her. Will had once told her there were no coincidences in this world. This did not have a good feel to it.

She knew about Trevor's problems with drugs, but Jared Peterson's name was new to her.

"Well, it's like this morning, she snuck out of school before lunch. And this afternoon, our friend saw her leave with Jared, and she didn't come back." Sara folded her arms as if to emphasize the seriousness of it.

"Yeah, she missed the big history test this afternoon."

"Missy wouldn't miss that test. She was getting an A in the class."

Tiffy's eyes brimmed with tears. "We just know something is wrong."

A couple of years ago, Missy had been reported missing by her grandfather. She was picked up halfway to Minneapolis trying to hitchhike on the freeway. Red couldn't remember why she had run away. Seeing how distressed Missy's friends were, she decided not to bring it up. Instead, she asked, "Was something going on with Missy?" Her tone turned serious. "Was she doing drugs, maybe?"

Both Tiffy and Sara looked at each other. "That's the thing. We don't know. She changed after she started going with Jared, the creep." Sara pressed her lips together. "We tried to talk her out of it, but she said it was all part of a plan."

"Plan?"

A tear trickled down Tiffy's cheek. "That's what she said."

The room was suddenly silent until a gust of wind rattled the windows. Red waited for the girls to say more, but the only sound was Tiffy sniffling.

Red patted Tiffy on the shoulder and said, "I'm glad you are worried about your friend."

"We made a deal," Sara said softly. "That we would always come here together to help. Missy never missed—until today."

Red glanced at Lou, who nodded. "Good plan. And now you think Missy has gotten involved with a bad crowd?"

"Like, that Jared Peterson is a piece of scum." Tiffy nodded emphatically.

Sara picked at lint on her sweater. "Yesterday she told me she wasn't going to see Jared anymore. She said she just had to clean up a mess first."

"Did she say what kind of a mess?"

Both girls shook their heads but wouldn't meet Red's eyes.

"But you don't know what she meant by that?"

The girls looked at each other. "Maybe it had to do with drugs. But we don't know for sure."

Another snowmobile droned on the lake. As if the noisy machine had awakened the deep winter, a chilly draft swept through the old building. Outside, the trees creaked.

Tiffy stared at her shoes. "I have to go. I told my mom I'd be home by six. She thinks I'm studying."

Red leaned even closer to the girls. In a voice that was almost a whisper, she said, "If I'm going to help Missy, I need to know what kind of mess she was in."

The girls remained silent.

"Where do you suggest I look?" Red prompted.

"She went places with Jared, but she never told us where." Sara shrugged, not meeting Red's eyes.

The muffled sound of Tiffy's cell phone interrupted the conversation.

Tiffy quickly pulled the phone out of her bag and turned her shoulders away from Red. "Hi, Dad." Her voice had a false brightness to it. "No, I'm in the car with Sara. I'm bringing her home. Sure, bye. See you in a bit."

She looked from Red to Sara. "I *really* have to get home. We'd better go."

Red pointed to Tiffy's cell phone. "Do you have a photo of Missy that you could text to me?"

Tiffy scrolled through her photos and found what she was looking for. It was a selfie of the three of them. Missy stood between Tiffy and Sara with a crooked smile. Her dark hair was cut in a pageboy style, and her face had filled out since the day Red had talked with her mother after Junior was found.

Red gave Tiffy her cell number, and Tiffy quickly texted the photo. "If you think of anything more about the trouble Missy was in, let me know. I'll do some poking around."

The girls nearly fled down the aisle, barely pulling their jackets on.

Red moved nearer to the heat duct to try to warm up her legs. It couldn't have been more than sixty degrees in the building. "Are you hoping your clients will preserve better if you keep it so cold in here?"

Lou shrugged. "The heat's expensive. We chill them out here but keep the exam room nice and toasty. They're so cold by the time we get them on the table that the speculum feels warm to them." She chuckled.

Scotty stood next to Lou. "I didn't know you had a sense of humor, honey."

Lou gave her the finger before turning to Red. "What do you think?"

Red crouched down to be closer to the heat. "I'm puzzled," she said, placing her hands against the warm register. "I think they know more than they are saying."

Lou agreed, squatting next to Red. Her white lab coat brushed the old wooden floor. "It's a hunch, Red. I know these girls—the cream of the crop, so to speak. But the two of them came in late today and almost missed the peer counseling session. Before today I could set my clock by the Missy, Tiffy, and Sara trio."

"We know they aren't telling us everything about Missy," Scotty added.

"No kidding." Red sighed. "I haven't heard anything from either the school or Missy's grandpa. That's the other reason I'm puzzled. It's usually the family that calls and the friends that cover up."

Red knew Missy lived with her grandfather on a wooded homestead in Whitefield Township. Her mother had left home shortly after Junior died. Red had heard that Grampa Jack was decent with her. Other than the one time when she ran away, the sheriff's office hadn't gotten any other reports on Missy.

"I'll give Jack a call. Hopefully Missy is home and tucked into bed."

The expression on Lou's and Scotty's faces told her they didn't think Missy was munching on potato chips in front of the television at home.

A gust of wind pressed a frozen branch from an elm against a church window. It sounded like a ghostly tap.

7

SHERIFF RED
SOMEONE'S INSIDE

Red sat in her car and watched as Lou and Scotty locked up. Scotty waved and shouted, "See you at Georgia's. I feel a win coming on."

Scotty was so bad at cards that she'd once folded with three aces showing. She later claimed it was only because she'd had two beers and a candy bar. Red knew it was because Lou had raised her ten dollars and Scotty could never figure out a bluff—not even a blatant one.

Red rolled down her window to an icy blast. "I'll be late. I need to follow up on the missing Missy. Save a hot buttered rum for me."

Even as air from the heater warmed her legs, Red felt a cold pressure in her chest. What were the chances that she would review Junior Klein's file and several hours later be told his daughter was missing? Like Will, she wasn't keen on coincidences. Tomorrow she would study Junior's file again. Hopefully, by then, Missy would be a found teenager.

As the car idled, she remembered another missing teenager—her brother, Lad. He first disappeared when he was fourteen. By then, something had changed in him. He slid from the goofy kid who was obsessed with model rockets to a brooding teenager who spent most of his time shut up in his room. Sometimes he talked in a low mumble while the wooden floor creaked beneath him as he paced.

He didn't come home from school on a Friday. She and her parents spent an anxious night pacing and listening for the phone. They called neighbors and classmates, but no one had seen him. They found him on Saturday when the weekend janitor at the school opened the door to the furnace room. Lad was curled up asleep in the corner.

Her parents brushed it off as a "little incident." But the "little incidents" became more frequent as Lad's mental illness became more obvious and his inner voices grew louder. One day, he simply didn't come home.

Red resolved that Missy Klein would not do the same. Before she pulled out of the Church lot, she called the dispatcher. "Can you patch me through to Jack Klein?"

The cell phone rang feebly until a barely audible mechanical voice asked her to leave a message after the tone. Red raised her voice and asked Jack to call her back. Hopefully Jack knew where Missy was, and this would be cleared up quickly. She really wanted to play poker tonight with her nurse friends. Listening to them talk about their day was like meditation for Red.

Once she ended the call, she set the phone down on the seat beside her and put the car in gear. The Forester complained as the wheels moved.

"Cold, are we? It will get worse before it gets better." January in Pearsal County was notorious for days of below-zero weather. A snowmobile zipped out and crossed in front of her, heading for the lake. She watched the dark-clad rider. Last year at this time, she'd stood in the entryway of Matt Carlson's parents' house. She and Father Paul from the Catholic church were bearing the news that Matt's snowmobile had gone down in the icy waters of Hammer Lake.

Matt's mother had looked at them with eyes that flashed with disbelief, grief, and anger. She'd said, "I told him. I said, 'Matt, you go too fast on that machine, and the lake will suck you in.' That's what I said. I said, it will take you."

"Be safe," Red said out loud as the snowmobile disappeared into the woody area that bordered the lake. It only took minutes in the icy water for the hypothermia to drug a person and send them into an eternal sleep—if drowning didn't kill them first.

Her cell phone rang. Jack Klein must have gotten the message. She hit the speaker button on the steering wheel of the car, thankful for the new technology.

"Sheriff Red."

The voice, a high-pitched, panicked tone that transcended the static of the phone and filled the car. "Fire, Sheriff. There's a fire at the Henderson cabin. Hurry! Someone's inside! Someone's inside!"

The line went dead.

8

SHERIFF RED
FIRE

It felt like the Forester was going in slow motion as Red pushed the gas pedal as far as she dared on the icy roads. She knew the exact location of the Henderson cabin because three years ago, Arnold Henderson had hanged himself from the rafters of the ramshackle wooden structure, and she'd been the first officer to arrive at the scene. Arnold's face was an ashen, purplish color, his tongue protruding and the rope biting into his neck. Beneath him a tipped chair. The cabin smelled of the urine and stool that dripped down his pants. Will had explained, "The sphincters relax in death. Hanging is never pretty."

Blinking hard, she turned her attention back to the road. This part of the county was sparsely populated, the land swampy and thick with underbrush. Old logging roads led to primitive hunting cabins set deep in the woods. The cabin stood at the end of a rutted logging road on the south side of Hammer Lake.

She sped down the highway, shouting directions to her dispatcher, praying he could handle this after only two months on the job. Red called for a snowplow, a fire truck, and an ambulance. All would take precious time. Meanwhile the eerie voice on the phone echoed in her head.

Someone's inside.

She believed the voice and the fire. Several homemade meth labs had exploded over the years in Pearsal County. She'd hoped that scourge was over with the cleanup of the trailer court in Pine Acres, but maybe not. The sheriff in a nearby county had just dealt with a meth explosion despite all the laws restricting the purchase of the drugs that were the main ingredients.

"Please, not a lab," Red uttered aloud.

Black smoke stained the sky above the treetops a quarter of a mile down the unplowed logging road to the Henderson cabin. She pulled over as far as she could on the plowed county road, leaving her emergency flashers on so the others could find it.

Taking a deep breath, she grabbed her heavy winter boots from the back seat and laced them up. She knew she should wait for backup, but the high-pitched voice repeated in her head. *Someone's inside!*

She opened the emergency box and pulled out a large flashlight. "Do your job, Red!"

She hit the road running, cursing the heaviness of her boots and the depth of the snow. At least two snowmobiles, perhaps three, had been down this road. The tracks appeared to be fresh. By staying inside the snowmobile track where the snow had been compacted, she could move faster. Still, she felt like her body worked in slow motion as her boots sank into the snow.

The thick scrub pines on either side of her cast shadows across the track. Ahead, the burning wood crackled.

"Please let this be an empty cabin," she gasped, trying to push her legs faster. She knew full well that cabins in the woods in the middle of January did not spontaneously combust. They either went up in flames from vandals—drunken teens in pursuit of a kick—or stupid winter campers who didn't know how to use a wood stove. Or the alternative—she pictured the tubes and cooking pans and plastic jugs from a meth lab.

Her lungs burned and beads of sweat poured down her temples as she neared the cabin. Her heart pounded and her chest ached from the exertion and the frigid air. She ran with legs that felt like giant, unforgiving logs. Urging them on, she vowed to get out cross-country skiing more. She spent too much time now in front of spreadsheets instead of keeping herself fit.

Ahead, the undergrowth and trees cleared. Already the heat from the fire warmed her face. As she neared, the intensity grew. In front of the cabin, a snowmobile lay on its side, engulfed in flames.

"Hey!" she yelled. "Hey, is anyone in there?"

The cabin's front door was blown out, a blackened slab on the snowy floor of the forest. Flames shot through the gaping doorway. Red shielded her face from the searing heat of the fire, searching through the orange glow for signs of a person—a body in the cabin. The intense heat drove her back.

No one would survive this. She pulled the collar of her parka up to cover her mouth against the choking smoke and made a wide circle around the cabin. The snow rose to her knees where it had drifted against the trunks of trees. Flaming pieces of debris shot out of a hole in the roof. It landed in the snow with a sizzling sound. At her back, the cold crept up her spine, while the heat tore at her chest. She called out, but her voice was lost in the roar of the fire.

In the distance, a faint siren wailed. Red doubted that the fire truck could do much at this point but keep the flames from spreading into the winter-dead trees and brush of the forest.

A small outbuilding, the outhouse, stood quiet and untouched a hundred feet behind the cabin. A deep-rutted path led from the outhouse to the back door of the cabin. The cabin had been in use this winter.

Someone's inside.

Something dark lay on the path near the door of the outhouse.

9

SHERIFF RED
JARED PETERSON

Red plunged through the snow toward the dark thing. Low brush scratched and whipped at her pants. Her foot caught a hidden root, and she fell forward, her flashlight flying from her hand.

One of her mittens slipped off and dropped beneath the snow. "Goddamn it!" She dug in the snow, her hand quickly becoming bone-cold numb. An ache crawled up her wrist and into her forearm.

"Aaaarp." A faint gasping sound rose above the noise of the fire.

Red looked up from digging through the snow. The black thing in the outhouse path moved, like the rippling of a tarp.

Oh, my God. She scrambled to her feet and lunged forward. As she neared it, the tarp transformed into a human figure, singed hands flapping against the snow. It writhed, crying in a high, trembling pitch.

Red leapt over a bank of snow to reach the figure. The flames from the cabin stabbed at them.

She leaned over to see a teenaged boy whose eyes were white and wide on the soot-blackened face. One pupil was larger than the other. "It's okay," she said gently. "Can you move? We need to get you away from the fire."

The figure stared at her with the look of a panicked animal caught in a fence.

"Can't find..." He choked and spit up blood. "Can't find her."

"Is someone else inside?"

He coughed again. "Wanna go home." His voice faded.

Inside the cabin, something popped, then exploded. Glass from a windowpane came flying at them. Red grabbed the boy and rolled away from the spray of broken glass. A jagged shard landed less than six inches from where they had just been. She got to her knees, grabbed under the boy's arms, and dragged him into the woods away from the cabin. Behind, in the sooty snow, was a red stain, a stain of blood from the boy.

"It's okay," she murmured again. "Is anyone else here?"

The boy opened his eyes. In the twinkling light of the clear, arctic night, his eyes shone with a glaze that caused Red to stop her pursuit of the other people. He was going into shock. Quickly, she pulled off her parka and wrapped it around him.

Leaning close to his face, she said, "It's okay. We'll get you out of here."

With her one mittened hand and her bare hand, she piled up snow beneath his feet to elevate his legs.

"It's okay," she repeated, tucking the parka around him. It wasn't okay, though. She felt the boy fading from her. Where were the fire truck and ambulance?

"It's gone. Can't find..." The boy tried to lift his hand, his words slurred. "Find Coke. Find her." He lapsed into a spasm of coughing that grew weaker with each breath.

"Hang on, there. Help is coming."

Beyond the roar of the fire came the siren and the rumble of heavy machinery. The snowplow and fire department had arrived.

She held the boy tight, pressing her body against his, willing her warmth into him. His carotid pulse was barely discernable.

"Hurry," she whispered. *This must be what it feels like when people call 911 and it seems like it takes forever for help to arrive. Hurry, I'm losing the boy.*

The sound of voices rose over the spit and roar of the fire.

"Here! I'm back here!" Her voice was hoarse from gasping in the cold air.

Two firemen came plunging around the burning cabin, their thick boots and thick coats slowing them.

"Red!" one of them called. "Are you all right?"

"Over here, near the tree."

The next few minutes were a flurry of activity as one of them ran for a stretcher while the other knelt over the boy. The boy's eyes were half-closed, revealing only the whites. The fireman looked at Red with a grim expression.

"We'll get him to the hospital." His voice had little conviction.

"There might be someone else. The caller said, 'Someone's inside.'"

The fireman shook his head. "No rescue now, I'm afraid. Maybe recovery when the fire is out."

Red stood while they loaded the boy, still wrapped in her coat, onto the stretcher. It wasn't until she watched them carry the stretcher through the deep snow, stumbling and weaving, that she realized how cold she was.

Joe, the volunteer captain, reached her carrying an extra parka. "Here, before we have to haul you off with frostbite."

Red slipped into the jacket. "Do you know who the boy is?"

Joe nodded. "Jared Peterson. He lives just down the block from me."

Red let out a long sigh, her breath like smoke in the frigid air. Missy Klein's boyfriend. "Damn." Too many coincidences.

10

SHERIFF RED

JACK KLEIN

Joe handed Red a cup of steaming coffee from a thermos. She took it in her shivering hands. The coffee, bitter and strong, warmed her as she swallowed it.

"They'll take him to the hospital to get him stabilized, then they'll send him to Regions in St. Paul. They've got a top-notch burn unit." He hesitated. "If he survives."

Red took another sip, breathing in the aroma, and shook her head. "My gut says he won't make it." She'd felt the life draining from the boy as she'd held him close. They would try to save him. They would pump on his chest and shock him with a defibrillator, but it wouldn't bring him back.

Red tried to absorb as much heat as she could from the vents. Thank God Lykkins Lake and Pearsal County had put up the money for a new fire truck. Between the chimney fires, the poorly installed woodstoves, and the damned meth labs, they'd needed it.

Outside the truck, four volunteer firemen pumped water on the ruins of the cabin. Three walls still stood, charred and smoldering, while the water from the hoses pooled and thickened into ice in the frigid air.

The firemen took short turns in the cab of the truck to warm up. Red looked down at the hand that had lost the mitten. Her fingers were turning a bright cherry red and throbbed with each beat of her heart. She hadn't noticed them until Joe nudged her into the fire truck.

"Any signs of another body?"

Joe shook his head. "I doubt there is one. Who knows, maybe the kid was high and thought someone else was with him when he ran outside."

"Did anyone find his cell phone?" Red was beginning to wonder if Jared made the call in his injured state. Could someone else have called it in?

She closed her eyes and saw the boy again, wrapped in her parka, his eyes wide open, mumbling, *Find Coke. Find her.*

Maybe Coke was the someone else. Or maybe she'd misheard.

Wearing a borrowed parka and mittens way too big for her, Red slid out of the truck and onto the snow strewn with charred debris. She walked around the perimeter of the cabin with a flashlight looking for tracks or the phone. The air smelled of wet wood and ashes, like a campfire that had just been doused with water. Behind her, over the growl of the fire engine, she heard snatches of conversation between the members of the fire crew.

"She's still hot, but I think we have most of 'er."

"Watch that hose. It's slippery as hell out here now."

Red kept to the deep snow inside the woods to make sure she didn't step on any tracks. If there'd been another person inside who'd gotten out, she wanted to find a trail. That person could have run blindly out of the burning cabin and collapsed in the woods. The forest beyond the cabin was dark and thick. She found no tracks leading away from the cabin and into the woods.

Bone-tired and running on nerves, she drove back to town. Her frost-nipped fingers still tingled as she gripped the steering wheel. Clouds moved in to cover the dim light of the stars. She prayed it would not snow and cover anything up until she'd had a better chance to look around in daylight. The ache in her jaw said she'd be lucky to get back to the site before the snow fell.

Her radio crackled to life with the dispatcher's voice. He was so excited, he squeaked when he talked.

"We got an official ID on Jared Peterson. He's a senior over at the high school. I know about him. They say he's a real slacker—you know, into the whole drug scene. He's in the emergency room now."

Had Missy been with him? If so, she prayed the girl wasn't a charred heap inside the cabin.

She worked to keep the urgency out of her voice. "Can you patch me through to Jack Klein again?"

"Wow, Missy Klein hangs around with him. Was she in that cabin?"

"Just put me through." For a dispatcher, he was far too inquisitive. She would have to do some coaching with him. But now wasn't the time.

Jack Klein answered this time. He had a gruff, abrupt tone. "Yes?"

"Jack Klein? This is Sheriff Red Hammergren. We've got a situation, and we're trying to locate Missy. Is she with you?" Red mentally crossed her fingers, hoping the girl was snug in bed.

Jack's voice softened. "What's this all about?"

Red hesitated and finally decided on the truth. "We had a fire up at the Henderson cabin. Jared Peterson was one of the kids involved. I'm told Missy was going out with him. We're wondering if she might have more information on it."

Jack cleared his throat. "She said she was staying in town with friends tonight. They're going to the wrestling tournament at the high school tomorrow." He paused. "I told her that if she was going to stay in town, I didn't want her out with that boy."

"Does Missy have a cell phone?"

Red heard an audible sigh. "What teenager doesn't?"

"Would you call her and make sure she's okay?"

"Sure, I'll have her give you a call when I reach her." Before he hung up, she heard him mumble, "Never liked that Peterson kid."

This was the kind of conversation she should have had with him in person. She could pick up so much more in a face-to-face conversation, but right now she needed to know whether Missy might have been in that cabin.

She drove, noting the ache in her neck and jaw. It was the kind of ache that went beyond tension. It was her weather forecaster that said that bad weather was on the way. And another sense that she had, a tightness in her chest, said that she was in for more than bad weather.

11

SHERIFF RED
JARED'S PARENTS

Jared Peterson's parents sat in a small conference room down the corridor from the emergency room at Lykkins Lake hospital. The hospital had a late-evening hush except for the whisking sounds of the nurses as they hurried through the hallway. The doctor had not yet been in to talk with them.

Mrs. Peterson was younger than Red, with jet-black hair and a face that had gone soft in the cheeks and chin. Her eyes were red and swollen from crying. Mr. Peterson sat stiffly in a chair, his fingers drumming on the armrests and his eyes darting between Red and the conference room door. He was a long-haul trucker who drove a rig for a company in Duluth. When he wasn't driving, he spent a lot of time at Cuttery's, the bar on the edge of town.

Red sat across from them, holding a pen and her small spiral notebook. Her fingers were stiff enough from the frostbite that it was hard to grip the pen. As she observed Jared's parents, she realized they had no idea how badly their boy was hurt.

Mrs. Peterson picked at her sweatshirt and apologized. "I must look a fright. I was in my pajamas when the hospital called."

"Oh hell, Donna." Mr. Peterson ran his hands through a greasy mop of hair. "The sheriff here don't care what you look like."

Mrs. Peterson continued to pick at the sleeve.

"Do you know why Jared was at the Henderson cabin tonight?" Red kept her voice low and calm.

With a puzzled expression, Mrs. Peterson said, "He wouldn't have any reason to go there." She looked at her husband. "Would he?"

"Out in the middle of nowhere? No." Mr. Peterson was emphatic.

"Was he hanging around some other kids? Maybe they would know something." Red kept her fingers on the pen even though she wasn't writing anything. The pen and notebook made her look more official, and with these two, official might keep them honest.

Mrs. Peterson looked straight at Red. "He was grounded because of his grades. He wasn't with other kids—I know that for sure." She paused and directed her voice to Mr. Peterson with an accusing tone. "He wasn't supposed to go out."

The Petersons were facing a difficult time in their marriage if Jared didn't make it. Red had seen this before. How do you survive the loss of a child? Especially an only child?

"What about Missy Klein? I'm told they were going together. Could she have been at the cabin with him?"

"She came to the house a couple of times with Jared, but she stayed outside—wouldn't come in." Mrs. Peterson sniffled and dabbed at her nose. "I asked Jared to bring her in, but he said she was shy."

Mr. Peterson shook his head. "He should have stayed away from that girl—with her crazy mother and all. Just trouble, I'd say."

Mrs. Peterson ignored her husband as she rubbed a tear away from her cheek. "He wasn't doing drugs. I know he wasn't because I asked him. Just like they say on those television commercials. 'Talk to your kids.'"

Mr. Peterson gripped the armrests, his lips pressed into a tight line. "Did you find the snowmobile? I told him he couldn't take it. Brand-new machine. I still got two years to pay it off. I told him he had to start being more polite to people at home, and he had to get his grades up before he could take it." He narrowed his eyes. "He's going to have hell to pay if anything happened to that machine."

Mrs. Peterson pulled a tissue out of her large handbag and heaved a long, shuddering sigh. "Jared is a good boy, but things really changed last year when he got in with that wrestling crowd."

"What do you mean?" Red put the pen down.

"It's just..." She hesitated. "Oh, I don't know...probably nothing."

Mr. Peterson glared at her. "Hitch Norgren is a good guy. Those kids he coaches are the cream of the crop."

Mrs. Peterson clamped her mouth shut and stared at her lap.

What were they hiding? Red sensed a long-standing tension between the two of them. Was Jared the cause? Before she could ask any further questions, the hospital nurse came to the door and motioned to Red.

She wanted to say something else, something reassuring like, *He's going to be fine.* But Jared Peterson was not going to be fine. Even if he survived. Instead, she said gently, "Take care. If I have any more questions, I'll get back to you."

The nurse guided Red to the emergency room. The ER in Lykkins Lake consisted of one room with an exam table, cabinets with supplies, and a crash cart. For critical cases, the hospital was a stopping point for stabilization before patients were sent to better-equipped and fully staffed trauma centers.

Jared was on the exam table covered with a sheet up to his neck. In the harsh light, the skin on his face appeared waxen. His eyes were partially open. The life had gone out of them, and his jaw hung slack. The crash cart next to the exam table told the story with the disarray as drawers had been yanked open to administer the drugs that wouldn't put the life back into him.

The nurse, middle-aged and worldly wise, looked stricken. "I'm sorry," she whispered. "I can never get used to this." She busied herself cleaning up around the exam table.

Dr. Vijay, the emergency room locum who made the rounds of the small hospitals in the area, looked equally distressed. "The injury was too critical." He bowed his head and held his hands together as if in prayer. "We did everything we knew to do." He turned away.

Red forced herself to look at Jared. She'd investigated deaths before. She knew what it looked like, but like the nurse, she never got used to it. In death, his face had taken on a childlike peace. At least his parents would have that as a memory.

She cleared her throat a couple of times before she could speak, thinking about how she'd tried to push life into the boy as she struggled to warm him in the snow.

"Was it smoke inhalation?"

Dr. Vijay walked over to the body and gently turned the boy's head to the side. "He was bashed." The hair on the back of his head was matted with blood. He pointed to the skull. "See how it's dented in. Like he was hit with a bat, maybe."

Red remembered the redness of the snow by the boy. "Could he have fallen against something?"

Dr. Vijay's tone was firm. "He has other bruises. Someone hit him in the head. I don't know if that's what killed him. The autopsy will tell us more. Probably was suffering from smoke inhalation as well." He grimaced. "I'll have to tell the parents. I hate to say someone broke his skull."

"You don't need to. Just tell them he died from his injuries related to the fire. As you said, we won't know more until we have the results of the autopsy."

Dr. Vijay's eyes were a soft brown, and he had a kind way of speaking. He would be gentle with the Petersons.

Red took a deep breath. "I need to be the one to explain to the parents why we have to do an autopsy." She touched Dr. Vijay on his arm. "But let's wait until Father Paul can get here. They'll need his support." The three of them would be the bearers of the bad news.

She thought about the boy's last words. *Find Coke. Find her.* Were they ramblings from the brain injury? Or had he said something like, "Find Cole, find her"?

When they entered the conference room with Father Paul, the expression on Mr. Peterson's face said that he understood already that something terrible had happened. Mrs. Peterson, on the other hand, looked at them with hope in her eyes.

Dr. Vijay sat down to be eye level with the Petersons. His words were straightforward. "I'm sorry that I have bad news for you. Jared died of his injuries from the fire." He stopped to let them react.

Mrs. Peterson's mouth dropped open in disbelief. "What?"

"We did everything we could." Dr. Vijay kept his voice soft.

In shock, Mrs. Peterson began keening. "Oh no. Oh no."

Mr. Peterson stared blankly at Dr. Vijay and then at Red. It was as if his brain couldn't process what had been said.

After a few moments, Dr. Vijay continued. "He wasn't in any pain. I can assure you of that." He paused again, and Red noticed how his hands shook. This must have been one of the hardest parts of being a doctor.

"How? How did this happen?" Mr. Peterson came out of his trance.

Red explained to them again about the fire and explosion at the cabin. They nodded, but they weren't really listening.

"I'm so sorry for your loss. I'm afraid we'll have to do an autopsy. It's standard with an unexpected death like this."

God, she hated herself for sounding so officious. Mrs. Peterson sobbed quietly into a tissue as Father Paul sat next to her, his hand gently on her shoulder.

Mr. Peterson said nothing for a few moments. Then he looked at Red with a confused expression. "Did you find the snowmobile? He wasn't supposed to take it."

Red quietly slipped out the door as Father Paul and Dr. Vijay sat with the parents. She sat in the doctor's cubicle by the nurse's station to make calls regarding the autopsy. She would wait there until the Petersons left to make sure they got safely to their car. It was a long journey home when something like this happened.

Within a few minutes, Father Paul accompanied them out the door. *Bless him*, she thought.

Her cell rang as they pulled away.

"Sheriff, this is Jack Klein calling back."

Red knew what he was going to say before he said it. She could tell by the tone of his voice even though it was tinny from being transmitted from cell tower to cell tower.

"She's not with her friends, and she's not answering her cell."

Red took a deep breath and said, "Jack, I'm at the hospital. Do you think Missy might have been with Jared Peterson?"

Jack was silent for a long time. "I...I don't know. I think she's been doing things and not telling me. Since last fall, she's been real quiet. That's when her mother died. I kind of lost track..." His voice faded.

"We'll find her," Red said, hating to leave the conversation with an empty promise.

12

SHERIFF RED

BLUE

Blue, the five-pound poodle, wiggled joyfully when Red let herself into the house. The green digital numbers of the clock on the microwave said 1:28 a.m.

She picked up the dog. He sniffed at the stale smoke on her clothes before his little pink tongue licked her nose.

"Yuck. Old poodle breath. When are you going to learn to brush your teeth?"

She carried him to the door, set him down, and gave him a gentle shove. He looked at her with eyes that said, "You sadist, don't you know it's freezing out here?"

"Hey," she said. "You're a dog. Remember? Dogs pee outside."

While she waited, she rummaged in the refrigerator for something to eat. The mostly bare shelves consisted of a quart of whole milk, a tub of yogurt with an expiration date from before Christmas, and one bottle of Summit Pale Ale left over from last summer.

"Pretty sad." She shook her head and sniffed the yogurt. "Edible, I guess."

In the two years since Will died, she'd spent little time at home. She told Georgia, "The place is so empty. If it weren't for Blue, I think I'd probably live in my office at work—you know, a sleeping bag in the corner. When I come home the place is a shell."

She didn't tell Georgia that sometimes in the middle of the shadowy night, she would catch glimpses of Will coming out of the bathroom wearing that ratty old flannel bathrobe that he'd inherited from his dad. She would blink and he'd be gone, a ghost in her house.

Her thoughts were interrupted by Blue's yip at the door. When he came back in, his paws were cold with the snow. Red collapsed into the worn brown recliner with Blue nestled in her lap. She closed her eyes and saw the boy flailing in the snow. *Find Coke. Find her.* He was injured and crying out. Maybe he meant, find the cocaine and you'd find her. Or maybe he was talking about someone named Cole.

"What was he saying, Blue? Who is the 'her'? Was it a clue or the rantings of a dying boy?"

Blue looked up at her and burped. She stroked the soft fur on his head and ticked off all the things she had to do in the morning. Interview the friends and schoolmates. Go back to the scene. Talk with the Petersons again. Find Missy Klein.

"He was just a kid, Blue. Who would kill a kid?"

The dog lifted his head, sighed, and settled again on her lap. As he closed his eyes, she thought about the day he had come into their lives.

Seven years ago, her third miscarriage turned into an emergency when the bleeding wouldn't stop. The doctors took her womb to save her life. She'd felt gutted, emptied of all life when they told her she'd lost the baby and her ability to have one. In her black hole, she closed the door to Will and everyone else. If they asked how she was, she said, "Fine. I'm fine."

Once home from the hospital, she lay in bed with the shades pulled. She told Will she was having cramps and that was why she didn't want to get up. The darkened bedroom was her safe place. She could wrap herself in the sheets and blankets and mourn the loss of the baby—far enough along to know it was a boy. She stayed like that for three days. On the fourth day, Will came home at noon and stood over her, his white uniform shirt ironed crisp.

"Okay, I know you want a little Hammergren to keep the family line going."

"What?" Red barely looked at him, her voice groggy with sleep and her hair greasy and tangled.

"Come on." He walked out of the room.

The bedclothes held her in a warm embrace. She turned on her side and closed her eyes.

"Out here," Will called. Then he began talking in a low, cooing voice as if he were rocking a baby.

Red sat up and listened. Will was not a "cooing" kind of a guy.

He continued to talk. "That's a good boy."

She rolled out of bed and stood up. The room spun, and she had to steady herself against the bedpost.

"She's coming." He raised his voice.

In the living room, Will squatted on the old oriental area rug, petting something. He continued to talk in a gentle, soothing voice.

She walked over and squinted down at him.

"Is that a rat?"

"Nope. I got myself a dog to replace the wife. She walked into the bedroom one day and never came out."

Red knelt beside him and pulled a finger across the soft, fluffy puppy hair. The dog looked up at her with round brown eyes and licked her finger. His little tongue felt like a fine-grade sandpaper. She stared at the creature for a while and finally said, "I don't think he'll iron your shirts like the wife does."

Three days later, she put on her deputy uniform and went back to work.

Blue's soft snoring lulled her aching body. She fought the heaviness that tugged at her eyelids, but sleep overtook her. The dream was filled with the shadows of great evergreen trees. Moss hung from the branches like thick spider webs. She was looking for Will's grave, but she couldn't see through the trees and the moss. Her flashlight glowed a sickly yellow, and when she banged it against the tree, it went out.

Will, where are you? Her voice was a mere croak. He emerged from the shadows a skeleton with Will's eyes. She drew back. No, she tried to say. No,

I don't want you like that. Her throat was dry, like someone had filled it with dust. As she backed away, she started to cough, and the coughing woke her up to Blue licking at her nose.

She pushed herself up in the recliner and slid the dog off her lap.

"Whoa," she said to him. "That was a bad one." The dreams where she searched for Will had faded over the two years, but the death of Jared Peterson must have conjured them up again.

She fought the dream by closing her eyes and picturing the healthy Will she'd married ten years ago. He was twenty years her senior, long divorced, tall and slightly awkward. In contrast to Red's mane of tangled hair, Will was nearly bald and kept his hair cut as if he were still in the military. He had light blue Nordic eyes similar in color to hers.

"Our eyes are the only thing about us that match," he once said.

"How about our big feet," she countered, pointing to his size fourteen shoes.

When she first started working as a dispatcher in the sheriff's office, she hadn't particularly liked Will. He struck her as officious and standoffish. But she needed the job to help pay for her mother's care. Later, over many interactions, she learned that underneath the officiousness was a smart man with a wry sense of humor who scored high on the introvert scale of the Myers-Briggs.

Will was the one that suggested she go to peace officer's training. She remembered her initial response to him. "I'm a lousy shot, and I hate guns."

"You don't need to shoot. I'll shoot for you. I need someone who can read people—that's what you're good at."

The memory of that conversation brought a smile. She knew he was lying about the "read people" part. He'd simply discovered that she knew how to build a spreadsheet. He didn't need a deputy as much as an office assistant.

She took his advice, got the schooling, and came back to the Pearsal County Sheriff's Department as a new deputy. The romance grew in fits and starts, beginning with a few beers at Cuttery's Bar to discuss cases. When they realized that they wanted more than casual conversation at a bar, she offered to resign.

"The commissioners shouldn't put up with you dallying with one of your employees."

Will's response was so quick, she had him repeat it. "Did you say marriage?"

After they married, the county was in such a tight spot for deputies that the commissioners decided to make an exception to the rule about hiring relatives.

As Will explained, "I didn't hire my wife. She was already an employee."

No one complained until Will died and Mitch Rafferty tried to make it an issue in the election.

Red brushed off thoughts of Mitch Rafferty and his campaign to unseat her as sheriff. She would have to deal with that issue in three years. Meanwhile, she really needed to sleep.

In the bedroom, she slipped into bed without brushing her teeth. Blue burrowed under the covers and snuggled close to her like a kid's teddy bear. As her eyelids drooped, she wondered what the Beldon and Mitch Raffertys of the world would think if they knew their sheriff slept with a smelly little fur ball.

She awoke in the predawn darkness. Green digits from the clock glowed 6:30. Blue wiggled on the floor beside her, his toenails clicking on the hardwood floor.

"Okay." Red stretched and eased herself out of bed. She let him out the patio door where he took mincing steps to the end of the shoveled area. Instead of lifting his leg to pee, he squatted. The big thermometer nailed to the tree beyond her patio registered ten above zero.

"Oh, such a macho dog." Red stood at the door watching in dismay as large flakes of snow sifted down from the sky. She'd better get back to the Henderson cabin before everything was covered up.

A hot shower succeeded in waking her up but did not help wash away the ominous feel of last night and the dream about Will. She once confessed to Georgia that the dreams not only filled her with dread but also with guilt.

"In the dream, I want to find him, and yet I'm afraid because I don't want him to come back as he was when he died. I can't go through it again."

Georgia, who was also a widow, assured her, "It's what grief is all about."

Red pulled a comb through her tangle of dark hair and stepped into a pair of thick corduroy pants. Because she was tall and had a sturdy build, she often shopped in the men's department, especially for winter clothes.

"I like big girls," Will had said early in their courtship, "because big girls don't cry." She'd whacked him on the shoulder when he started singing the Four Seasons' song in falsetto.

Red smiled at the thought and laced up her size ten boots. Blue looked at her as she stood at the door with an expression that said, "You're leaving me again?" She made a mental note to ask her neighbor to come over later and let the dog out.

"Sorry, pup. I have a missing teenager to find, and I desperately need some coffee."

Blue turned and walked into the living room.

"Good dog," she said as she closed the door behind her. At least something in her life was predictable.

13

SHERIFF RED

FOOTPRINTS IN THE SNOW

The streets of Lykkins Lake were empty of the usual Saturday morning activity. When Red opened the door to the Town Talk Café, Scotty looked up from the paper. "At last, a customer."

"People will drive miles in a snowstorm to avoid your coffee. They're probably out on Highway 63 right now hightailing it to Brainerd for a decent latte."

"Ha! Imagine the waste—driving all that way for a five-dollar coffee that's more milk than caffeine. What is this country coming to?" Scotty folded the newspaper and stood up. "Missed a great poker game last night."

Red slid into the booth by the kitchen while Scotty poured her a steaming cup of weak brown coffee.

"Sorry. I got caught up in sheriff's business."

"So I hear. Another meth lab gone awry?"

Red grimaced, sipping the coffee. "God, Scotty, this coffee is worse than usual. Been cleaning the coffee urn with Drano lately?"

"All the better to keep our sheriff from getting dependent on it. Coffee's bad for your blood pressure, your stomach, and your teeth. Besides, I don't use Drano anymore. It's an environmental hazard."

"I wish the meth cookers felt the same way."

Scotty scrambled eggs with broccoli and spinach and set the plate in front of Red.

The door to the café opened with the jingling of bells. Two men walked in, speaking Spanish.

Scotty called out, "You want the usual?"

"*Por favor.*" The men sat down in a booth near the window, talking in low Spanish.

Five minutes later, Georgia and Lou arrived, sliding across from Red. Georgia, a retired nurse, used to be the Commissioner of Health for the state. She understood the complexities of being county sheriff because of her years in executive levels in state government. "It's all a balancing act, Red," she'd once told her. "You balance what you need to do with the politics and hope you come out doing the right thing."

Georgia retired the year the anti-abortion conservatives took over the legislature and passed a law that the Department of Health needed to inform women who were considering abortion that it could cause breast cancer. "That's when things went out of balance for me. I told the governor my department wouldn't comply with a law that would force us to lie. He fired me."

Red picked at her eggs. When she was sure that Scotty wasn't looking, she grabbed the saltshaker and tried to introduce some taste to her breakfast.

"I hear a high school boy died in that fire." Georgia pushed up her glasses. The hearing aid in her left ear was barely visible behind her chin-length silver-gray hairstyle. Georgia had an air of sophistication even when chewing on a charred piece of toast.

"But Missy wasn't with him," Lou added.

Red grimaced. "It's amazing how word gets around this town."

Lou smiled. "We're here to serve."

"Are we talking meth with the Henderson cabin?" Georgia took another bite of her toast, dabbing a small crumb off her chin.

Red added more salt to her eggs, then sprinkled on some pepper. "I don't know. I'm going back as soon as I finish my eggs to see what I can find. Since we cleaned up the lab at the trailer court, meth hasn't been much of a problem here."

"I hear the drugs are coming in from Canada now." Scotty stood over Red, pointing to the saltshaker. "By the way, that can be a lethal weapon, you know."

Before Red could reply, the bell over the door jingled, and a gust of fine snow swept in. Horace Winstead and Lester Thomas, two of the county commissioners, settled into a booth on the other side of the café.

"I hope they keep their mouths shut," Scotty muttered. Horace and Lester were known to talk loudly about the "illegals" taking all the jobs in town whenever the Vincente brothers were in the restaurant. Lester thought his commissioner position gave him permission to express his opinions wherever he felt like it.

Red raised her eyebrows at Lou and Georgia. "Keep Scotty under control. It's against the law to hit a customer over the head with a frying pan—even if he deserves it. My jail is packed with druggies, crazies, and drunks. There's no room at the inn. The last thing I want is Scotty using up what little space I have."

Georgia picked up her coffee cup. "We'll keep an eye on her, dear. And if she has to whack those boys around a bit for insulting her clientele, we'll testify in her favor."

Politically, Red should have greeted her commissioners. They were the ones who held the purse strings for her department. They were the ones who would grill her next week about budget overruns. But, today, as she thought about the dead boy and the missing girl, she simply didn't have the heart to make small talk.

Julio and Tomás Vincente nodded at her. Last summer, they'd re-shingled her house. They were two of the hardest working guys in town.

Red leaned closer to Georgia and Lou. "Do you know of anyone in town they call Coke or Cole?"

Lou wrinkled her eyebrows. "Doesn't sound familiar, but let me think about it."

Scotty walked over and began clearing plates. "What are you guys doing? Conspiring without me?"

"Red's looking for someone named Coke." Georgia handed her plate to Scotty. "Ring a bell?"

An elderly couple walked in as the bells over the door rang. Scotty laughed and said, "No, but it looks like someone rang my bell. Gotta go."

Red stood up, nodding at the Vincentes before leaving.

Find Coke. Find her.

Snowflakes wafted from the sky as Red drove to the Henderson cabin. Right now, the roads were clear, but she worried that if the snow continued, travel would become difficult.

At the cabin, Red stood outside with her hands on her hips. When she closed her eyes, she saw the boy in her arms, mumbling and flailing. The lightly falling snow created a gauzy gray curtain. By the feel of the snow beneath her boots, she estimated that the temperature had risen another ten degrees.

With the warming temperatures and an ache in Red's jaw, she suspected a low-pressure system with plenty of snow was moving in. She guessed they would have six to ten more inches on the ground before the skies cleared. Enough to wipe out any footprints.

Charred debris and soot from the fire stained the snow and invaded the pristine woods that surrounded the cabin. The wreckage was bathed in a layer of ice from the fire hoses. Red took sliding steps as close to the entrance of the cabin as she dared. Little remained from the intense heat. A piece of blackened metal from the wood stove, congealed lumps of unknown origin, the cast iron sink.

She studied the wreckage, looking for signs of a body, hoping she would find none. The fire had consumed nearly everything and left nothing behind that could tell her whether this had been a lab and whether someone else had perished in the fire.

With her phone, she snapped photos of the interior and the exterior before she slid her way to the back of the cabin and to the path to the outhouse. She saw where she had pulled Jared off the path. The bloodstains in the snow were barely visible because of the trampling by the firefighters and paramedics. She took more photos of the area, feeling a sense of rage at whoever had clubbed the boy. The viciousness of the blow said that if Missy had been part of this and was still alive, they would not spare her. An involuntary shiver ran up Red's back.

The little wooden outhouse stood intact, far enough away from the fire to survive with a little scorching on the door. It tipped slightly to the right, caving over the years into the soft forest floor.

Had anyone checked the outhouse last night? She winced at herself for not doing her due diligence once the fire had been tamed. The boy had been headed in that direction. Did he think someone was in the outhouse, or was he simply fleeing the fire?

Red walked to the door. A large crow landed on the rotting roof of the building and cawed. A second one joined him. It was as if she had invaded their territory and they were warning her off. When she pulled on the wooden handle, nothing happened. The door was either wedged or locked shut.

"Is anyone there?"

Red pulled harder on the door.

"It's the sheriff. Is anyone inside?"

The crows cawed again.

Red braced her back leg and wrenched hard at the door. The top part of the door gave, but the bottom was stuck in the snow. Kicking at the sill with the heel of her boot, she chipped away the icy snow. The door rattled in her hand and finally let go, flying open and sending Red scuttling back, flailing her arms to keep from falling.

Inside, the one-seater was empty. The only movement was the rippling of a piece of toilet paper frozen onto the edge of the seat. Red stepped inside and pulled out the flashlight from her pocket. With a grimace, she clicked it on and peered into the hole. Six feet below, in the icy lumps of urine-stained sewage and toilet paper, was a pile of cans and plastic bottles. A stench of waste rose from the pit. Red held her breath and continued to peer into the pit.

Out of the corner of her eye, she saw a bright pink piece of cloth. It was stuck on a nail protruding from the inside of the door. Red pulled off her mitten and gingerly held the fabric between her thumb and forefinger. It appeared to be the shiny outer fabric of a down jacket. She dropped it into a plastic bag and stuffed it in her parka pocket.

Outside, the falling snow formed a light gray veil. Red walked back toward the cabin before she took a deep breath. The air smelled like charred wood, not the telltale ammonia odor of a meth lab.

Had the boy dumped the meth ingredients down the outhouse? Was that why she'd found him in back?

Something about the scene was all wrong, but she couldn't put it together. The falling snow landed on her shoulders, building up quickly. If she didn't check out the perimeter of the cabin within the next half hour, it would be covered in an inch of new snow.

Reluctantly, she went back to the outhouse. She'd have to call the environmental health boys to get some samples to see if the site was contaminated. Damn. This stuff could do terrible things to the groundwater and to the lake water. Who knew what other chemicals were down there and what had been scorched into the earth with the fire?

For a second, the budget spreadsheet ran through her head. Another unanticipated expense. Before he died, Will had extracted a promise from her to run for sheriff in his place. "Red, you are the best person for the job."

"Really?" she'd said with raised eyebrows. "Why?"

"Because you know how to use an Excel spreadsheet. Could you imagine anyone else on my crew that can create formulas?"

If her boot hadn't caught on a downed tree branch, she might have missed the tracks. As she stumbled and righted herself, she saw the small indentations in the snow. They appeared to lead away from the outhouse, northwest toward Hammer Lake. From the distance between the tracks, it looked like the person was leaping, perhaps like a deer. Or maybe she was reading more into the tracks. They could have been a deer, the hoof marks obscured by the new snow.

Red followed them, feeling like an ungainly animal lumbering through the unspoiled quiet of the snowy woods. After ten yards, sweat from the effort soaked into her Gore-Tex underwear, and she panted like a bear.

"Not in the best shape, are we?" she gasped.

The woods and underbrush behind the outhouse were blurred from the falling snow. The little prints were quickly filling in, and the wind was picking up. Red stopped, peered into the grayness, and took a deep breath. She needed snowshoes to follow these tracks, and she knew that by the time she picked those up and returned, the tracks would be buried. At least she knew they led toward Hammer Lake. Reluctantly, she turned back.

14

SHERIFF RED

WALT LAFRANCE

By the time Red reached her car, the snow was coming down hard and fast. She took the township road to the highway, noting that it was already becoming slippery with the newly fallen snow. Red stopped at the highway, praying the snow would let up before her office was flooded with calls about cars in the ditch and stranded snowmobilers. She was about to pull onto the highway when a black Escalade hauling a trailer with two snow-mobiles on it zoomed by, going far too fast for the conditions.

"Give him five minutes and he'll be in the ditch," Red muttered. The Forester's wheels grappled with the ice beneath the blowing snow. Red was glad she'd bought the four-wheel-drive vehicle despite the protests from her commissioners. It was economical, handled well, had space, and most of all, the seats heated up in the winter.

"Did you buy another one of them foreign-made cars? What is it, Japanese? My dad didn't fight overseas to have 'em steal our jobs," Lester Thomas had barked at her when he saw the car in the courthouse lot last summer. Was he rude to everyone? If so, who voted for him? Of course, she knew the answer to that. Lester came from a big family, long established in Pearsal County. He was related to almost everyone in his commissioner district.

"Gee, Lester," Red had replied. "Speaking of stealing jobs and ruining the local business, isn't that a Wal-Mart bag you're carrying? Been shopping in Brainerd? Ginny Blake told me they closed their store here on Main Street because everyone was driving to Wal-Mart."

Lester had mumbled something about prices and slunk away. Dealing with some of the dumbass commissioners was one of the biggest pains of her job. Fortunately, Pearsal County had elected its first female commissioner in history. Ginny Blake, despite the store closing, was smart, tough, and managed money well. She didn't care that Red drove a Subaru as long as she got the job done.

Last fall, after Ginny was elected, Scotty had overheard some of the ole boys who rolled dice and drank coffee at her back table grousing. "Damn women taking over the county. Them and those illegals are ruining the country." Yup, definitely more than a hint of red state here in Pearsal County.

It was amazing how quickly the weather changed from a gentle snow to pouring out of the sky, like the weather goddess had just dumped a whole bucket on Pearsal County. The wind whipped it around, reducing visibility to a few yards. Red slowed to twenty miles an hour, tension building in her shoulders. She needed to get back and meet with Jack Klein before talking with the high school kids about Missy and Jared Peterson, and it was getting harder and harder to tell where the pavement ended.

If Missy Klein was out in the woods somewhere, could she have survived the frigid night? And if so, would she be walking in circles now, lost in the storm? Snowstorms were known to disorient even the most expert outdoorsmen. With the wind picking up, the wind chill would be dropping below zero.

She cursed the dizzying snow and concentrated on staying on the road. At least most people in Pearsal County had the good sense to stay home on days like this.

Most people—but not all.

Down the road, Red passed the blinking red taillights of a snowmobile trailer tipped in the ditch. She slowed, the anti-lock brakes controlling a skid. The Subaru stopped well beyond the flashing lights. She inched the car as far onto the narrow shoulder as she dared.

When she stepped outside, the first thing she noticed was the sting of the icy snow against her cheeks. The texture had changed from loose, fluffy flakes to a fine icy pellet. The snow would not be letting up anytime soon.

The SUV had skidded and plunged nose-down into the ditch with the trailer poking out onto the shoulder. The wheels of the Escalade churned, digging further into the ditch as the driver gunned it trying to back out. The trailer jiggled with the movement but didn't budge.

People who handled their vehicles like this in the snow were either inexperienced drivers or drunk. Red walked over to the driver's side, hoping this person was just stupid and not stupid and drunk. It was too early in the day to deal with someone who had been drinking all night.

She tapped on the window with her flashlight. "Hey. Stop. You aren't going anywhere." At least not without a tow truck.

The window whined as it slid into the door panel. A man with a cell phone in his hand looked at her. His mouth was set in a thin line. He appeared to be in his late thirties or early forties and wore a North Face down jacket that still smelled of the store. His hair was carefully cut to hide the balding patch on the back of his head, and his teeth were brilliantly white against the tan of his face.

"Need some help?"

"I'm fine." His smile had a Hollywood dazzle to it.

Red shook her head. "Your front end is sunk up to the bumper. You're going to break the trailer hitch at this rate, and you have a good chance of dying from carbon monoxide if you don't dig that tailpipe out. You're not going anywhere without a tow." She paused. "Unless you want to wait for spring to come."

The man frowned. "They told me this would get me through anything. It's four-wheel drive."

He was clearly not a local. Anyone with experience in the snow and ice knew that the big, high-riding SUVs had no handling ability on ice. And because they were so far off the ground, any kind of crosswind would whip under the chassis and throw them off. Add a trailer with two snowmobiles, and this was a disaster in the making. These SUVs were vehicles for the suburban dreamers who thought that someday they'd drive to the top of a mesa and view the Grand Canyon just like the ads said—not for careening through the ice and snow.

The driver with his perfect hair and teeth had a familiar look, but she couldn't put her finger on why. The words *Entertainment Tonight* came to mind.

"I'll call 911 and get some help." He flashed her another smile and held up his cell phone. "No problem."

The wind whipped through Red's jacket, and she shivered in irritation. She needed to find Missy Klein, not deal with this urban warrior. If she didn't get back on the road soon, she'd be stuck with him until the plows could get out.

She shook her head. "You won't get a phone signal out here, and I'm the 911 you'd call."

"What?"

Red fumbled for her identification and showed him her badge. "I'm the sheriff. Could I see your driver's license?" She really didn't want to know who he was, but her training told her to always check. Fortunately, she did not smell alcohol on his breath.

"Walt LaFrance?" She compared the photo on the California license to him.

He nodded.

"I've seen you in something, haven't I?"

"*General Hospital*, maybe."

It was too cold to be having the conversation.

Walt LaFrance was wearing loafers, another indication that he wasn't prepared for winter weather.

She pointed at his shoes. "Got some boots with you?"

"In the back. I'm meeting some friends to go ice fishing and snowmobiling. I've got the boots, the snowmobile suit, and the whole outfit." He grinned at her.

He had dimples, for God's sake.

"Where are you meeting your friends?"

Walt waved vaguely at the passenger side of the car. "Hammer Lake. I'm meeting my friends at a resort."

The only place open on Hammer Lake in the winter was Eddie's Resort. Mac Morris, who owned the place, rented furnished fish houses. Most of them were primitive—a fish hole, a heater, a couple of cots. But he had one deluxe trailer complete with carpeting, a wood stove, and two bedrooms.

"Staying on the lake?"

He nodded again.

A gust of wind blew through her jacket and down her back. "Well, you're headed in the wrong direction, then. Mac's place is north."

"Oh? I was following the GPS."

GPS, Google Maps, and MapQuest were notoriously inaccurate in this part of the country.

"Next time, I suggest you use an old-fashioned map." She handed the license back to Walt. "I'll radio Darcy's. He's got the best tow truck. Meanwhile, I suggest you put those boots on. Don't leave your vehicle, run the engine for ten minutes at a time, and shut it off. Get out and check your tailpipe to make sure it's not covered before you run the engine. Got it?"

Walt smiled, but his brow was wrinkled. "Ah, okay. Any idea how long it will take for the tow?"

She shrugged. "Could be a while. Make sure your tailpipe is uncovered. Carbon monoxide can sneak up on you."

"Um, okay."

"I'll check back with Darcy to make sure he got you out."

Red took one more look inside the SUV. On the floor of the passenger seat was a crumpled plastic Wal-Mart bag. In the North Country, even Hollywood actors shopped at Wal-Mart.

The radio in her car squawked.

"Good luck fishing. And don't drive that snowmobile into the open water on the lake. Okay?" She remembered the grieving mother's words— the lake will suck you in. Hollywood actors from California probably didn't know about the danger of an iced-over lake in a Minnesota winter.

"Thanks." He flashed her his five-star smile once more.

"Be safe," she added as she walked away. What was a California guy like that doing in Minnesota in January? Ice fishing? Somehow it didn't add up, but he was the least of Red's worries as she pulled back onto the slippery highway and headed back to town.

15

SHERIFF RED
MISSY'S LETTER

Red sat at the chipped Formica kitchen table kitty-corner from Jack Klein. He lived in a log home south of town near the river. As she talked with him, she kept an eye on the snowfall outside the warmth of the house. It was not as intense in this part of the county as it was up by Hammer Lake. Still, if the snow kept up, they could get blocked in.

She cupped her hands around the mug of strong Scandinavian coffee and inhaled the deep aroma. Too bad Scotty didn't have Jack's recipe for coffee, maybe she'd have more business.

"It's the eggs," Jack said. "That's the way my father taught me—throw in an egg, shell and all, with the grounds. It keeps 'em settled." His lips twitched into a half smile. "And it gives us a little protein."

Red sipped the coffee and nodded. "Your father knew what he was doing."

"Without fancy espresso machines."

Although Jack Klein had the rugged face of a man who spent as much time in his life as possible outdoors, he appeared frail. His face had a gauntness as if he'd recently lost weight. A fall from the roof of his studio last summer left him walking with a cane. His main business, designing and making wooden patio furniture, had suffered with his injury.

His face also carried the etching of a man worn down by tragedy. Even before his son had been shot to death, his wife had died of breast cancer. Before she got sick, Missy's grandmother, Serena, created artistic quilts. One of them once won a grand-champion ribbon at the state fair and was on display at the Minnesota State Historical Society for several years.

Red took another sip of the coffee, recalling what she knew about Jack's son and Missy's father, Junior. He had worked a variety of summer construction jobs and helped Jack with both his furniture and guiding business. He was known locally as a gifted craftsman with wood.

Red thought about the file on her desk. Will had reviewed the report on Junior's death with her and shrugged. "Hunting accidents in the North Country happen all the time when you have a forest full of amateurs armed with powerful weapons they only fire once a year."

In the four years since Junior's death, multi-round assault rifles had seeped into the county. Red remembered one old hunter say, "Why the hell would you want a weapon that would turn a deer into hamburger?"

Before she ran for sheriff, she became a card-carrying member of the NRA, one of her few concessions to politicking in a small conservative town. She believed in their gun safety programs, but after Sandy Hook and the NRA's insane Second Amendment rights lobbying, she'd dropped her membership. Looking back, she was still ashamed that she'd ever given that organization money. Too many people, including children, had died because of them. This, however, was not something she would share with the general electorate. Gun rights still held a heavy sway on the voting public in Pearsal County.

Outside the kitchen window, snow darkened the skies. "Tell me everything you can think of about Missy. Friends, interests, any changes in behavior recently." Red saw a flash of pain in his worn blue eyes.

He frowned. "That's the hard part. I can't say I know much about Missy. She stopped talking the beginning of this school year." Jack turned his head and stared out the window at the steady cloud of falling snow. "I'm ashamed to say, but it was easier for me, really."

A radiator in the kitchen clanged as the hot water circulated through. The woolen stockings on Red's feet gradually dried in the radiant heat as Jack talked.

"So, everything was pretty normal until fall?"

Jack nodded.

"What happened?"

He sighed, a long, steady outpouring of air. "Mayme, Missy's mother, showed up out of the blue—skinny and worn like a dog with mange."

Jack shifted in his chair, wincing as he moved.

"Missy was born six months after Junior married Mayme. They were both right out of high school. Hell of a way to start your adult life."

He was quiet for a moment, then said, "Junior was smart. His mother and I hoped he'd go to college. He loved putting things together...he would have made a good engineer."

A wind gust rattled the plastic covering the window in the entryway. At this rate, the highway would be drifted in soon. And the little tracks behind the outhouse were probably long gone. At least she'd taken photos.

"But never mind that. Mayme wasn't quite right in the head, and it was clear after they married that Junior was going to have to take care of the little girl."

"What do you mean, 'not quite right in the head'?"

"Well, I'm no psychiatrist or what have you, but that woman was crazy. Heard voices some of the time, crept into weeks of dark silence. Junior brought the little girl over whenever Mayme went off the deep end."

"Was she ever diagnosed?"

Jack smiled without humor. "What kind of diagnosis was she going to get around here? First, we don't have anyone to do it, and second, even if we had someone, Junior worked temp for the highway department and didn't have insurance or money for it." He shook his head. "No, she sank deeper and deeper, and we stood around and watched."

Red nodded, thinking about her brother, Lad. How many times did the same story play out? Sadly, she or her deputies were the safety net for mental health problems. Look at her jail. At least sixty percent of those poor souls had some kind of mental illness or chemical dependency. Georgia said many of them used the drugs to numb the pain from the mental illness and quiet the voices in their heads.

Jack stood up, limped over to the stove, and picked up the battered coffeepot. "Warm you up?"

Red lifted her mug to him.

Jack poured the coffee and remained standing, leaning against his clean and polished countertop. "Two days after Junior's funeral, Mayme trucked Missy over here and asked if I would watch her for a few days. She emptied the trailer where they lived and disappeared. Gone for almost four years—until this fall."

"When she made the surprise visit?"

Jack didn't answer.

"What happened?"

"She was banging on the back door. Looked like death warmed over. Skin and bones, teeth missing, hair tangled into a nest. Shivering like a wet puppy and she smelled bad—like she'd rolled in something dead. But she was talking nonstop, almost yelling." He looked down at Red. "I thought I was going to have to call you and have her hauled off."

Red nodded. "What did you do?"

"I tried to get her settled before Missy came home from school. Looking back, I'm sure she was on drugs of some kind. Anyway, at least I got her to sit. She kept saying, 'It's time to get them. They gotta pay for what they did.'"

"Rantings of a paranoid?"

"Maybe. I think she was talking about Junior because she rattled on about guns and hunting."

"Then what happened?"

"She was shivering so hard, I went into Missy's room to find a sweater for her. When I came back, she was gone. I stood right here in the empty kitchen and wondered if I'd imagined the whole thing. Except she left an envelope behind with Missy's name on it. The words were scratched in pencil, and they said, 'private and confidential.'"

"Missy got the envelope?"

"And I never asked her what was in it. That's when things changed."

Red took a deep breath and let it out with a little whistle. Her head ached, and she cursed her sluggish brain for not being able to connect any of these dots.

Jack interrupted her thoughts. "A few weeks later, we got word that Mayme was in a hospice house in Minneapolis. Missy visited her once. I didn't. Mayme died right after that. They say it was cancer, but I think she had AIDS. I saw needle marks on her arms."

"Do you think this has anything to do with where Missy might be now? Or with Jared Peterson?"

"Yes." Jack's voice was flat. "I keep thinking about that letter she left for Missy. I should have asked her. I think Mayme put her on to something."

Maybe, Red thought. Or maybe Missy simply got herself mixed up with the local drug scene because she was grieving or because she was doing the teenage rebellion.

"Jack, a couple of years ago, I recall that Missy ran away. Could she have done the same thing again?"

Jack reached across the counter and grabbed a prescription bottle, shaking out two tablets into his hand. He washed them down with the coffee.

"I don't think so." He shook his head slowly. "That was a misunderstanding, and we worked it through."

"Where was she going?"

Jack hobbled over to the table and sat down again with a sigh. "I had a sister in Minneapolis. Missy thought she wanted to live with her."

"Would she go there again?"

"No. My sister died last year...another goddamn loss for Missy."

"She's seen a lot in her sixteen years."

Jack did not reply.

Red thought about Jared's words. "Jack, did Missy ever say anything about someone named Coke or Cole? Maybe a friend or a teacher? Someone she might go to if she was in trouble?"

Jack gazed beyond her and scratched his chin. "I'm sorry. I can't think of anyone. Before she got hooked up with that boy, she was always with those other two girls."

Red set down the coffee mug and stood. "Can I see Missy's room?"

Jack led her through the old house, its floors creaking beneath their footsteps, the wind rattling the windows. She was surprised by the neatness of the small rooms. Sparsely furnished with heavy old oak tables and chairs and thick colorful area rugs. As she passed through the living room, she was struck by the quilt hanging on the wall.

In it, a shimmering fog rose over a small pond. On the opposite side of the pond appeared to be an animal, perhaps a deer. What made this stand out was the contrast of colors. The gray tones and subdued earth tones next to brilliant yellows of the full moon and piercing silvers from the stars in the sky.

Red studied the hanging. Something about it was unsettling. Perhaps because it didn't quite fit a pastoral landscape, perhaps because the animal in the distance seemed so skewed.

"The wife did it. This is the one that won the grand prize."

"It's beautiful." *Beautiful* was the wrong word—*haunting* would have been better. "She was quite an artist."

Jack cleared his throat. "Serena died six months to the day before Junior."

In contrast to the neatness of the living room, Missy's room was cluttered with furniture, stuffed animals, movie posters, discarded clothes, and all the detritus of a teenaged girl.

"Did she have a laptop?"

Jack winced again as he leaned against the doorframe. "She only had the cell phone. I've called it, and it goes right to voicemail."

"The room looks teenage typical," Red commented.

"After she ran away that time, I promised her room was her own space. I don't step inside the door unless invited. And she hasn't invited me much lately."

Red picked through the room. She found an empty prescription bottle with the label peeled off filled with thumb tacks. Otherwise there were no signs of drugs or drug paraphernalia.

"Do you know if Missy kept a journal or a diary?"

"After Mayme died, I took Missy to a grief counselor in Brainerd. She suggested Missy write what she was thinking in a journal. I bought her one with a cloth cover—you know, something nice. It was the best I could do for her." Jack's voice shook.

Red remembered how she'd talked to a counselor after Will died. The counselor had said something similar. "Write him a letter and tell him how you are feeling." She'd even purchased a journal with a leather cover. It was still in its box next to all the estate papers.

Red closed her eyes, trying to imagine where Missy would have kept a journal. It wasn't on her little bedside table or the bookshelf.

"Do you know if Missy might have had a hiding place?"

Jack shrugged. "I kept out of her room."

Red checked under the bed and even lifted the mattress to see if she'd kept it there—assuming it existed. She thought about the teenager alone in her room with a blank book. If she'd written in it, where would she put it? A safe place.

After going through the small closet and the chest of drawers, she asked, "Jack, did Missy ever spend time in another place? Like another room?"

He frowned, massaging the back of his head. "You know, sometimes when it got really quiet in the house and I wondered where she was, I'd find her in her grandmother's sewing room. I never go in there—too many memories."

He led her to a small room off the living room. It was filled with neat stacks of fabric and several sewing machines. Red studied the room. It had a small writing desk in the corner. Unlike the rest of the room where every horizontal space was covered with sewing materials, the top of the desk was empty except for a glass jar holding pens and pencils.

"Serena used to do her books in here. Kept a ledger in the drawer and told me to 'mind my own business' when I asked to see it." Jack chuckled. "She made a fair piece of money on her quilts."

Red pulled the drawer open. A newspaper with Junior Klein's obituary was tucked in the drawer. Underneath was a blue cloth notebook.

She showed it to Jack. "Is this what you bought her?"

Jack nodded with a grave expression.

Opening the book, she read a letter dated last fall. It was written in a careful cursive:

Dear Mom:

I can't forgive you for leaving me and then coming back at the end. I try and I know you were sick in the head all those years. But it makes me mad that at the very end you said Dad got shot because he was trying to stop you from getting drugs. But you didn't tell me who did it. Now I have to find out myself. But, I'll fix it, just like Dad was always fixing things for you

The letter stopped abruptly as if Missy had been interrupted. Rereading it, Red saw both anger and innocence in the words. Missy was on a mission to avenge her father's killing.

"Jack, did Missy ever say anything to you about Junior's death? Like asking questions or suggesting her father had been murdered?"

Jack blinked, startled by the question. "Not that I recall. As I said, she really stopped talking to me this fall. It was like she was really angry." He paused, tapping his leg. "And I haven't been in the best of shape."

"If Missy was going to go somewhere safe, do you know where she'd go? Or who she'd contact?"

Jack slowly shook his head. "I'll think on that and give you a call if I come up with something."

As they walked to the door, Red remembered the piece of fabric she'd taken from the outhouse. It was still in her pocket. She pulled it out and held the clear plastic bag out for Jack.

"Does this fabric look familiar?"

"That's the same color as her winter jacket." He wrinkled his brow. "Where did you find it?"

"The outhouse of the Henderson cabin."

A pained look crossed Jack's face, but he said nothing.

Outside, two inches of snow covered the top of her car. If Missy was somewhere in the woods by the burned-down cabin, God help her.

16

SHERIFF RED
THE ESTATE CLAIM

Powdered sugar speckled Jason's dark brown corduroys as he finished his second donut. Red watched him swipe away the sugar on his pants and smiled, thinking about Scotty and her campaign to have better nutrition in the community. Someday she would sic her on Jason. But today, she needed to concentrate on Jared Peterson and Missy Klein.

"They're transporting the body today for the autopsy, assuming the roads are passable. I doubt we'll see any results, though, until early next week." She rubbed her temples, hoping the nagging throb in her head didn't turn into a full-blown headache.

"Someone beat him up and clubbed him in the back of the head?"

Red took in a deep breath, picturing the boy in the snow, and let it out slowly. "Looks that way. Dr. Vijay thought the head injury probably contributed to his death. We'll see what the coroner has to say." If he had drugs in his system, it would take several weeks to get the results back.

"Bad news all around." Jason wiped donut crumbs off his face. "Do you think Missy did it and took off?"

Red blinked, wrinkling her brow. "To be honest, it didn't occur to me."

She took out her phone and scrolled to the photo of Missy with her friends. She was smaller than the other two girls. Inwardly, she shook her head. No, the scene was wrong. The tracks in the snow told her Missy had fled—most likely in fear.

Red handed Jason a list of names. "Jared's parents gave me this list of friends. I'd like you to check them out. We're looking for who might have been in that cabin yesterday, who he was hanging around with, and whether he was connected with any drug dealing."

"Got it." Jason studied the list. "These aren't the kids who usually cause trouble."

"I know. I think Jared had been fooling his folks for quite some time. I don't think they really knew who he'd been around other than Missy Klein."

Jason brushed the crumbs off his lap. "Missy Klein. She and Jared seem like an odd match. My little sister is in her grade. I remember that she and Missy had some kind of school project together a couple of years ago. Missy did the posters for it—very artistically done for a kid. I'll ask if she knows anything."

When Jason stood up, a light snowfall of powdered sugar dusted the floor. Red wanted to say, "Don't let Scotty see you like that," but she refrained. She might be her deputy's boss, but she wasn't his mother.

"Good luck checking out Jared's friends. I'm going to have a chat with Trevor Farnsworth. Even though his mother claims he's been clean for five months, I'm guessing he still knows the scene."

After he left, Red sat quietly at her desk for a few moments, trying to clear her head. Too many missing parts. Too many things happening.

Cal, the dispatcher, walked in carrying a cream-colored envelope. "This came for you, Sheriff. Registered and everything." He dropped the letter on her desk and walked out. Cal was not one for small talk.

It was from a law firm in Minneapolis. Red recognized the name, Raymond and Raymond. The return address indicated that their offices were in a marginal part of downtown filled with empty storefronts. Expensive stationery but cheap rent, she surmised. They advertised during the local nightly news—twin pitchmen in polo shirts and khakis.

Letters from lawyers did not usually intimidate her. As sheriff of Pearsal County, she had a pile in her inbox. Mostly she turned them over to the county attorney. This one was different, though. It was addressed to Mrs. Will Hammergren. This was personal.

"Dear Mrs. Hammergren," it began. "This is to notify you of our claim on the estate of your late husband, Will Hammergren."

"What? Who else would have a claim on Will's property?" She stared at the words. "Damn it! I don't need this on top of everything else. Especially not from a sleazy city law firm."

After reading it, she put the letter back in its expensive envelope and stuck it in her pocket. She didn't want it to be lying around for prying eyes —like young Billie, the night dispatcher. She suspected that on quiet shifts he did a lot of snooping in her office. That was why she kept the key to the filing cabinet on her key ring.

In the parking lot, Red brushed off the snow that had accumulated on her car since returning from talking with Jack Klein. If the snow kept up at this rate, they'd have a foot or more by the end of the day. When she was in high school, a snowfall like this was exciting. Maybe the school would close. Maybe she could stay home and read by the warmth of the electric heater in the living room. Now it only meant more work for her staff. Fortunately, Nate, her second deputy, was back from his vacation in Mexico. Unfortunately, he was battling a case of "turista." He thought he'd be able to patrol tonight, but he was iffy. Jason might have to do a double. Or worse, she might have to spend the night patrolling.

One of the aspects of her job she disliked the most was staffing. As she scraped the snow that had frozen onto her windshield, she thought about those months after Will died when she'd put in sixteen-to-twenty-hour days just to keep the department running. When the commissioners appointed her the acting sheriff instead of Mitch Rafferty and he'd abruptly quit, she'd been left with a gaping hole. Her first thought when he had thrown his resignation on her desk was, *Good riddance.* Her second was, *Now what do I do?*

Behind her, Ed shouted, "Cold enough for you?" He was shoveling the steps to the courthouse even though the building was closed for the weekend.

"I'm afraid it's going to get colder," she called to him.

He nodded and turned back to his shoveling. Despite not getting paid to work the weekend, Ed was there whenever a flake of snow dropped. Red smiled as she slid into the car. Talk about a work ethic.

17

SHERIFF RED

TREVOR

The sidewalk to the Farnsworth house hadn't been shoveled since the last snowfall. Icy footprints in the old snow were filling in with bright white powder. The outside of the house itself looked tired—peeling paint, a sagging eave in front, and a sparse string of Christmas lights that hadn't been taken down.

Red knocked on the door several times before Wendy answered. Her hair was a disheveled tangle that needed a good shampoo. She was still in her bathrobe even though it was close to noon.

She blinked the bleariness out of her eyes. "Is something wrong?"

"Could I come in?"

"Is Dad okay? They said he was fine when I called the hospital." Wendy's voice rose.

Red smiled and reassured her. "He's fine as far as I know."

As Red walked by Wendy, she noted the odor of stale cigarette smoke. A walker and a commode sat in the corner of the living room by a worn recliner. The coffee table in front of the sofa was piled with magazines and advertising circulars as well as empty dishes.

Red unzipped her parka but stood in the entryway. The disarray in the living room reminded her of how the mess had accumulated in her living room during Will's illness.

"Sorry, I haven't picked up this morning," Wendy said in a soft voice as she sat down heavily on the sofa. Hugging her robe together, she said, "The hospital said they have to discharge Dad. Medicare rules and stuff."

Red sat on the edge of an easy chair that was missing its cushion. "Wendy, you and your husband need to talk with the hospital social worker. Albert should be in the memory care unit at the nursing home."

The bass rhythm of hip-hop music thumped upstairs. Wendy looked up at the ceiling for a moment and then at Red. She had tears in her eyes. "I promised Dad I would never put him in a nursing home."

Red nodded sympathetically. "I know. I made the same promise to my mother. But I couldn't take care of her anymore." She looked at Wendy. "The truth is, Mom did much better in the home. By then she didn't know me and thought I was her sister. Talk with the social worker. You know the staff at the home will be good to him."

Upstairs the beat grew louder. Red pointed to the sound. "Actually, I'm here to talk with Trevor if you don't mind."

Wendy hesitated. "He hasn't done anything."

"I know." Red folded her hands. "He's not in trouble. I just have a few questions for him."

"He's clean," she repeated.

Red stood up. "I'll just go up and see him for a few minutes."

Wendy pushed herself off the sofa so fast that a stack of magazines on the coffee table tipped over onto the floor. "I'll go get him." She wasn't able to disguise the wariness in her voice. Wendy did not want her son alone with Red.

As Wendy hurried up the stairs, Red slipped out of her parka and laid it over the back of the easy chair. She assessed from the state of the living room that Wendy was exhausted and probably depressed. She also wondered if she was drinking to ease the pain of her situation. She hoped the hospital would help her get Albert placed before something bad happened.

After a few minutes, Trevor lumbered down the steps looking even more disheveled than Wendy. He wore a pair of gray jogging pants and a dark blue hoodie. Red guessed that if she got close enough to him, she'd smell the odor of an unwashed teenaged boy.

"Hi, Trevor," she said.

Trevor stood by his mother, round-shouldered with his lower lip pursed out. "I'm clean."

Red nodded. "Can we sit down and talk for a minute?"

Trevor gave Wendy an uncertain glance. She nodded. With a soft grunt, he slumped down onto the sofa. Wendy positioned herself next to him.

"I'm wondering if you can tell me anything about Jared Peterson. I understand you are friends."

Trevor stared at his bare feet. His toenails needed clipping. "Haven't seen him."

"But you are friends."

Wendy interrupted. "Trevor hasn't associated with anyone from school since he was suspended. He's been home with me."

Early last fall, Trevor had been caught by the vice principal selling joints to a couple of junior high boys. This was the third time he'd been caught, and the school suspended him for the semester and the court put him on probation.

"Do you know who he hangs with?"

Trevor continued to stare at his feet. He shook his head.

"He doesn't know anything," Wendy insisted.

Even with her parka off, Red was getting overheated. The room with its papers and dirty dishes and the odor of cigarettes and grease tried her patience.

Find Coke. Find her.

"Do you know anyone they call Coke?"

Trevor stiffened but said nothing. Red leaned toward him, suddenly tired of the mopey adolescent and the protective mother. "Listen, I know you were dealing, and I know Jared's been dealing. I need to know the source." She peered at Trevor with such intensity that he drew back.

"I don't know anything." His eyes darted back and forth between Red and his mother, like a caged animal.

"Back when you were caught, you said you got your stuff from a guy in Duluth. You were covering for someone else, weren't you?"

Trevor's eyes widened, and his voice rose. "I don't know anything."

Red noted that his hands shook as he picked at something on his jogging pants. His response told her that someone local had been supplying him and that whoever it was had instilled fear in the boy.

"Trevor, Jared died last night. It's important that we know who he associated with."

Trevor's jaw dropped, and the fear in his eyes was almost palpable.

Wendy gasped. "What? What happened?"

"We don't know yet."

"Was it drugs? Did he overdose?" Her voice was so intense that Trevor moved away from her. Her eyes bored into Trevor. "That's so stupid!"

Red ignored her and directed her question to Trevor. "Does the Henderson cabin mean anything to you?"

He wouldn't meet her gaze. Instead, he dropped his head in a gesture of defeat and stared at his lap. In a bare whisper, he said, "Sometimes we'd go there, you know, to smoke and stuff."

"And?" Red prompted him.

"Nothing. I haven't been there since before…"

"Before?"

Trevor let out an irritated grunt. "Before I got kicked out of school. Okay?"

Wendy reached over and patted him on his leg. "It's okay, honey."

Trevor pushed her hand away. His expression was a combination of adolescent anger, irritation, and fear. He said no more.

The silence in the room was broken only by the hum of the refrigerator. Red asked a few more questions and received vague answers. The defiant-teen look had been wiped from his face, and Trevor had the expression of a scared little boy.

"Okay then." Red stood up and pulled on her parka. On her way out the door, she said to Wendy, "Trevor's been involved with some very dangerous people. If he says anything to you, please give me a call."

She knew she wouldn't hear from Wendy, but she wanted to leave the door open.

In the half hour she'd been at the house, another inch of snow had accumulated on the car. The wind was picking up, and it wouldn't be long before they would have whiteout conditions.

If Missy was out there somewhere, Red prayed she had found shelter.

Red stopped at home to let Blue out. The dog wiggled in excitement, his nails scrabbling on the tiled floor of the kitchen when she walked in. It reminded her that she needed to get him to the groomer. He was long over-due. Another thing she had neglected.

"It's nice that someone is glad to see me." She picked him up, stroked his chin, and brought him to the door. "Out you go."

Blue took tender steps outside into the fresh snow. "Next thing you know, you'll be asking me to buy you winter boots," she called after him. She watched him, glad that most of Pearsal County didn't know she had such a wimp for a dog. Sheriffs were supposed to have big German shepherds.

While she waited for Blue, she took out her cell phone and called Cam Sunderman, sheriff of Green Lake County. Last year, his county had three deaths from a tainted synthetic fentanyl. They'd eventually found the source to be an underground mail-order website. Maybe he could tell her more about the drugs in Pearsal County.

"Red Hammergren, what a surprise." Cam's voice boomed over the tinny cell line. "How's the weather?"

Cam had a reputation for being easy-going, straitlaced, and thorough. Red had worked with him a couple of years ago when they tried to get a joint two-county grant to hire a shared deputy. Red dropped the effort when Will died and she became buried in too much of the day-to-day activity. She was still a little embarrassed that she had left Cam in the lurch on the project.

"Weather is terrible and getting worse here. And yours?"

"Same. We'll probably pull the plows in an hour or so." He waited a few moments. "So, I'm guessing you didn't call to talk about the weather. What can I do for you?"

"I've got a dead teenager who was mixed up in drug dealing. But I can't get a handle on it—where the drugs are coming from and who is involved. Have you heard anything about Pearsal County?"

Outside, Blue scratched at the door. She let him in, and a blast of the wintry air sent a chill up her neck.

"There's been talk..."

Red waited.

"But nothing that I can confirm. One of my CIs said something about high school kids in Lykkins Lake."

And you didn't share this? Red stayed silent.

"However, he's about as credible as the sponge in my kitchen sink."

They talked a little longer, but Cam had nothing more to share. "Good luck with the weather," she said before she hung up.

"You too. By the way, you sure do look good in that cowboy hat and buckskin skirt."

Red groaned. "You saw it? Is that all you guys do in Green Lake—surf the web?"

"No crime here. It's either watch cartoons or check out social media. You must have had a helluva designer."

"That's the quality website you get with your three-figure contract. Please tell me you can't get to it anymore."

"You're in luck. It's gone..." He laughed. "But not forgotten. By the way, you owe me a beer."

Cam was divorced and a couple of years younger than Red. For a moment, she weighed the thought of seeing more of him. Blue looked up at her with searching eyes. She felt a moment of guilt. No. This was not the time.

"Can we wait until after the blizzard?" Red chuckled and patted Blue on the head.

"Okay, but I never forgive a debt."

"Right." Maybe someday...

After she hung up, she poured nuggets into Blue's dish. "Have a nice lunch, old pup. I have work to do."

Before putting her parka back on, she pulled out the letter from the lawyers. She really needed to sit down with it and study it more carefully, especially the photocopy of a birth certificate. Instead, she walked it to the second bedroom that doubled as an office and set it on top of all the other papers. Blue trotted in behind her.

"Some other time, Blue. I have people to find and crimes to solve." Blue danced at her feet until she picked him up. "You stay warm now, okay?"

Zipping up her parka, she headed out the door. "Drugs and high school kids," she muttered. "Damn."

18

SHERIFF RED
GEORGIA'S ANTIQUES

Red eased into a chair in the back room of Georgia's Antiques. The wind whipped at the windows of the old building, rattling the frames and pushing icy air through the edges of the thick plastic that covered them. A gas space heater in the corner radiated warm air. Her toes tingled as they sucked up the heat. On the wall above the table was a large tapestry of garish-colored dogs at a poker table. Beneath the tapestry was a neatly printed laminated sign that said, *Rules of the Florence Nightingale Memorial Poker Club:*

- *Must be a nurse to play*
- *If not a nurse, must be a county sheriff*
- *No talk about bowels or other bodily functions allowed during game*
- *No smoking and no spitting*
- *Winner will donate proceeds to the betterment of humankind*

Georgia moved to Lykkins Lake fifteen years ago after a long career in health care. After she was fired by the governor, she worked as a health care consultant. When her husband died, she retired and then decided to run the ramshackle antique store just off Main Street in downtown. Her hours varied depending on whether she felt like opening the store.

"It's a hobby," she once said. "A very expensive hobby."

The back of the store was the gathering place for the poker club. Red's initiation into the club came three years ago after Will was first diagnosed with the lung cancer that took him. Red got to know Lou, the nurse practitioner from the clinic, and eventually she was invited into the group as what they called, "their token outsider."

"We need a fourth because Carol retired from the hospital and moved to Texas," Georgia explained.

"Can you imagine anyone deliberately moving to Texas?" Scotty added.

All three of them had helped Red when Will became so sick. As Scotty once declared, "Absent a real hospice program here in the northern hinterlands, we are it."

Gusts of wind blew through the cracks of the old building. Nothing would be moving in Lykkins Lake for at least the next eight hours.

"So." Georgia set a bowl of chili in front of Red. "What's new since breakfast?" Her jaw was set in an expression that said, "Don't give me any crap."

"Let's see." Red blew on the soup. "I've come up with nothing new on Jared Peterson, Missy Klein is still missing, and an actor with a ridiculously expensive jacket is sitting in a ditch waiting for Darcy to tow him out. On top of that, my headache tells me this snowstorm is working its way into a full-blown blizzard."

As if to emphasize her words, a blast of wind sent a cold draft through the back room, strong enough to ripple the hanging on the wall. Red looked up at the card-playing dogs. "You need better windows and insulation here."

Georgia ignored her comment. "Did you say an actor? What actor?"

"Walt LaFrance. He says he was on *General Hospital*."

"Square jaw, dimples, good teeth?"

"Yup."

"I remember him from when I was stuck on the couch after my knee surgery. I watched that soap faithfully. Good-looking. Probably gay. What's he doing here?"

"Ice fishing."

Georgia rolled her eyes. "Sure. Hollywood people flock to Minnesota in January to ice fish."

Red shrugged. "Maybe he's scouting a location for a film—something like *Frostbite Falls ER*."

Georgia chortled. "Yah sure, you betcha."

Red finished her soup. It was meaty and spicy and definitely not cooked by Scotty.

Georgia nibbled thoughtfully on a soda cracker. "I've heard about a California connection."

"What are you talking about?"

"Meth, heroin, and even prescription opioids."

Red scraped the bottom of her bowl. Last summer, she'd attended a law enforcement seminar talking about the Mexican cartels and their pipelines. One of the ways that drugs got into Minnesota was up the California coast and north into Canada.

"Walt LaFrance isn't our drug mule. For one thing, he was wearing loafers in the middle of a snowstorm in January. For another, his teeth are too white."

Georgia leaned back and chuckled. "I'm just saying..."

They were quiet as a spray of snow pelted the front windows of the store. The wind was moving the snow into drifts that would cripple the roads.

Georgia broke the silence. "How are Jared's parents handling this?"

Red blew on green tea that Georgia brewed with honey and lemon. It felt soothing as it washed the hot chili down. "They're in shock. All the dad could talk about was the snowmobile. And the poor mom kept saying, 'He wasn't doing drugs. I know because I asked.'"

"So, he died of smoke inhalation?"

Normally Red wouldn't reveal that kind of information to the general public. However, she trusted Georgia to keep things confidential.

"We won't know until they do the autopsy, but I think he died of a head injury. Dr. Vijay described it as being 'bashed.'"

Georgia shook her head. "Someone 'bashed' him?"

Red nodded. "When the call came to me, the caller said, 'Someone's inside.' He wasn't alone in that cabin. Someone else was there."

"Could it have been Missy?"

"She might have been in the cabin at one time, but I think whoever hit him was big and strong. Still…"

Find Coke. Find her. Red stopped herself from saying more.

Outside, the city plow rattled by. They would pull the plows in another hour or so if the visibility got worse.

As she thought about the worsening weather and about the possibility of a sixteen-year-old out in it, Red looked at Georgia. "I'm a little puzzled. When I talked with Jack Klein, he didn't seem as distressed as I expected that Missy was missing. I didn't get a sense of urgency. You know, the 'we've got to find her' urgency."

"Do you think he knows something he's not saying?"

Red shrugged. "I don't know. I couldn't read him."

"I've learned, living here amongst the Swedes and Norwegians, that people can be hard to read. Especially the older ones. They were trained in 'understatement.'"

"Maybe." Red wasn't so sure.

They sat in silence for a while. Red reflected on how comfortable she felt in this cluttered back room with its garish tapestry. She wished she felt this relaxed in her own home. Too many memories, maybe.

"I need your wisdom on another matter." Red told her about the letter from the Minneapolis lawyers. "They say someone else has a claim on the estate—the daughter of Rolf Hammergren. Even sent a copy of the birth certificate."

"Rolf? Will's brother? Didn't he die many years ago?"

Red sighed. "That's been part of my problem in getting the estate settled. Will never took his brother's name off the forest acres, and I can't find a death certificate or any information on him."

Wind shook the front door, making a sound as if someone were knocking. Red walked over to the door and peered through the wavy glass. Outside, little eddies of snow danced down the newly plowed street. Inside, the windy draft caused dust to swirl over the clutter of old furniture, china, and glassware of the store.

"Well, that's a dilemma."

Red continued to stare outside. "You'd think as sheriff I'd have these great investigative skills, but I haven't had any success in finding Rolf or where he might be buried." She turned to Georgia. "Those woods are sacred, and I don't want some interloper messing with them."

Georgia, Lou, and Scotty all knew what was at stake in those 160 acres of woods. They also knew that settling the estate and getting the deed straightened out had been a sore spot with Red. They'd stopped talking about it with Red the night Scotty had asked, "Any progress in getting your name on the property up north?"

"Is that all you can talk about?" Red's snappish reply had caused an unnatural silence to fill the room. She'd later apologized and said quietly, "I wish the whole thing would go away."

She was still sorry she'd lost her temper with Scotty. Friends like her were hard to come by.

Georgia nodded with an understanding expression. "First off, you need to make sure this birth certificate is genuine. Even if it is, people can lie on them. The mother can put down whatever name she chooses. It's not like the state is demanding DNA proof."

"I suppose you are right about that."

Georgia continued. "What do you know about this brother, Rolf? I thought you told me he died in an institution."

Red sat back down and took a sip of the tea. "Unfortunately, that's all I know. I don't even have the information on what institution or where he died."

Georgia closed her eyes and thought for a moment. "If we can find out where he was, maybe we can dig up his medical records from when he was institutionalized. They might tell us whether he was even capable of producing a child."

"That's a strange thing to say."

Georgia massaged her neck with a pained expression. "Back in the forties, fifties, and even sixties, it wasn't uncommon for people who were institutionalized to be sterilized. It's a sad chapter in our history, going back to a theory of eugenics that was popular in the 1920s."

"Eugenics?"

"Basically, a movement to prevent those who were undesirable from procreating. This included the mentally ill, the 'feeble minded,' and many impoverished women. It lost its luster after the Nazis and World War Two but was still used well into the sixties."

"Will never gave me a clue about Rolf, other than that he died in a state hospital. I suspected from his tone that it was a big wound for his family and that his parents didn't share much about him."

Outside, the whine of a snowmobile penetrated the howl of the wind. Red glanced at the window. "Who the hell would go out in this?"

She pushed her chair back with an air of resignation. "I'd better get the idiot off the street. If he doesn't crash the thing into a parked car, he'll probably get lost, and I'll have another missing person."

"Relax." Georgia poured her more tea. "What are you going to do? Chase the machine down on foot and tackle the driver?" She waggled her finger at Red. "You are a bundle of nerves."

The snowmobile cut its engine in front of Georgia's building. Moments later, Scotty came in, stomping snow off her boots. Her cheeks were ruddy from the cold and the wind.

"Tain't a fit day out for sheriffs or cooks." She piled her coat, hat, and mittens on the floor by the space heater.

Georgia pulled another bowl from her shelf and scooped out chili for Scotty. "You've been out on your snowmobile? Who's minding the store?"

"We close early during blizzards." She rubbed her hands to bring back warmth. "I did my chef's duty by making up a dozen pizzas and delivering them to the school. They've got wrestlers holed up in the gym. Fortunately, the boys were so hungry, they didn't notice that I covered the pizzas with veggies."

"You are a subversive, aren't you?" Georgia sat down next to her. "Our ex–public health nurse is going to introduce good nutrition whether Lykkins Lake likes it or not."

Scotty shrugged. "Now that I got the pop machines out of the school, it's time to talk to them about the lunch menus. Mrs. Knutson needs to retire. She's been cooking tater tots and fish sticks a few decades too long. I figure in the fall we can use fresh local produce, and in the winter and spring we can buy from the whole foods co-op in Duluth."

Red pictured Scotty haggling with the school board over an increase in the cost of the meals. She had a major fight last year over the pop machines because the school had come to rely on the profits to fund school activities. Funny, though, when they replaced them with fruit and milk machines, the coins still rolled in.

Scotty turned to her. "I heard some gossip this morning before the snow chased all my customers away. Thought you should know that the anti-immigrant faction is getting vocal again. They've already convicted the Vincente brothers of running a meth lab out of the cabin that burned last night."

Red shook her head gloomily. "It doesn't help to have the right-wingers of Pearsal County rile everyone with their quasi-white-supremacist rhetoric." She finished her tea. "I'm going to have to put the drug dealing on hold until I find the missing teenager."

"So." Georgia leaned forward, her elbows on the table. "Have you found evidence of a meth lab at the cabin?"

Red pictured the charred remains and shrugged. "I don't know." The cabin hadn't struck her as a meth lab site, but with everything burned and blackened, it was hard to tell.

"During my brief tenure as Commissioner of Health, the meth labs were finally getting noticed. Funny, it wasn't a concern over the meth users or their children that drove the discussion. It was the environmental health people asking what all those chemicals were doing to the groundwater. Until then, no one saw it as a public health problem. 'Let the local sheriffs take care of it.'"

"Sure enough—but cut their funding first."

"Don't you love politics?"

Red stretched, shaking her head. "When Will died and they appointed me sheriff, I never expected to win the next election. By then the voters should have figured out that I was a *Mrs.* Hammergren, like Mitch Rafferty said at every gathering."

"He was certainly reaching for the lowest common denominator. Remember who we once elected as president and Minnesota came close to going over to the dark side." Scotty raised her hand. "But never underestimate the intelligence of the voting public."

"Don't go expounding on your liberal leanings, lady, or you might find yourself out of business around here." Georgia waggled a finger at Scotty.

"Pshaw, my liberal leanings are no secret. And the customers keep coming."

Georgia laughed. "That's because they have no choice unless they want to eat hot dogs and Cheetos from the Gas and Go."

"Enough of this stimulating conversation." Red wiped her hands on a napkin and stood up. "I've got to find a kid. Thanks for inviting me to lunch."

Outside, bundled against the driving snow, Red pushed her way through three-foot drifts to get back to the courthouse. Not a vehicle stirred on the street. The town was buttoned down for the duration of the storm. Red hoped no one broke a hip or had a heart attack shoveling today. She wasn't sure that, even if following a snowplow, an ambulance could make it outside the town boundaries.

Her cell phone buzzed against her hip. Pulling off a heavy mitten, she punched the answer button. Her bare hand immediately ached with the cold. The voice over the staticky line said, "Sheriff? It's Darcy. I got that SUV out of the ditch. Did you know that was Walter LaFrance in there? I got his autograph for Lois. She's going to be tickled pink."

"Thanks, Darcy. Take care in this weather." At least one problem was solved.

19

SHERIFF RED
HITCH

A gust of icy wind slammed the high school gym door shut behind Red. Inside the auditorium, three wrestling mats were laid out on the polished wooden floor. The competition had ended two hours ago, and students sat in clusters, eating Scotty's pizza. Chico Vincente, short and muscular, played cards with a group of teammates from Lykkins Lake. He laughed and shuffled the cards. It was hard to watch him with his friends and imagine that he was dealing drugs. In fact, it made her angry that people were pointing fingers at the Vincentes simply because they were Hispanic.

Hitch Norgren, the coach, paced, watching the clock when she approached him.

"Hi, Hitch," Red said. "Got a minute?"

"I've got lots of minutes. Can't get these students out of here until the weather clears." His tone was clipped and humorless. "We should have canceled the meet when we heard the forecast last night."

Hitch was a big man and had put on pounds since his short career as a professional wrestler. In those days, the promoters dubbed him "Hometown Hitch," and the women fans chased him down for autographs. His wrestling bio didn't mention that he was married to Bobbi, his high school prom date, or that he had a daughter named Tiffany. His handlers wanted to portray him as available. They knew it would sell more tickets. His fifteen minutes of fame had ended with a neck injury that put him in a brace for six months.

He still retained some of the boyish good looks, including a lopsided smile. But his face was scarred from severe acne, and he randomly blinked as if to wipe away a nervous tic on his right side. Over the years, he had developed an odd cadence in his speech. Sometimes the words tumbled out, and sometimes there were spacey gaps between thoughts. Brain damage? Steroid burnout? Red wasn't sure. She did know that when it came to wrestling, Hitch was one of the best and most beloved coaches in the state.

"You seem to be watching the clock."

He shook his head and smiled. "Sorry. I was supposed to meet a friend."

The poker club was not fond of Hitch, who was behind the push for the "positive alternatives" abstinence-only sex education in school. Red found it to be an interesting position, considering that he'd knocked Bobbi up right after prom. She was sure he didn't know of his daughter's involvement with the Church.

He and Father Paul from the Catholic church were the most vocal proponents of the curriculum. It was rumored that Hitch was considering running for school board to push his agenda.

Georgia had shaken her head during a poker club discussion last summer about Hitch and Father Paul. "You know what the research says? Those kids that get abstinence-only education are more likely to end up with unwanted pregnancies and sexually transmitted diseases."

"Why?"

"Because they don't know any better. No one told them about the alternatives."

Lou had added, "Like how to have safe sex and where diseases like gonorrhea and HIV come from."

"Oh."

After high school, Hitch made it out of Lykkins Lake on a wrestling scholarship and had done well enough at the University of Minnesota to be chosen for the Olympic team. A large picture of him on the podium with his bronze medal and tears streaming down his face hung in the courthouse. He was the hometown boy who made good—sort of. After a couple of years on the regional professional wrestling circuit, he'd packed up Bobbi and Tiffany and moved to California. Main Street Lykkins Lake was abuzz with talk that he was going to star in a big Hollywood movie with Arnold Schwarzenegger. Two years later, after the injury, the Norgrens quietly returned to Lykkins Lake, and Hitch took over as the high school wrestling coach. Nothing more was said about his Hollywood career. But the townspeople still loved Hometown Hitch. For five years now, the Lykkins Lake High School wrestling team had sent at least one wrestler to the state tournament. In the summer, Hitch ran a wrestling camp up on Cass Lake that drew boys from all over the United States.

If Red's memory was correct, Hitch's return to town happened the summer before Junior Klein died in the hunting accident.

Hitch interrupted her thoughts.

"Any news on when this storm might blow over?" He tapped his finger on his watch. It was a Rolex. She didn't know that high school coaching could be so lucrative.

"The latest word I have is that it's moving very, very slowly. You might be hosting a pajama party here."

Hitch's face darkened, and he was silent for a long moment. "Damn." He turned from her, paced a couple of steps, then turned back. When he looked at her again, his eyes held a bland expression.

Red was taken aback by the quick change in temperament.

"Well," he shrugged, "it'll be like summer camp, except I won't get paid the tuition."

Red motioned for him to sit down on the wooden bleacher. "Could we talk about Jared Peterson?"

Behind them someone laughed and called out, "Ay, caramba! Chico tanks again!"

Leaning close to Hitch, Red kept her voice low. "I'm sure you heard that he was in an explosion and died last night."

Hitch took a deep breath, shaking his head. "Such a waste. Such a waste."

"Do you know if he was involved with drugs?"

Hitch's response was immediate and hard-edged. "None of my boys have anything to do with drugs. I tell them and I tell them. Any hint of drugs and you're off the team."

"Do you know why Jared didn't sign up for wrestling this year?"

A muscle in Hitch's cheek twitched. "The kids are clean."

Red gazed steadily at Hitch, taking her time. His face twitched again. "Are you telling me all you know?"

Hitch blinked hard. "There was some talk about Jared. I don't know if it was true."

"What kind of talk?"

Hitch looked over his shoulder at the boys. "That he was dealing—mostly marijuana. I told him that if he was doing drugs, I didn't want him on my team."

"And?"

He shrugged. "He didn't sign up this year."

Red looked beyond Hitch to the wrestlers. They seemed so young with their baggy jeans and sweatshirts. How many of them were doing drugs behind the coach's back?

Two boys wearing Lykkins Lake Tigers jackets stared at her from halfway up the bleachers. They both had burly builds and long, scraggly hair. She caught the eye of one of them for a moment and noted the Neanderthal-like features of his face, a heavy boniness to his brow and thick, slack lips. He waved at her and grinned.

She did not wave back. "Who are those guys? I haven't seen them around before."

"You mean the Kazurinski brothers?" Hitch's voice slowed down and dropped off as if he had lost his train of thought. After a silence punctuated by more laughter from the kids playing poker, he said, "They help me with the equipment and spot the boys when they do weight training. Both love wrestling. But, they're pretty slow, if you know what I mean. Special ed. The school had to keep them until they were twenty-one. They stay out of trouble."

Interesting thing to say, Red thought. "I don't recognize the name."

Because Pearsal County was small, Red knew a lot of the families. Kazurinski didn't sound familiar to her.

Hitch shrugged. "They're cousins on Bobbi's side. Moved here a couple of years ago." Hitch yawned, looking bored and out of sorts. He twisted the wristband of his watch.

Find Coke. Find her.

"Hitch, do you know anyone called Coke or Cole?"

He frowned, showing a little of the tic. "Can't say it means anything. Why?"

Red shrugged. "Just a name someone mentioned."

Hitch glanced quickly at his watch. "Hope the storm lets up. I'm getting calls from the parents."

"Looks like you have it under control here. If you hear anything about Jared, will you let me know?"

He smiled at her, and in that moment, she could see why people liked him. "Sure will." As he walked away, Red noted a whiff of cologne, similar to what Mitch Rafferty wore at town meetings during the campaign. It brought back bad memories of the sneering way he'd challenged her.

A couple of girls in cheerleading sweaters and short skirts sat on the bottom row of the bleachers, texting and watching the boys play cards.

Red walked over to them and pointed to the card players. "Who's winning?"

The two girls giggled.

She sat down next to them and asked, "Do either of you know Missy Klein?"

They both nodded at the same time, as if their answer had been choreographed.

"We heard she ran away."

Red smiled at them. "Oh. Where did you hear that?"

The girl with the French braid down her back said, "I saw her skipping class with Jared Peterson yesterday morning."

"Oh?"

The other girl, with blond hair and purple streaks, added, "Yeah. Everyone said they were running away together."

"Can you tell me more about it?"

One of the boys looked up at them from the card game. "We heard they got into some kind of trouble."

"More than trouble," another boy added. "I heard Jared blew up in a cabin. Like, he's dead."

"That's so sad," the girl with the French braid said before turning back to her phone.

No one seemed particularly upset that Jared had died. Red found this strange.

"You guys must feel pretty bad that he died."

"I guess..." The other girl spoke. "But he was bad news. Like, drugs and stuff."

The conversation was interrupted by a familiar voice. "Are you interrogating my kids?" Red raised her eyebrows as Mitch Rafferty, complete with a heavy scent of his cologne, sat down. Mitch was in his early thirties, wore his hair in a military buzz cut, and carried himself with body language that said, "I'm so tough."

"Mitch." She kept the surprise out of her voice. "What are you doing here?"

"I help Hitch with the coaching when I have the time." He half smiled, and the expression was less a smile and more a smirk.

Hitch and Mitch. What a combination. She would never say it out loud, but Mitch had a smarminess about him that made her feel like she should go home and take a shower after talking with him. She didn't understand why she had such a visceral reaction to him, but she was glad he wasn't part of her staff anymore. Will, when he was healthy, made it a point not to talk about personnel with her, but he'd once blurted out, "There's something wrong with that guy. I just can't figure what it is."

Red's cell phone vibrated against her hip. "Excuse me." *Saved by the vibe*, she thought, walking away from Mitch.

"Sheriff? It's Ed. Jennie couldn't get in to handle the lines, and Cal needed a break. He asked me to watch the phones." She guessed that Cal was taking a long cigarette break in the courthouse entryway. Red cringed thinking that the dispatch was being handled by the janitor—a really nice guy with limited talents. *Yup, we've got* Mayberry R.F.D. *here today.*

"Sheriff?"

"Yes, Ed."

"I answered this call from the hospital. They lost a lady or something.

She was supposed to come in for something, and she never showed." Ed's voice shook. "I can't find Cal, and I don't know what to do."

Red said calmly, "It's okay, Ed. I'll take care of it. Who did you talk to at the hospital?"

"I forget."

"Stay there until Cal gets back. I'm sure he won't be gone too much longer. I'll call the hospital."

She punched in the number for the hospital. It took several rings before a breathless voice answered. "Lake Memorial, Carmen speaking." Carmen Cruzan was the director of nursing. Lou once described her as an old-fashioned battle-ax, but just the nurse you'd want in a crisis.

"It's Sheriff Hammergren. Did someone call in about a missing woman?"

Carmen skipped any polite patter. "Listen. We got a call over an hour ago from Sammy Brady that her water just broke. Contractions five to ten minutes apart. Said her husband went out to Hammer Lake, so she thought she'd drive herself in. They live a couple miles east of town. Even in this weather, she should have gotten in by now. And no one answers at the house."

"Can we get the ambulance to head out that way?"

Carmen's voice was sharp with exasperation. "No. Damn it. They're stuck an hour away. They had to transport a patient to the psych unit in Duluth—can't get back here with the rig until they can get the snowplow to them."

Over the last couple of years, rural ambulances spent more and more time out of the area transporting mental health patients. If it wasn't the ambulance, it would have been one of her deputies taking someone in for a psych evaluation. Red guessed she could count that as a blessing.

"I'll see if the Explorer can get through on the roads. Hopefully, she's not stuck in the ditch somewhere. Anything I should know about the pregnancy?"

"Nope. Sammy is an LPN here. She knows labor and delivery. When I talked to her, she said she thought everything was okay. Contractions were spotty. Doesn't sound like serious labor. And," she added, "this is her first."

First babies tended to take their time.

Red got directions to the Brady place from Carmen and clicked off the phone. When she walked by Hitch, he was talking intently on his cell.

"They haven't shown yet?" His voice rose in a harsh whisper.

Red would have liked to have known more about Hitch's conversation, but she had to get on the road. She glanced at the stands on her way out. Mitch was sitting close to the two cheerleaders, sharing something on his cell phone. She hoped it wasn't something salacious.

"Yuck," she muttered as she let herself out into the cold.

20

SHERIFF RED
SAMMY

Outside the high school gymnasium, the wind whipped the snow into ghostly sheets. As the icy snow slammed into her face and swirled around her, Red understood how people could become disoriented in a storm and walk in circles until they lay down and froze to death. She wondered if Missy Klein was wandering out there, struggling against the hypnotic rhythm of the snow. With a shiver, she also wondered if Sammy, the soon-to-be mother, was out trying to find her way to the hospital.

She plunged through the snowdrifts and fought her way the two blocks to the courthouse. Nothing moved in Lykkins Lake except the wind and the snow. The six vehicles in the parking lot were buried, mere outlines against the whiteness of the storm.

How was she going to find a woman in labor in this? She prayed that Sammy Brady had the sense to stay with their car—or better yet, had the sense not to start out in the first place.

Ed greeted her at the door with a relieved expression. Drops of melted snow ran down her face. She wiped them away, glad she'd had the laser surgery on her eyes, so she didn't have to deal with fogged, wet glasses.

"Cal got back right after I called you." He looked out into the parking lot. "It's gonna take more than my snowblower to get this place shoveled out."

Red nodded and trotted up the inside steps, leaving pools of snow behind her. Ed would have them mopped up immediately.

Cal looked up at her from the console. "Sorry." Cal was a man of few words.

"Well, we've got trouble." She filled Cal in.

Immediately he started making calls. First, he reached Jason, who had the Pearsal County Sheriff's Explorer. He was in town and could be over in five minutes. As Cal tried to track down a snowplow for them to follow, Red grabbed an emergency first responder kit and several blankets. She also checked to see that she had her Swiss Army knife and a box of latex gloves.

Cal called out to her from the other room. "No snowplow for at least forty-five minutes, boss. They're north on 25 trying to clear the road by the Golden Deer Casino. Lots of people in the ditch up there. I've got Gordon turning around, but it's going to take him a while."

"I haven't got a while. Unless you hear from me, send him to the Bradys' as soon as you can."

Red cursed the stupidity of the gambling public who couldn't stay away from their slot machines during a raging blizzard. What compelled them to get in their cars during near whiteout conditions to go throw their money away?

Georgia once said, "Lenin was wrong about religion being the opiate of the people. It's slot machines. Turns everyday, upstanding citizens into zombies."

Red was ready when Jason pulled up to the entrance of the courthouse.

"Grab a shovel," she shouted to him as she threw the blankets and supplies into the back seat. "I'll drive. You ride shotgun and keep me out of the ditch."

Jason was a reliable deputy but a hot dog when it came to vehicles. In his three years with the sheriff's office, he'd totaled two patrol cars. Red needed a steady hand at the wheel.

Red filled Jason in on the situation. "We don't know if she's stuck somewhere or safely tucked into her bed. No one answers at the house."

"Ever delivered a baby before?"

Red shook her head. Already, only two blocks from the courthouse, her shoulder muscles were knotted as she hunched over the wheel, trying to see ahead. "I only know what they've taught us in first responder classes." She chuckled. "And from watching *Call the Midwife*."

Jason suddenly cried out as a car fishtailed out of a residential street. "Watch out! Goddamn it!"

A black SUV skidded toward Red. For a moment, time slowed. Red resisted the urge to swerve and pump her brakes. Instead, she applied a slow, steady pressure and let the anti-lock brakes read the road. The driver of the SUV looked straight ahead, oblivious to the Explorer. Red turned the wheel slightly, just enough to ease by.

"Stop! I'm going to arrest that son of a bitch. What the hell does he think he's doing? He missed us by six inches." Jason looked incredulous. "And I don't think he even knew we were there!"

Red kept the Explorer moving forward. "She."

"What?"

"She. Looked to me like Bobbi Norgren driving."

"She could have gotten us killed."

Red took in a deep breath and let it out, glad that she had gloves on so Jason wouldn't see how her hands were shaking at the wheel. At this rate, Sammy Brady would have her baby and the child would be in kindergarten before they rescued her.

The Explorer crawled. Red kept steady pressure on the gas pedal while Jason directed her.

"Keep her left, you're headed for the ditch."

In places the road was completely obliterated. Only the occasional road sign and the fence posts on the other side of the ditch let them know they were still on the highway.

Red checked the odometer and the clock. They'd traveled three miles in forty-five minutes.

"I think I see something." Jason pointed to his right as the wind let up for a few moments. The red top of a pickup truck disappeared behind the swirl of snow.

"Do you see a road? Can I turn?" Red's hands clenched the steering wheel. Her fingers and wrists ached all the way up to her shoulders.

Jason shook his head. "We're going to have to hike it."

"Call in and let Cal know where we are. I'll slog in and see if Sammy is with the truck."

Red settled the first responder kit in the backpack and hoisted it onto her aching shoulders. Already she was sorry about her haste in the office. They should have loaded a rescue sled and snowshoes into the Explorer.

"I won't get any medals for this one." She plunged ahead, sometimes sinking into snow up to her knees. The pickup was at least two hundred yards ahead, and she fought for every foot of progress. Halfway there, she stumbled and fell over on her side. The snow welcomed her, and for a moment, she felt embraced by its warmth. Maybe she could close her eyes for a little while, rest up, and then move on. Sammy could wait.

A horn blast pulled her out of the hypnosis of the storm. Jason was warning her.

Red scrambled upright and plunged forward.

The pickup was tilted at a fifteen-degree angle, partly in the ditch, and the engine was running, its tailpipe buried in the snow.

"Shit."

Red ripped the passenger-side door open, letting in a blast of icy, clean air.

Sammy lay on the seat, curled up, her arms limply hugging her pregnant belly.

"It's okay, Sammy." Red reached over and switched off the engine. "I want you to take some good deep breaths."

Sammy groaned and whispered groggily, "I didn't mean to go off the road."

"Can you sit up?" Red reached across her and cranked down the window on the driver's side. "I know it's cold, but you need the fresh air."

"My water broke."

"It's okay. We'll get you to the hospital."

Sammy tried to sit up. Her face contracted with pain. "Something's not right." She whimpered. "It doesn't feel right."

Red took a deep breath, letting the frigid air singe her lungs. *Stay calm. People have been delivering babies since the dawn of the earth. You can do this.*

"Sammy, I'm going to take a peek and see how the baby is doing. I need you to roll onto your back."

"I can't!" Sammy cried out. "Something's down there that isn't right. I can feel it."

Red stroked the girl's forehead. Sammy's denim maternity jeans were soaked. Red eased them down, praying that Jason would arrive soon with the blankets. The skin on Sammy's legs was cold and mottled. "Relax, and take a deep breath. Can you pull your legs up a little?"

Red pulled on the latex gloves from her pocket and snapped on the flashlight. She was prepared for a glimpse of a little head about to crown. She thought back to her first responder class. If the baby was crowning, let the head ease out, then use gentle counter pressure so the shoulders came slowly. She took a deep breath. How hard could this be?

"Oh God." The words slipped out before she could stop them. Instead of a baby, a loop of the umbilical cord undulated out of the birth canal, moving with Sammy's contractions.

Red touched it and felt it throbbing to Sammy's heartbeat. The blood inside the cord was free flowing. She had to keep it that way or the baby would die before it was born.

"Another deep breath, Sammy." Silently Red cursed her numbed brain. What do you do when the cord comes first? Outside, she heard the crunch of snow and hoarse breathing as Jason made his way toward them.

"Red? Is everything all right?"

Think, Red. Her hands broke out in a cold sweat underneath the gloves. *Think.*

Sammy groaned with another contraction. Automatically, Red said, "Keep breathing. Take deep breaths."

Think. Sammy groaned again, and the cord moved. Suddenly Red remembered her paramedic friend, Tim, telling her war stories about delivering babies.

"Two things you don't want to see—a baby's butt coming through first, or the cord."

Keep the baby from pressing on the cord. That's it. Protect the cord. Red slipped her index finger and her middle finger into Sammy's vagina, holding the canal open and away from the cord. Now to keep the baby from coming down.

"Okay, Sammy, I need you to do something for me." She willed the calm into her voice. "I need you to get on your hands and knees."

"Can't," Sammy gasped. "Too tired."

"Sammy." Red's voice was sharp. "On your hands and knees!"

Jason arrived at the pickup. Frost sparkled white from his mustache. "What's going on here?"

Red concentrated on keeping the cord stable. "Help Sammy onto her belly. I need her butt up in the air. I need the baby to be pulled away from the birth canal."

Thank God for the way the truck tilted into the ditch, lowering the driver's side.

Jason, to his credit, didn't hesitate. In the cramped front seat of the pickup, arms, knees, heads colliding, they worked to get Sammy onto her hands and knees.

"You've got to radio this as an emergency. We need help. Get that plow out here now! We don't have much time." *And I don't know how to do a C-section*, she added to herself.

"Sammy, I know this is miserable, but you have to stay like this until we can get you to the hospital. The cord has come first. Do you understand? Rest your head and arms on the seat and keep your butt up. Can you do that?"

Sammy panted but kept her butt up.

"Breathe and don't push."

Between her fingers, the cord pulsed.

"What's Joe going to say when I tell him I was stuck in the pickup with my ass pointing to the sky?" Sammy said softly.

Red chuckled. "Definitely not like they show it on television."

Another contraction gripped Sammy. Red's fingers ached as they protected the cord.

Jason tucked the blankets around Sammy. "You need some heat in here."

"No kidding."

"Shovel. I've got a shovel in the back," Sammy gasped.

"I'll see if I can get the tailpipe clear so we can start the engine." Jason stepped back, radio in hand.

With the truck engine running and the heater sending out warm air, Red relaxed slightly, still guarding the cord. Jason reported that the plow was fifteen minutes out and that they'd gotten the old ambulance rig staffed and ready.

"How long?" Sammy gasped. "I'm so tired."

Outside, the sky lightened. The storm was passing, but the winds continued to sweep across the open field, and the temperature was dropping. The gas gauge on the truck registered empty.

"I can't hold on!" Sammy's thighs quivered. "I can't do this."

Stay calm, Red told herself. Her shoulders and arms ached from the cramped position, half on the seat, half kneeling. She talked to Sammy in a low, steady voice.

"Is it a boy or a girl?"

"Don't know. Contraction." She began to pant. The cord continued to pulse in a steady rhythm.

Stay up there, baby. "Where's Joe?"

"Got a call from Jack Klein."

"Oh?"

"Fish house. Fish house up on Hammer Lake, near ours. Wanted Joe to check it out."

"Did he say why?"

"Granddaughter. Something about her." She took a sharp intake of air and gasped. Outside, over the howl of the wind, was a faint siren. "Can't do this. Too hard."

"They're coming. Hang on. You're doing well."

Sammy groaned and started to shiver. "How long?"

"Soon. I hear a siren."

"I can't." Sammy sighed. "Please, just let me lie down. Can't you let me lie down for a minute?"

The siren and the scraping of the plow grew louder. "Sammy, what are you going to name the baby?"

"Don't know. Don't care."

Keep her talking. "Tell me about the fish house."

"You gotta know the lake. Not easy to find. In a cove." Sammy started to growl, trying to stifle the urge to push.

"Pant, Sammy. You can pant." Red huffed along with her. "We don't want to push the baby."

The cord pulsated, unimpeded. How long could they keep this up before the baby cut off its own lifeline? Lad, her younger brother, almost did that. Born purplish and limp. But Doc Carver brought him back. Red wondered if that was the start of Lad's descent into mental illness or if it was preordained.

Light-headed from the huffing and from concentrating on the cord protected by her fingers, Red was surprised when the passenger door to the pickup creaked open.

"Hey, Red. Let's get Sammy to the hospital." Mike Schumer, Lykkins Lake banker and volunteer EMT, smiled at her.

Ten minutes later, with some tricky maneuvers that were sure to leave Red with a strained back and shoulder, Sammy was in the ambulance. The cord pulsated between her fingers, still a lifeline to the baby. Very carefully, Red slipped her fingers away from the cord as Mike took over.

She climbed out of the ambulance. "Godspeed, Sammy. Godspeed."

21

MISSY

She couldn't tell if it'd been hours or minutes. The snow poured down, meaner and meaner. What happened to the fluffy flakes that she could catch on her tongue? Instead, the icy snow bit at her cheeks. She pulled the hood of her stupid pink parka closer, finally glad that Grampa Jack made her buy it.

She remembered how she'd glared at him in Fleet Farm Supply, hoping that no one she knew saw her there. But Grampa, she'd complained, I don't need something that warm.

Honey, you never know.

Well, Grampa Jack was right. Grampa Jack was always right about some things—like Jared Peterson. Honey, you sure you want to hang around with him? She hadn't answered him.

The woods were on her left and the lake on her right. Keep to the left, keep to the left, she repeated over and over. To her right, the lake grumbled like it was shifting in its sleep.

The snow swirling ahead of her made her dizzy. Her stomach growled, and her legs felt like giant logs.

You can do it. You can do it. She chanted out loud. Two steps more. Two steps more. A bramble grabbed at her foot, and she stumbled and fell to her knees. The snow enveloped her like her thick comforter at home.

Maybe she could lie down and sleep for just a while. She was so tired. A little nap would help. She closed her eyes and imagined sitting on the sofa at home under Gramma Serena's quilt, watching the play of the flames in the fireplace. The wood sizzled as sparks floated up the chimney.

A loud crack jolted her from her daze. She wasn't at home. No, she was on the lake, and the lake was angry with her for tramping on it. She pictured it rippling toward her like the ocean in a movie she saw last year. An ice-cold stab of fear caused her to gasp. The *Followers* would be searching, and they would spot her in her stupid pink jacket. Pushing herself up, she began the slow slog through the drifting snow.

Later, many chants later when her voice was hoarse and her legs felt like jelly, the snow cleared for a moment. Ahead, she saw a gray shadow, the outline of Grampa Jack's fish house. She lurched toward it with a last burst of strength. The house was near, and it had a stove and food, and Grampa Jack would know where to find her.

She stumbled on caked-up ice, righted herself, and ran. Snowmobile tracks, filling in from the storm, circled the little building. *Followers.* The ones who did the dirty work. Maybe they've come and gone and I'm safe.

Breathless, her chest aching from running, she grabbed the door and twisted at the knob. It wouldn't open. It was locked. Of course it was locked. And she couldn't remember where Grampa Jack kept the key. Her brain a wad of jelly just like her legs. She collapsed at the door, too tired to even cry. The icy snow slammed against her face as she closed her eyes.

22

SHERIFF RED

MRS. JENKENS

Red sat with the phone pressed against her ear as the snow danced in ghostly patterns across the courthouse lawn. Her back, neck, and arms ached even after a double dose of ibuprofen. Inwardly, she still shivered with a cold that even the old, overheated courthouse couldn't touch. Would Sammy and her baby be all right?

Jack Klein's voice cut in and out on the phone line.

"Yes," he said. "I asked Joe to check the fish house. It was a long shot, but I thought she might go there..."

The line crackled.

"He didn't find any evidence that she'd been there?"

"Locked up tight, he said."

Red paused, trying to find the right words. "Jack, why didn't you tell me about the fish house this morning?"

The line was silent. For a moment, Red thought they'd been cut off.

"If she was there, I wanted to talk with her first...you know..."

In case she was mixed up in drugs like her mother, Red added to herself. "We'll keep looking for her, Jack."

She wrote up the timeline on Sammy and finished the report. They had taken Sammy directly to the little hospital operating room, but Red hadn't heard anything more.

As she printed the report for the files, her thoughts moved back to Missy Klein. If Missy was in that cabin last night and if she escaped, would she survive the storm and the dropping temperatures? What teenage girl has those kinds of skills? She remembered her own stupidity as a sixteen-year-old walking to school in the bitter cold. Defying her mother, she wore black slip-on shoes with thin socks because boots weren't cool. Her toes were numb and felt like stumps by the time she reached school. For several hours her feet burned as they warmed up, and her great toe on her left foot was so swollen, she finally went to Mrs. Jenkens, the school nurse.

"Mild frostbite," Mrs. Jenkens had declared. "You girls. Every year I go through this with you. Bundle up or you will lose your toes and your ears!"

Mrs. Jenkens had been the school nurse since Will's time twenty years before Red. He once admitted that she scared him. "I swear she knew you were coming before you walked into her office."

At ninety-five, she still lived in the little bungalow across from the courthouse. In the spring, multicolored tulips lined the walk to her house. In the summer, the flower beds in front of her house were a mass of oranges and yellows from giant marigolds. Red enjoyed watching her yard change as the seasons changed.

A light was on in the front room of the bungalow, and the outside light over the door glowed a soft yellow in the diminishing snowfall. Red regarded the house and wondered if Mrs. Jenkens could tell her something about Will's brother, Rolf. If she'd known Will, she might have known Rolf.

A little break from the missing Missy couldn't hurt. "Why not?" She picked up the phone.

Mrs. Jenkens answered the phone on the seventh ring. "Yes?"

"Mrs. Jenkens, it's Red Hammergren, the sheriff. I'm across the street in the courthouse and was wondering if I could stop over for a minute? I'd like to ask you about Rolf Hammergren."

The phone went *clunk*, and Red heard a muttering sound. Red shouted into the receiver, "Mrs. Jenkens, are you all right?"

"I'm old, but I'm not deaf, dear. Just dropped the phone. Come on over before it gets dark. I never answer the door after dark."

Cal walked in while Red was pulling on her parka.

"Sheriff?"

"Yes, Cal."

"I thought you'd like to know. The hospital called. It's a girl. Six pounds. Doc says she's doing okay. Says it's the quickest C-section he's ever done."

Red took a deep breath and let it out with a smile. "Thank God."

Cal looked at his feet. "Hope Ed is okay. I didn't mean to scare him."

"I'm sure he's fine."

Red zipped up her coat. Too many problems. Missy Klein and a dead boyfriend. Why did they all decide to create a crisis on a weekend with a snowstorm? Wasn't one baby in distress enough?

"I need to check something out. I'll only be gone a few minutes. Call me if you need me."

Feeling only slightly guilty about taking a break, Red crossed the street. Muscles in her lower back spasmed as she took careful steps through the snow. The last thing she wanted to do was fall and wrench her back. Or worse, break a leg.

The snow was easing up, which meant the temperature would be dropping soon. The sidewalk to Mrs. Jenkens's front door had been shoveled earlier in the day, and it had already partially drifted in. Red knew that Ed looked out for Mrs. Jenkens. No one said anything when he used county time and county equipment to keep her sidewalk clear. She was, after all, a Lykkins Lake institution.

As Red approached the little porch with the bright blue paint, she wondered why she didn't know more about Rolf Hammergren. Had he lived, he would be seventy-five years old now. In the only family photo she had of him, he was probably about ten years old and sat in a rocking chair holding the baby Will. He gazed down at his brother with a Mona Lisa smile on his face. One eye was slightly crossed, but otherwise he looked like a normal ten-year-old.

She rapped on the screen door and heard the metallic sound of Mrs. Jenkens's walker.

"I'm coming." Her voice was high and tremulous.

Red remembered Mrs. Jenkens in her navy skirt, pressed white blouse, and sensible white shoes. She always had a scowl on her face, which the students interpreted as disapproval. The kids called her "Nurse Ratched" from the movie *One Flew Over the Cuckoo's Nest*. Only later, when she finally got thick glasses, did the scowl go away.

The door opened to a blast of warm air from inside.

"Well, come on in, and leave the cold outside. And don't track snow on my floor." She chuckled. "I could slip and break a hip, you know."

She still wore a navy skirt. Red wondered if it was the same one she'd worn thirty years ago. It was too long now for her shrunken frame, almost touching the floor. The white collar of a blouse was folded neatly over a thick red cardigan sweater. On her feet were the same kind of clunky white shoes that she'd worn to school. The only thing that had changed about Mrs. Jenkens over the past thirty years was her height.

Red unlaced her boots and took them off, careful to leave them on the throw rug.

Once inside the overheated little living room, Red sat on a richly uphol-stered couch covered with crocheted afghans. Immediately, a white cat jumped onto her lap.

"Prissy is a good judge of character, so I guess you'll do." Mrs. Jenkens eased herself into a recliner.

Red tensed. For a moment she was back in the nurse's office with her frostbitten toes, embarrassed and chastised.

Before she could ask, Mrs. Jenkens leaned forward and said, "Funny you should ask me about Rolf Hammergren."

"Oh?"

"Somebody called me a few weeks ago and said they were from a lawyer's office and could they ask me some questions about him." She pursed her lips and shook her head. "I said, 'No, thank you,' and hung up."

Red stroked the cat. It purred, shedding white fur on Red's heavy corduroy pants.

"What's this interest in Rolf Hammergren all of a sudden?"

Red thought for a moment about how to approach this and decided to simply tell Mrs. Jenkens the truth. "I received a letter from a law firm yesterday that someone claiming to be Rolf's daughter is seeking a portion of the Hammergren estate. I'm trying to find out if it's legitimate." She paused while the cat arched its back and stretched. "My husband, Will, didn't talk much about him, and I can't find anyone who seems to know anything."

Mrs. Jenkens looked thoughtfully at Red. "You mean they want some of that land up by Hammer Lake."

Red blinked in surprise. "You know about the Hammergren acres?"

A clock ticked loudly in the room off the living room. Its cadence was matched by another clock in the kitchen.

"Oh, that was a story thirty years back. Out-of-town speculators thought there might be oil or natural gas or something under the forest. It never came to much."

"I don't remember hearing about it."

When Mrs. Jenkens laughed, her eyes sparkled behind the thick glasses. "Of course not, you were that careless teenager with frostbitten toes."

Heat rose up Red's neck to her cheeks. "You remember that?"

Mrs. Jenkens smiled and pointed to her head. "I remember lots from way back. Unfortunately, I don't always remember what I did yesterday...or where I put my glasses."

On the end table next to Mrs. Jenkens, an alarm pinged.

Mrs. Jenkens didn't appear to hear it.

"Your watch alarm is going off. Do you need to do something?"

"Oh, is it? I can't hear those high tones anymore." She picked up the watch. "My nephew brought it for me and set it so I'd remember to take my pills." She pointed to her head again. "I don't need it, though. I take the pills when the postman drops off the mail. He's like clockwork."

Red decided not to ask her about Sundays and when the postman was on vacation. She changed the subject back to Rolf Hammergren. "You were the school nurse back when Will was there. I thought you might know something about his brother."

Outside down the block, a snowblower roared to life. With the storm tapering off, the town would soon be abuzz with the blowers and plows.

"Yes, I remember him. They say he wasn't breathing when he was born. He lived, of course, but he wasn't right."

Red thought immediately about Sammy. She hoped her baby would be all right.

"But," Mrs. Jenkens continued, "he looked normal except for his eyes." She blinked and stared at the wall beyond Red as if trying to remember.

Prissy the cat continued to purr loudly on Red's lap. Blue would not be happy when he smelled cat on her.

"My girlfriend used to babysit the two boys. She said Will was such a sweet boy. Smart, loved to build things with blocks. I guess Rolf was fourteen at the time, too old for a sitter, you'd think. The last time she was there, he was in the backyard swinging, and my girlfriend was in the house reading a book to little Will. When she looked out the window, Rolf had disappeared." She squinted through her thick glasses. "He probably had the mind of a four-year-old. Will was the one who said, 'We need to find Rolf.' He was scared.

"My girlfriend looked all over the house and was just about to call her mom for help when Will pointed to the tool shed way in the back part of the yard. Somebody came running out and jumped the back fence. My girlfriend found Rolf in the shed with his pants down. He was crying and saying something that she couldn't understand." Mrs. Jenkens blushed.

The cat stopped purring as she looked at her master.

"After that, she wouldn't babysit there anymore."

"Do you know what happened to Rolf?"

Mrs. Jenkens shook her head. "There were rumors. The Weavers next door had a bunch of kids. Someone said that he did something to one of the girls. Others said that Mrs. Hammergren couldn't take care of him anymore. I guess the Hammergrens finally put him in the state hospital." Her voice trailed off. "Those were different times, you know. People like Rolf were put away, not kept at home."

They sat in comfortable silence only interrupted by the sound of the snowplow. Red needed to get back to the office. On the off chance that Mrs. Jenkens still kept up with the goings-on at the school, she asked, "Do you recall anyone named Coke or Cole?"

Mrs. Jenkens pursed her lips, drumming her fingers on the chair arm. "Hmmm. I don't remember a Coke, but I do recall a Cole."

Red leaned closer as Mrs. Jenkens nodded. "Oh yes, Cole Treuer. He was a student teacher back—oh, I can't remember back when. Nice boy. I heard he went on to become the principal at one of the schools in the cities. The kids liked him."

"How long ago was this?"

Mrs. Jenkens laughed. "Long enough that he's probably retired to Arizona by now."

Red's cell phone rang, and the cat stopped purring again. "Excuse me." She lifted the cat and set her on the floor before walking into the hallway to answer it. As she spoke into the phone, she noted that all her interviews lately seemed to have been interrupted by phone calls.

"Red, it's Georgia. I think we have another problem."

"Please don't tell me we have more missing teenagers."

"Can you come over to the store? Lou and Scotty are already here."

"What is this about?"

"I'd rather show you—in case..."

When she returned to the living room, Mrs. Jenkens dozed with the cat on her lap. Red slipped quietly out the door.

"Oh, Will," she said, taking a deep breath of the chilled air. "What family secret did you hide?"

23

SHERIFF RED

THE CHURCH DONATION BOX

Outside, the late afternoon sun sent pink rays across the deep blue sky. Without the cloud cover from the storm, the heat drained out of the earth. Snow crunched beneath Red's feet with the icy brittleness of at least five degrees below zero. It would get worse with nightfall. She shivered and hoped Missy had found shelter—if she was out there and if she was still alive.

Georgia, Scotty, and Lou greeted her from the round oak table in the back of the antique store. The space heater poured warm air into the room, but it was no match for the bone chill of the air outside. Everyone wore thick sweaters.

"What's so important that you called the poker club together on this nose-numbing night?" Red half expected them to bring out a cake and shout, "Surprise," but she quickly changed her mind by the worried expressions on their faces.

"Look." Georgia pointed toward the open wooden collection box on the table. It held a few dollar bills and some loose change. Georgia lifted the dollar bills to expose a thick, tightly rolled wad of money secured with a rubber band.

"Is this the donation box from the Church?"

Lou nodded. "I grabbed it last night when I closed the clinic, but I didn't open it until this afternoon."

"How much money is in there?"

"I didn't unroll it in case you needed to check it for fingerprints or something."

"Like on those television crime shows," Scotty added hopefully.

Red pulled off her parka and sat down. "I think it's safe to count it. We aren't going to fingerprint all those bills. For one thing, we don't know if a crime has been committed. For another, unless the bills are brand new, they'll have dozens of prints on them. And lastly, my crime scene investigation budget got spent on dental services for a couple of meth heads in my jail."

Scotty laughed. "Is that why you don't have those handsome investigators running around with guns and portable labs?"

"Yup. Instead, I have a fat dentist from Brainerd who whines about payment every time I send him a prisoner."

The tea kettle on a hot plate whistled. "Tea?" Georgia called out.

The room filled with the spicy aroma of herb tea. Lou and Scotty pulled the money out of the box and sorted it into separate piles for each denomination.

"I wish we had this to play with at our next poker game," Scotty said.

"Shush. The law might hear you."

Red stirred honey into her tea and contemplated the pile of money in front of her.

"It's drug money, isn't it?" Lou looked at Red.

"Best not to jump to conclusions."

"But who? And why?" Georgia pulled out a one-hundred-dollar bill and examined it. "Were they hiding it or donating it?"

All the weariness and stress of the day gathered into Red's shoulders. She ached from her ankles to the top of her head.

"When did you last check the box?"

"We empty it once a week or so. Didn't you check it last time?" Lou turned to Georgia.

"A week or so ago, I think."

"But you're not sure?"

"I'm sure I emptied it before the new year. For the books." Georgia looked chagrined. "We don't pay much attention to the box because there's never much in it. I think the most we've ever counted out was fifty dollars."

"Until today," Scotty added.

"So." Red sipped her tea. It was too sweet. "The money could have been left anytime in the last two weeks." She set down her mug. "Who knows about the box?"

Georgia put the one-hundred-dollar bill into the pile. "Only the people who use the clinic. We keep it at the back on a table behind the last pew."

"And the Church is locked between clinic sessions?"

Red's worry grew as they totaled up the cash. If it was drug money that someone was hiding, then they'd be after it, which put the Church and everyone who used it in danger. If it was put in the box as a donation...No, she didn't believe someone would stuff this much cash in the box out of good will.

They counted in silence as Red watched them. By the time they finished, Red's tea was cold.

"Five thousand and some change," Scotty announced.

"Enough to stock up on our supply of no-cost birth control pills."

An uncomfortable quiet filled the room as they stared at the piles of money on the table. Down the street, the town plow scraped the road, its engine rumbling above the whine of the wind.

Up until ten years ago, the drug problem in Pearsal County had been limited to some of the usual suspects, the families with long histories of drug and alcohol abuse, the dumb teenagers experimenting, and a few "upstanding" citizens who got caught. Methamphetamine was a home-grown operation. For a while, the labs were everywhere from isolated cabins to the trunks of cars.

Something happened, though. When the law passed making it hard to buy pseudoephedrine over the counter, the home labs dried up. But the meth problem didn't go away.

Her contacts in the Bureau of Criminal Apprehension and Drug Enforcement Agency warned her. "It's organized now. They're bringing stuff from the big labs in Mexico in through the Canadian border. They pack it up in ways that the drug-sniffing dogs can't detect. Those guys at the top have nothing more to do than figure out ways around the law."

Instead of home-grown meth, northern Minnesota was dealing with opioids and heroin brought in across the borders. Every decade, it seemed like something new became the enemy—marijuana, cocaine, PCP, speed, and now prescription drugs. As Will once said, the craving for a high was universal.

Red wondered when the money in front of her would be missed. She had a bad feeling about this.

Find Coke. Find her.

She was sure this was tied to Missy Klein and Jared Peterson.

"Hundred dollars for your thoughts, Sheriff." Scotty waved a bill in front of Red.

Shrugging, Red stirred her cold tea. "If you don't mind, I'll take your donation box over to the courthouse and lock it up."

"Aw, can't we use it to buy a new wall hanging first?" Scotty pointed to the gambling dogs behind her.

Red stood up and said in a tight voice, "And don't tell anyone about this. Let's just say that if this money is illicit, someone is after it."

Lou, who was quietly knitting a multicolored shawl, looked at Red. "I'd talk to Tiffy Norgren and Sara Weick again if I were you."

Before Red walked out with the box, Georgia motioned to her from the little kitchenette in the back of the store. "I've been thinking about that letter from the lawyer claiming Hammergren land. Why would anyone want a stake in those acres? It's nice wilderness but hardly prime property. It's not even on a lake."

Red shrugged. "There was some talk about minerals in the soil. That's the only thing I can think of." She pulled her cap on. "I don't know. When it comes to inheritance, people can get weird."

She once broke up a fight in the hospital between two brothers over a life insurance policy. She arrived in time to stop the younger one from hitting his brother with the telephone while their mother breathed her last. It turned out they were fighting over an $800 policy, not even enough to post the brothers' bail.

Red waved to the group and stepped out into the frigid winter.

Carrying the collection box under her arm, she surveyed the empty street in front of Georgia's Antiques. Even though the plow had been through, snow was drifting back over the road. It would be at least a day before things began moving again in town. The clock was ticking on finding Missy.

24

MISSY

A cold blast of icy snow scraped at Missy's cheek, and she opened her eyes with a start. She was huddled against the door of the fish house, snowflakes freezing on her eyelashes. She had been dreaming of her father and her mother. In the dream, they were bathed in a bright light, like an angel she'd seen on television. They held their arms open to her.

Maybe she could close her eyes and find her parents again. Except that something was poking into the side of her knee. She reached down to touch an icy chunk of snow. When she pulled it away from her knee, she remembered.

This wasn't a chunk of ice; it was the key's hiding place. Her father had made it in his pottery studio to look just like snow-encrusted ice.

"No one will guess the key is in here," he'd said.

Her fingers were numb stumps inside the mittens. In the distance, she thought she heard the low roar of a snowmobile. Or maybe it was just the wind, or maybe it was the lake roiling beneath the ice.

Missy fumbled with the chunk of pottery. She knew it was supposed to pull apart, but her fingers were like paws. Tears popped into her eyes.

Hurry. Maybe the *Followers* were out there. Or maybe the lake would rise up and seize her in its icy water. She couldn't think straight, her brain frozen like her fingers.

Sometimes you just have to get mad to get the blood flowing. That was what Grampa Jack once said after he banged his head on an open cupboard door.

She pictured Jared and how he slapped her in the face, and then she closed her eyes and saw the murderer pulling a trigger that sent Junior to heaven and left her without the dad who played in the snow with her and took her fishing and hiking.

Anger rose, hot around her cheeks. I. Hate. You. She cried out at the one who put the bullet through her father's heart. With fury, she smashed the pottery against the door and felt it shatter. The key fell to the ground near her foot. She clawed at it with frozen, aching fingers.

Come on. Come on.

She scooped the snow and the key and stared at it in the palm of her hand. For a moment, dark blobs floated in front of her eyes, and she felt dizzy, like she was falling over. With a deep breath of the icy air, the blobs and dizziness disappeared. Her fingers were so stiff she could barely hold the key. She poked it into the lock.

What if it didn't fit? What if the lock was frozen? Sometimes Grampa Jack had to use his lighter to get the key to turn. In her pocket, she had two matches left. Should she use them or save them to light the camp stove in the fish house?

Can't think. Can't think.

The roar in her head grew like a black cloud coming to squeeze the life out of her. She twisted the key. Nothing. Gripping the key, she tried again. It wouldn't move.

She closed her eyes and thought about her father and her mother and the white halo around them. They'd want her to be safe. She knew that was what they would want.

Then she remembered. Grandpa Jack had to pull the doorknob when he turned the lock.

She tugged at the doorknob and twisted the key. The lock clicked open.

Missy burst into tears as she staggered inside the fish house and locked the door behind her.

Outside, the wind rose as the clouds moved on and the temperature dropped.

25

SHERIFF RED
BOBBI NORGREN

After locking the box of money up in her office, Red thought longingly about going home. The recliner with Blue settled on her lap and a glass of red wine called to her. Except she needed to talk with Tiffy Norgren again. She suspected that Lou was right; Tiffy and Sara knew something more. Sighing, she trudged to her car. Overhead, the stars twinkled in frozen clarity. The temperature would plummet. Was Missy out there somewhere in the deathly cold?

Hitch Norgren's house was located in a heavily wooded area on the southeast shore of Hammer Lake near Highway 63. Someone had plowed the driveway with a military precision. Red guessed that at the rate the snow was drifting, the driveway had been re-plowed at least once, if not twice. Red pulled to a stop in the turnaround. Wind cut through the Forester as if the car were made of paper. Overhead, a fingernail moon emerged from a ghostly cloud.

The Norgren house had been the talk of Lykkins Lake. Designed to be earth friendly, it had thick walls of a special concrete developed in Sweden. The metal roof came to a peak, then came partway down onto a wall of windows facing south. It was built in such a way to shade against the high summer sun but allow the angled winter sun to add solar heat. The architect, someone famous in California, had built it to California specifications.

The old wags at the Town Talk had laughed and said it was the only earth-quake-proof building in the upper Midwest.

Off to the side was an industrial-sized pole building that looked neither earth friendly nor like it belonged in *Architectural Digest*. The building housed Bobbi Norgren's quilting business. It was dark against the forest wall.

A light popped on over the front door as Red knocked. She shivered inside the heavy parka. The temperature would descend to at least fifteen-below tonight. Red hoped no one in the rural area would run out of propane. She didn't want to go out on any more emergency rescue calls—unless it was to find Missy Klein.

Bobbi Norgren opened the door and greeted Red. "Come in, Sheriff. Don't stand out in the cold." She had large, wide-set brown eyes and a mouth that held a perpetual "Oh?" expression. Her straight brown hair was pulled back into a bouncy ponytail.

"Thanks, Bobbi."

Once inside, Red quickly slipped out of her heavy coat and boots. She did not want to become overheated before she had to face the grim cold again.

Bobbi hovered and chattered. "Quite a storm. I've had to get the tractor out three times to keep the driveway open. Have to keep it open for my business, you know. Hitch isn't here. Would you like some coffee? I've got home-baked banana bread, too."

Bobbi ushered her into an open, two-story living area with a large field-stone fireplace. Still talking. "I heard it's going to get down to twenty below tonight. I hope people can get to church tomorrow. We're having a potluck. I heard the wrestling teams got home okay. Hitch isn't here right now. I'm making a tuna casserole."

A dark brown leather couch sat in front of the fireplace. Gas flames licked around a perfect fake log. The Norgrens burned no wood in this impeccably clean house.

"I'm here to talk with Tiffy." Red stood close to the fireplace.

Bobbi frowned. "Tiffy?"

"We're trying to find her friend, Missy Klein. We thought Tiffy might have some ideas."

Bobbi brushed away invisible lint from her blue jeans. The jeans were ironed with a sharp crease. "I don't like Missy. She's trouble. Hitch isn't here, you know. Can I get you a cup of coffee and a piece of banana bread? It's warm."

Red raised her hand. "Thank you, but I don't want to put you to any trouble." She kept her voice calm. This wasn't the Bobbi she'd seen at the grocery store calmly checking off items from her list. This wasn't the Bobbi that ran one of the most successful quilting businesses in the state.

"Are you all right?"

"What?" Bobbi blinked and shook her head.

"Is everything okay here?"

The "Oh?" lips pressed together for a moment into a pout that slowly widened into a smile. "I'm fine. I've been too busy today. We have a potluck at church tomorrow, and Hitch isn't here right now, and I need to keep the driveway open." She stopped. "You must think I'm silly, going on like this."

Not silly—looney, maybe. Or high. Red looked at Bobbi for telltale signs of meth use. Sometimes the users were good at hiding it. But Bobbi wasn't thin, her teeth were perfect, and her hair looked healthy.

Red tried again. "I'm looking for Tiffy. Is she here?"

Bobbi pulled nervously at her cashmere sweater. "I'm sorry, Tiffy is spending the night with Sara. They were going to watch old movies. Can I get you some coffee and banana bread?"

Bobbi was halfway to the kitchen before Red could reply.

"Do you have any idea where Missy might have gone?" Red followed her into the kitchen. A loaf of banana bread cooled on top of the stove. Like the living room, the kitchen was scrubbed clean, not a dirty dish in sight, not a stray appliance on the counter.

Bobbi stopped in front of the sink and turned to Red as if she'd forgotten what she'd come for. "Missy Klein. Junior's daughter. I knew him in high school. Poor girl. Losing both her mother and father. Junior was such a nice person..."

Her voice trailed off, and her eyes emptied as if she were suddenly in a trance.

"Do you know where she might be?" Red prompted. What was wrong with this woman?

Bobbi blinked. "What?"

"Missy Klein. Do you know where she might have gone?" Red raised her voice.

A slight shudder ran through Bobbi's shoulders. "I told Tiffy to stay away from her. Bad crowd. Junior was such a nice man. Did you know he wrestled with Hitch in high school? They were such good friends. Too bad about his wife. Mayme was a little odd."

So are you. Red wondered again about Bobbi and drugs.

Bobbi pulled open the cupboard door near the sink and grabbed two mugs. "Did you say you wanted some coffee? Come to think of it, I'm out, but I could heat up water for tea, or I could offer you a glass of orange juice."

"Do you think Missy was mixed up in drugs?"

One of the mugs slipped from Bobbi's hand and crashed to the floor. Bobbi stared at it, her fingers twitching.

"I hear things sometimes. From the boys when I go with Hitch to the meets."

Red squatted down and picked up the broken pieces of the mug. Bobbi did not move.

"I hate when things break." A tear trickled down her cheek.

"What kinds of things do you hear from the boys?"

Bobbi wiped her eyes. "Oh, nothing really. Silly boy stuff. No, I don't know anything about Missy. Junior was such a nice man. Did they ever catch the hunter who shot him? Would you like some banana bread before you go? I could wrap up a few pieces for you."

Red tried one more time. "Do you think Missy might have been mixed up with drugs?"

Bobbi continued to stare at the floor, working her lips. "I don't know. Bad crowd with that Peterson boy. He should have stayed on the wrestling team. Hitch won't tolerate misbehavior. No drinking, no drugs. Those boys are good boys. Would you like some banana bread?"

Red smiled at her. "No, thank you. Save it for your family. I'll see if I can catch Tiffy at the Weicks' house."

"Yes, that would be nice." Bobbi's voice turned vague. "Do you think I should plow the driveway again? Will it drift in tonight?"

. . .

Back in the Forester, with the heater blasting tepid air into her face, Red rubbed her forehead as if to erase the craziness of Bobbi Norgren. All the circuits weren't firing inside that woman's head. She wondered what she'd find in the Norgren medicine cabinet. She had that skittish demeanor of someone who has been beaten. Was Hitch Norgren an abuser?

Georgia once told her that she thought Bobbi was a lot smarter than she acted. "She's odd, but she's got *some*thing. Who would have thought there would be money to be made in quilting?"

"She makes quilts? Doesn't that take time?"

"No." Georgia shook her head. "That's the beauty of it. People sew together their fabric and patterns and send them to her. She adds the batting and the backing and does the actual quilting. They're the artists, and she's the quilter."

"I think we have a crazy quilter," Red muttered as she threw the car in gear and gave it some gas. The tires slipped on the newly plowed snow, then caught with a skidding sound.

The reception at Sara Weick's house was a little more normal. Sara opened the door wearing a Lykkins Lake Tigers sweatshirt, sweatpants, and fuzzy yellow slippers. She carried a bowl of popcorn. The only thing that wasn't normal was the look of disappointment on her face when she saw it was Red. Obviously, Tiffy and Sara were expecting someone else.

"Hi," Red said. "Can I come in?"

"Sure, I guess." She looked beyond Red.

"Don't worry. I won't take up too much of your time. Are your folks around?"

"They went to the Golden Deer for a while."

"In this weather?"

Sara shrugged.

Sara's parents were known for spending a lot of time at the casino. She wondered how much money they left behind at the poker machines. The house hadn't been updated in twenty years—complete with dark brown carpeting and cheap paneled walls. Quite a contrast with the Norgren house. Still, its shabbiness felt far more comfortable than the sterile perfection of the Norgrens'.

Tiffy sat on a sagging sofa in front of the television. When she saw Red, she quickly grabbed the remote control and clicked off the movie. Red stood in front of the couch and motioned for Sara to sit down. She decided that "official" would be the best way to see if the girls had anything more to say.

"You aren't telling me everything you know about Missy."

Both girls stared at their laps.

"We know this is about drugs."

Tiffy's mouth dropped open. "How..."

Sara glared at Tiffy.

"Come on, ladies. You know Missy is in trouble or you wouldn't have said anything yesterday." Red was getting hot inside her parka, but she didn't want to change her stance. She knew the girls were on the verge of talking. She silently counted to five.

"Jared Peterson is dead, and I believe that Missy is in danger. If you don't want to talk with me, I suppose I'll have to bring you two in." She reached inside her pocket for her cell phone.

"Wait." Sara pulled her knees up to her chest and wrapped her arms around them. "If we say something, will you have to tell our parents?"

"Depends." Sweat was now dripping down Red's back. If she unzipped her coat, she was sure steam would come out.

"Sometimes," Tiffy said in a small voice, "kids would buy stuff from Jared."

"Like what?"

"A little oxy, some marijuana, the usual stuff."

The usual stuff. What were these two teenagers, sitting on the couch with popcorn, wearing fluffy slippers, doing talking about the usual stuff? Red unzipped her coat, pulled it off, and sat down on a creaky upholstered chair.

"Tell me about it."

"Well, that's the thing," Sara said. "Missy didn't do drugs. She said she didn't want to be like her mother..." Her voice dropped away.

"Yes, and?" Red prompted.

"Well, this fall when she started hanging out with Jared, we thought she'd lost it."

"Did she say why?"

Tiffy and Sara exchanged a look, both clearly distressed.

"We promised we wouldn't say anything." Sara hugged herself harder.

"Who did you promise?"

"Missy," Sara said into her knees.

Tiffy shifted on the couch and accidentally hit the play button on the DVD. Suddenly the room was filled with the sound of Julie Andrews singing about a "spoonful of sugar." The girls really were watching old movies. *What a contrast*, Red thought. *Talking illicit drugs while watching Mary Poppins. Who knew?*

Quickly, Tiffy grabbed the remote and clicked the movie off. With a sheepish expression, she murmured, "I like *Mary Poppins*."

Red nodded. She couldn't stand Julie Andrews's voice. "What's the deal with Missy? This is important."

"She didn't tell us everything."

"But it started with her mom being sick in Minneapolis." Tiffy's face showed relief, as if keeping this secret had been a great burden.

"We went with her once to see her mother at the hospice place." Sara stared at the gray television screen that was holding *Mary Poppins* at bay. "Missy wouldn't let us go in. It looked like a really nice place, too. She told us to go get coffee and come back."

"Yeah, we found a coffee shop and sat for a long time." Tiffy turned to Sara. "Missy was real weird when we picked her up. She said she was going to find out who 'did this to her.'"

A gust of wind rattled one of the living room windows, sending a cold draft of air across Red's back. The girls moved closer together. "Do you know what she was talking about?"

Tiffy shrugged. "Kind of."

"We think it was about who sold drugs to her mom and that she thought her dad's shooting wasn't an accident. But Missy wouldn't tell us anything else."

"Was she looking for that person?"

"We kinda think so, but Missy wouldn't tell us." Sara pushed her bangs out of her eyes.

"We think she found something out, but this last week or two, she wouldn't really talk to us."

"You're still sure she wasn't doing drugs?"

They both looked uncertain.

"What about someone named Coke or Cole? Does that mean anything to you?"

Both girls frowned, shaking their heads. Tiffy spoke, "The kids call my dad Coach, but I've never heard of anyone named Coke."

Red asked a few more questions, but Tiffy and Sara had nothing more to add.

Red stood up and pulled on her coat. "Do you know where she might go if she was trying to hide?"

Tiffy shrugged. "That's the thing. We are her best friends. I think she'd come to us first."

"Yeah, that's another reason we're worried."

Just before she let herself out the door, Red turned to the girls. "Do you know anything about all the money that was put in the donation box at the Church?"

Tiffy and Sara stared at her with expressions that said, "Huh?"

Red believed them.

26

SHERIFF RED
ANNIE

The clock on the wall of her office ticked with its battery-powered precision. Eight fifteen and Red was no closer to finding the missing Missy. It had been a hell of a day with so little to show for it outside of Sammy's baby. The corner streetlight glowed crisply in the frigid night air. In the warmth of the office, with the wind whistling through the old courthouse windows, her eyes drooped.

The room darkened into a gray haze, and Will appeared in front of her, gaunt from his battle with cancer. He spoke to her, but he had no voice. The words came inside her head. "Look for the connections. It's like a quilt, patterned and sewn together."

She opened her mouth to ask him what he meant when a blast of wind beat an icy spray of snow against the window behind her. Red's eyes snapped open.

"Oh boy." She rubbed her forehead and took a deep breath. "Time to wake up."

She stood up, stretched, and reached for her parka when the words of her dream came back to her. *Look for connections.*

What did she know? Missing Missy, dead boyfriend, undercurrent of drug dealing, money in the Church donation box. Added to that, Junior Klein's unsolved death. Connections?

She picked the file on Junior Klein out of her inbox and read through it again. Were there connections? She walked over to the large county map hanging on her wall. It took a little squinting with her middle-aged eyes—and yes, she knew she needed reading glasses—before she found the spot where she thought Junior had been found. She remembered the little wooden hunter's shack. It was surprisingly close to the Henderson cabin. The footprints in the snow headed in that direction. Would Missy plunge through the snow to get to someplace familiar? Did she know that area? If she had gone in that direction, then what? If she was running from someone, would she go to the shack and hide?

If it hadn't been dark and late and extremely cold, Red might have headed out to where Junior had been found. But the only way to get to the shack in the winter was with a snowmobile or snowshoes. If she tried to find the place tonight, she might end up being the next missing person in Pearsal County. Tomorrow, she decided. Tonight she needed to rest her aching muscles.

Outside, the snowplow scraped against the pavement. She watched it throw the new snow to the growing bank at the side of the road. Time to go home. Before she locked up her office, she grabbed the Junior file and stuck it in her bag. Maybe a sit-down with it and a glass of wine would help.

When she arrived home, she found that her neighbor, Oscar, had already plowed out the driveway. She made a note to bring him a six-pack of Summit Stout next week as thanks. In the winter, Oscar plowed her driveway, refusing to accept money. In the summer, he mowed her lawn, again refusing to accept money.

"I'm a retired old duffer. I ain't got nothing else to do," he'd said the first time she tried to pay him. After that, she brought him beer and an occasional bottle of Jameson. She also gave him a key to her house to let Blue out on the days she was too busy to stop by.

"Me and that dog of yours, we get along just fine."

Blue greeted her with happy yips, his butt wiggling and his toes scrabbling against the hardwood-floor entry.

"Did you miss me?" She picked him up as soon as she shook off her coat. Frost was building on the inside of the kitchen window above the sink.

The thermometer outside the window registered ten degrees below zero. Another reason not to try to find Missy in the middle of the night.

"Time for you to pee, you old pup." She put the little poodle down and held the door open for him. He sniffed and backed away. "Oh, no you don't. Minnesota dogs pee outside even when it's thirty below. That's the rule." She nudged him out the door with her foot, thinking about Will and Blue.

Blue had stayed faithfully by Will's side during the summer and fall of his illness, and even now, two years later, he still looked hopefully from his spot on Will's old recliner every time someone walked in the door. The recliner's fabric arms were frayed and stained from spilled coffee. It was on her to-do list to have it hauled away, but every time she thought about doing it, she saw Blue curled up on the seat as if protecting it for the time Will would come back.

The dog yipped and scratched at the door just as her cell phone rang. Red scooped him up and pulled her sweater around him to warm him up as she answered the phone.

"Red, it's Lou. You asked me this morning if I knew anyone named Coke."

"Yes, and I haven't had much luck finding such a person."

"Well, I wondered about the name, and something finally came to me."

Red pressed the phone closer to her ear. "And?"

"Back when I was in junior high, the school musical was going to be *Annie*. I tried out to be one of the orphans, but I remember an older girl at the auditions—they called her Coke."

Red was surprised the name hadn't been familiar to anyone else.

"She wasn't at our school very long—maybe a couple of weeks. If I recall, she was living with a foster mother." Lou paused. "Of course, I can't remember the foster mother's name. The only reason I remembered about Coke was because it was such an odd name. At the tryouts, I asked her about it, and she nearly took my head off. Said her stupid blankety-blank parents named her Cocaine."

"Oh, bad choice. Do you know if she's still around?"

"She wasn't in the play, and I never saw her again. Sorry."

Red set Blue on the floor with a gentle pat. "Well then, next important question. Did you get the part?"

Lou laughed. "They were desperate—so yes. And Mayme Klein played Annie." Her voice dropped. "Poor Mayme."

"Maybe someone from the cast would remember her."

"Well, let's see. Mayme played Annie, and I think Bobbi played Miss Hannigan. She was terrible, by the way. Hammed it up so she sounded hysterical, and she couldn't carry a tune."

Red thought about the crazy Bobbi she'd just seen. She couldn't imagine her in the part. "Anyone else?"

"Now that I think of it, what a sad cast. Junior Klein was Daddy Warbucks, and boy did I have a crush on him. Now he's gone, too." She made a tsking sound. "And Hitch was in it as well. He couldn't sing. Worse than Bobbi. No wonder he crashed and burned in Hollywood."

Red remembered that she'd asked Hitch about Coke, and he had said he didn't know anyone with that name. Was he lying? She made a note to ask him again.

After she finished the call, Red settled into the recliner. Blue whined and wiggled at her feet until she picked him up and put him on her lap. He nestled in and rested his chin on her thigh.

She opened the file on Junior Klein. Nothing stood out. Jack Klein had found him in an open area near the old hunting shack. Junior was wearing blaze orange, and his rifle was unloaded.

Connections? Tomorrow she'd get someone out to the hunting shack.

She slipped the file back into the canvas bag. A wave of sadness swept over her as she thought about Missy. "I can't imagine the pain she's had in her short life." Blue yawned in reply.

Jack had given her a school photo from this year. Missy looked a lot like him, with piercing blue eyes and high cheekbones. In the photo she smiled, showing a small dimple on her cheek. The smile appeared to have a tightness to it, like she didn't quite know how to be happy.

"And now, if we find her...when we find her, we'll have to tell her about Jared."

Unless she already knows.

This was one of those rare times when Red wished she'd stayed in Minneapolis teaching middle school science instead of running a backwoods sheriff's office.

27

SHERIFF RED
ROLF HAMMERGREN

Red took a long, hot shower. The steamy air and warm water rolling down her back drew the tension out of her neck and shoulders. The Tylenol eased the pounding behind her eyes. As she relaxed, she began to make a mental list of what she had to do in the morning. She needed to get someone out to the hunting shack, and she needed to talk to Hitch again. If she could connect Jared to the wrestlers, maybe she would know where to start in the search for Missy. And she needed to track down this mysterious Coke.

By the time she'd thought through all the problems of the day, the water began to turn tepid.

"Great," she said to the steamed-up mirror. "I've drained the hot water heater. Not very green." Scotty, who used garbage bags made out of soy or some damn thing, wouldn't approve.

She pulled on green flannel pajamas decorated with Santa and his reindeer and padded to the kitchen, glad her house was isolated enough that neighbors couldn't see her. The pajamas had been an after-Christmas bargain at a time when her bank account had been drained by Will's illness. The first time she put them on, she was sure she could hear his ghost laughing over her shoulder.

"I know. I know. I look like a giant elf," she'd said to the empty house. "But it's all I can afford."

She thought for a moment about the number of sheriff's sales on foreclosed property she'd done in her career. Most were related to medical expenses, not extravagant living. Her best friend in high school lost her home after her husband was diagnosed with ALS. Her paltry job as a cashier at the Super Value didn't pay health insurance benefits. When her husband could no longer work, the bills piled up. When he died, she was left with massive debt and no place to live.

Will's illness took most of their savings despite having health insurance. Co-pays, out-of-pocket charges, and equipment rental all added up. Cryptic bills came in for months after he died. She remarked to Georgia one poker night after writing out yet another check, "Our system is too complicated. I don't even know what I'm paying for anymore."

"You're paying because the medical-industrial complex has very effective lobbyists in Washington. Medicine is big business."

It still galled Red that some of her conservative commissioners railed against Obamacare. Easy for them to say, as long as they were commissioners, they were on the county health insurance policy.

She shook that thought out of her head and concentrated on whether she should have a cup of hot tea or a glass of red wine. The wine looked promising, but she decided she needed a totally clear head for tomorrow.

Despite the relaxing shower and the tea that advertised itself as "sleepy time," she was still wired. Maybe going over the Klein file once again would put her to sleep.

"No, Blue, I don't want to do police work right now. Can't I have a break?"

The dog sat on her lap and licked the back of her hand.

She set him down and walked into the second bedroom that was once going to be a nursery and now was an office. One of the bulbs in the ceiling fixture had gone out, and when she flipped the switch, weak light emphasized the chaos in the room. Two large bookshelves were crammed with paperbacks that Red would never read. Will was a voracious fan of pulp crime fiction. Red preferred nonfiction and even then hardly read anything beyond the *New York Times* that Georgia passed on to her.

Will once said, "One of the first things I do when I'm investigating is notice whether there are books in the house. You can tell a lot about a person by what they read or don't read."

Smiling, she wondered if you could also tell a lot about a person by the pajamas they wore.

A big wooden desk that Will had reclaimed from the courthouse took up most of the floor space in the small room. The desk was piled high with papers and files. Some of the piles were old medical bills and utility bills paid long ago.

Whenever she had anyone over, she simply closed the door to this room. Intellectually, she knew that her inability to clean and organize this room was part of her grief. A nagging voice in her head reminded her to "get over it." Next summer, she resolved, she would clean the room and paint it a different color.

She picked up the letter from the lawyers about Will's acreage and laid it in front of her. The letter was filled with legalese, but the basic message was that someone else might have a claim on the Hammergren estate. Enclosed was a photocopy of a birth certificate for Louise Mary Weaver. The father was listed as Rolf Hammergren.

Shaking her head, she rummaged through the papers until she found the thick accordion file labeled *Hammergren Estate*. She pulled out the section on Rolf. All she had in the Rolf file was his birth certificate and the form to order a death certificate. If worse came to worst, she would need to go through the red tape to have him declared dead. Tonight was not the night to think about that.

"This is not helpful."

Blue pawed at her ankle. It was past his bedtime, and he was tired of her roaming around the house. The thermostat had automatically switched to night temperature, and the house quickly cooled down.

"Okay, okay. This doesn't tell me anything."

She put the file back on the messy desk and was about to leave when the tackle box that had originally held Rolf's birth certificate caught her eye. She'd left it on the floor in the corner of the room, where it had been gathering dust for the last six months. With a sense of shame for how she had neglected this room and all the paperwork, she picked up the box and brought it out to the kitchen.

Blue whined as she sat at the table and finally trotted off to bed in disgust. He knew the electric blanket on the bed would be warm.

She sat in the chilly kitchen and pulled out the papers in the box. Back when she'd discovered the Hammergren family papers in a dusty tackle box in the basement, she'd skimmed through all the documents looking for a death certificate. When she couldn't find one, she closed the box and put it in the corner.

One thick envelope contained what looked like official commitment papers. Red set it aside. She felt like she was intruding on something that had brought great pain to Will and the Hammergren family. Still, it might have information on where he was placed.

The box also contained old insurance policies for Will's parents, including a life insurance policy on Rolf taken out after he had been committed. It paid out a $1,200 death benefit, and there was nothing else in the box to indicate that it had been claimed. Maybe the life insurance company had documentation on Rolf's death.

Knowing all the insurance company mergers and acquisitions, finding this information might be more impossible than finding a death certificate. Why had Rolf's parents bought a life insurance policy on him, anyway? Probably for funeral and burial expenses.

Red groaned. This wasn't helping her sleep, and it wasn't getting her anywhere with the mysterious person who claimed to be Rolf's daughter. As she piled the papers back in the tackle box, a note slipped out. It was written on cheap grade school lined paper.

The message was scrawled in pencil. She had to squint to make out the words:

Dear Sherif. Rolf didn't do nothing. Bruther did it and blamed Rolf. You shoodn't send him away.

The note was not signed or dated.

"Curious." Red kept the note out and put everything else back. What did Mrs. Jenkens say? She thought something might have happened with one of the neighborhood kids. The neighbors next door had a large family. Could it have come from one of them?

It was time to join Blue under the electric blanket. As she always did, she took her cell phone with her, hoping not to hear from it.

Fifteen minutes later, after tossing and turning in bed, Red slipped out from under the warmth of the blanket. Blue looked up at her with sleepy eyes but stayed nestled in the bed. He wasn't much good for keeping her company on her many sleepless nights.

In the kitchen, with a steaming mug of tea, she fingered a file labeled *Funeral.*

Will was very clear as soon as he was given the lung cancer diagnosis that he didn't want a fuss.

"Just throw me into a pine box and bury me under a tree." He'd said it in a half-joking manner, but Red knew he was serious.

"Is that what you want?" The question was hard to ask. If they didn't talk about it, maybe it wouldn't happen.

He'd grabbed her wrist and pulled her down to sit beside him on the sofa. "Remember last year when we spent that week seeing Olympic National Park in Washington? The rain forest with its fallen logs?"

Red let out a long, slow breath. "You mean the nurse logs—they fall and feed the new growth."

"I want to feed the new growth, too. At least I will leave some Hammergren behind."

Red flinched. Because she couldn't have children, the Hammergren line would die out.

In those last days, under the care of her poker club, Will repeated his wish. By then, he was in bed most of the time. They'd gotten a hospital bed and set it up in the living room so he could look over the lake. Lou, Georgia, and Scotty took turns caring for him while Red held the sheriff's office together.

In his haze of sickness and drugs, he would look out the window and say, "My woods, I want to be in my woods."

Red knew that the Hammergren land north of Hammer Lake meant something sacred to Will. As a boy, he'd hunted the land with his father and camped alone on starry summer nights.

It was Scotty who suggested it.

"Why not let him rest in his woods? I've been reading about green burials."

The suggestion numbed Red. You don't just bury bodies wherever you feel like it. Besides, a beloved sheriff needed a community funeral.

That was when Scotty talked with Ryan, the undertaker from the funeral home. They'd gathered around Will's bed and made a plan. At that point, he wasn't always coherent and often dropped off to sleep in mid-sentence. But one evening, while the fall air filled with the sweet smell of fallen leaves, he sat up, looked at Red, and smiled.

"I'd like that. Tell Pearsal County you cremated me. But put me under the great oak behind our little cabin up there."

Will died a week later. Lou sewed a shroud, and the four women laid him into the pine box Will had chosen weeks before.

Ryan helped them dig the grave.

"I hope no one is videotaping this with their iPhones." Scotty grunted as they used ropes to lower the casket.

Red hardly remembered the rest except they were sworn to secrecy. Will's final resting place was hallowed ground.

Two days later, an urn filled with ashes from Georgia's fireplace was displayed at the funeral and later buried next to Will's parents.

Red wanted those acres to stay wild and sacred.

Her tea grew cold as she stared at the note in front of her. Was it true that the Hammergren blood had continued?

Suddenly dead tired, Red crawled back into bed. Blue snored, nestled against her.

28

SHERIFF RED
TREVOR MISSING

Red dreamed she sat at her kitchen table awaiting Thanksgiving dinner. Will stood at the stove with his back to her. The air should have been filled with the humid aroma of roast turkey. Instead, it smelled like morning mouth of someone who never brushed his teeth. The timer for the oven chimed, and she wondered why he didn't turn it off. It sounded just like a cell phone.

She woke up with a start, her phone ringing and vibrating on the bedside table. The digital clock glowed 11:28 p.m. She'd only been asleep for twenty minutes. Blue's head lay on the pillow next to her. "Dog breath," she muttered, then answered the phone.

"Red, it's Cal. Wendy Farnsworth called in. She said she can't find her son. She wants you to call her."

Red's stomach growled as she sat up. She'd forgotten to eat supper. "Put me through to her."

Wendy's voice shook. "I was sleeping on the couch this afternoon when I heard him talking on the phone. He sounded upset, but I didn't hear what he was saying." She let out a trembling sigh. "I must have fallen back to sleep. When I woke up, his room was empty, and he was gone. I saw the footprints on the steps."

"What time was it when you noticed he was gone?"

"Maybe five. He wasn't supposed to leave the house. That was our rule."

"Did you try calling his friends?"

The laugh that came across the line was half-desperate and half-cynical. "He doesn't have any friends—not since he got kicked out of school and stopped hanging around with that wrestling crowd."

"Do you have any idea where he might go?"

Wendy was silent.

"Any place he liked to hang out?"

"Maybe the bowling alley. He liked to play the video games there."

Red stretched with one arm to shake the sleep out of her tired muscles. "Wendy, stay by the phone. I'll check the bowling alley. Call dispatch if he turns up."

She set down the cell phone and stroked Blue. "Sorry, my day isn't quite over. Now I have another missing teenager."

Just before she pulled on her parka, she called Lucky Strike Lanes. Usually late on Saturday nights they had "Moonlight Bowling." The call went immediately to voicemail. It was a good guess that they had closed early because of the storm.

The snow crunched with a brittle squeak beneath her boots as she walked to her car. The windshield was covered with a thin layer of frost. Judging by the feel of the snow, the temperature was still dropping. She made a note to plug the car into the engine heater when she got home. Although the Subaru was as reliable as any car manufactured, even it could balk at starting when the temperature went down to fifteen below.

As she sat in the cold car waiting for the windshield to defrost, she recalled how she and Will had talked about adding a garage to the house. All they had was a covered carport. As with many other things, they had never gotten around to having a garage built. They both agreed that it was stupid not to have one in Minnesota winters.

"Next year. I'll do it," she said out loud, shivering in the cold car.

Lykkins Lake was dead. No traffic, no signs of life. And at near midnight, most of the houses were dark. Red drove slowly through the main road, noting that it had drifted in again after the plow had been through. "Let me not get stuck."

Out on the highway, a lone semi lurched by, sending a spray of snow behind it. She followed its tracks about a quarter of a mile to the bowling alley, which sat on the edge of town next to the used RV dealership. The lights outside the alley cast a yellow glow over the empty lot. Two cars were parked near the entrance to the building. Both were buried in snow, looking like giant white elephants against the background of the blue cement block of the bowling alley. Neither had been moved in the last few hours, and no tracks showed cars either coming or going to the bowling alley.

Red pulled over to the side of the road and put on her flashers. She didn't want anyone to slam into her car even though visibility was relatively clear. With her flashlight, she surveyed the area around the bowling alley. She saw no footprints. It was deserted.

Back in her car, she sat for a few moments trying to put herself in Trevor's shoes. "He's seventeen, drug seeking, not in very good physical shape. Where would he go?"

The drug houses she knew about were scattered throughout the county. Many of them were trailers set up on lonely acreage outside of town. Not somewhere a teenager could get to on foot—unless someone picked him up. Too many places to hide in the county.

Another semi roared past her. As it headed north, she thought its head-lights caught a glimmer of something in the RV lot. The last thing Red wanted to do was get out of the heated seat of her car and plunge through the snow to the RV lot. Yet, she was sure she'd seen movement.

Carefully, she pulled back onto the highway and crept forward, her flashers still on. A lighted sign announced "Belnor RV. We buy, sell, and trade." Behind the sign, the lot was enclosed by a chain link fence. The RVs stood like small monuments to winter with snow piled on their hoods and tops.

Red rolled down her window and peered into the lot where she thought she'd glimpsed something. She saw nothing but snow that had drifted up to the tops of the wheels.

"This isn't getting me anywhere."

Another semi drove by, its horn blaring as it passed Red's car. For a few seconds, the lot was again in the lights. There it was, behind a smaller Winnebago. An orange cap half-in and half-out of the snow.

Red stepped out of her car, flashlight in hand, and slogged through the driveway to the gate of the lot. The gate was open wide enough for a snowmobile to pass through, and tracks indicated at least two had entered within the last couple of hours.

"Hello?" Red called out. "It's Sheriff Hammergren. Is anyone there?"

Two cars whipped by on the highway, going too fast for the road conditions.

She called out again, "Trevor, are you there?"

A whimpering sound came from the direction she'd spotted the orange cap. As she plodded through the snow, she focused on the sound. The lot had a trailer that functioned as a sales office behind the first row of RVs. She closed her eyes to visualize the area.

Several years ago, she had investigated a break-in here. It turned out to be a drunken local who thought he'd been cheated out of a fair price for his camper trailer. He'd done some damage to the office, but the manager had declined to press charges.

"Old tipsy Carl. He'll pay for the damages. If he doesn't, you'll be the first person I call."

Red had been happy not to have to arrest Carl or do the paperwork.

She followed the tracks to the office, and in the dim cone of light from a streetlamp, she saw the orange cap. She hurried to the cap, praying that she wouldn't find a body to go with it. Shining her flashlight on it, she noted that it was a blaze-orange fleece-lined hunting cap, complete with earflaps. She couldn't imagine Trevor Farnsworth wearing it. This was the cap of a hunter from bygone days.

"Trevor?"

Inside the office, something tumbled over, crashing to the floor. As Red moved toward the door, it suddenly opened. Trevor staggered out, staring at her with glazed eyes. He was wearing an unzipped green down jacket that was half off his left shoulder. Red grabbed his arm. "Are you okay?"

"Dunno." His voice was slurred.

"Are you high?"

"Dunno."

She braced herself to steady him.

"Who else is in that office?"

"Huh?"

She pulled him so close to her that she could smell his breath. Trevor wasn't high, he was drunk.

"Who have you been drinking with?"

Above her, a sliver of a moon nested in the sky. She believed that a full moon created an energy that caused women to go into labor and men to hit their girlfriends. However, this moon wasn't full, and Trevor Farnsworth was suffering from something else. She saw it even in the drunken eyes. He was afraid.

Trevor suddenly reeled backward, ripping away from Red. He lurched to the side of the building, bent over, and vomited.

While he retched and gagged, Red stepped up to the door of the office. She shone her flashlight inside the little building. Other than the chair that Trevor had knocked over coming out of the building, nothing seemed to be disturbed. She saw no evidence of a liquor bottle or beer can. The door did not look like it had been kicked in, and the lock did not appear to have been jimmied.

Trevor was now down on his knees, coughing and sobbing. He looked at her, and in the moonlight, she saw the face of a terrified child.

"I didn't say anything."

She stooped beside him. "Who were you with?"

He shook his head. "Said, 'Drink. Keep drinking or we'll hurt your mom.'"

"Trevor, look at me. Who was with you?"

He picked up a handful of snow, sucked on it, and spit it out. He shook his head. "Bad people." His eyes grew big. "They want to find her."

"Who do they want to find?" Red already knew the answer. *Missy.*

Trevor's face turned ashen, and his eyes closed as he passed out.

An hour later, at the hospital, Red talked with Dr. Vijay. "Alcohol poisoning. I see it with teenagers. Twenty-one shots and then they are dead. This boy will be all right."

Wendy Farnsworth rushed in. She'd thrown a coat over her nightgown. At least she had the sense to put on her boots before leaving the house.

"You found him at the RV place?" She looked incredulous. "What was he doing there?"

"I don't know, Wendy, but he had enough alcohol in him to stop his breathing."

"Trevor doesn't drink." Her brow wrinkled in confusion. "I know he doesn't drink. We have liquor in the house, and he's never touched it."

Red patted her on the shoulder. "We'll get it figured out. I'll try to talk with him tomorrow. He's scared of something."

Red left instructions with the night nurse to call if anyone tried to visit Trevor. She would have posted a deputy to sit with him, but her crew was so short-staffed that she only had one patrol on tonight. Hopefully it would be a quiet night.

As she walked out into the moonlit deep freeze, she thought about Wendy. Her father and her son now had adjoining rooms at the hospital. Then Red thought again about Trevor's words before he passed out. They want to *find her.*

Find Coke. Find her.

29

SHERIFF RED

BLUE

A shadow person trudged through the woods toward her. He wore an orange hunting cap with earflaps and carried a hunting rifle. A skull dangled on the end of the rifle. The skull had a perfectly round hole in its forehead. She stared at the hole, knowing that if she could get close enough to see inside, she would have the answer.

The shadow person squeezed the trigger, and the skull's jaw shattered like glass.

~

Red woke up with her heart pounding and her face bathed in sweat. Had she heard glass breaking, or was it a dream? The image of the skull faded as she took a deep breath and pushed her damp bangs away from her forehead. Something about the dream pricked at the back of her eyes. What was it? The dream was gone, but a sense of foreboding permeated the dark bedroom.

Maybe the foreboding had been triggered by Trevor and the fear she'd seen on his face. Maybe by the missing Missy. Or maybe by the unfinished business with Will's estate. Whatever the case, she was awake now.

Blue stretched under the covers and inched his way up to her face. He licked her and looked at her with anxious brown eyes.

"Need to go out, old pup?" She smiled at him. In some ways, he was like an old man with prostate problems. It seemed like he needed to go out at least once in the middle of every night.

How did I end up with a dog with a bladder the size of a pea? The cold of the bedroom hit her as she crawled out from under the covers. She sat up, closing her eyes for a moment, and tried to conjure up the image from the dream. Leaves crackling as the shadow person neared. What was it?

Will used to tease her about her "spidey sense." "Sometimes I swear you know about trouble before trouble itself knows. It's either your jaw aching or that ache in your chest."

She'd shrugged him off by saying, "It's common sense, dear. Nothing mystical about it."

Still, something didn't feel right. Red threw off the blanket and shivered as her feet touched the hardwood floor. Blue looked up at her with an expression that said, "Yes, I have to pee, but, no, I don't want to go outside. It's freezing out there."

"Come on, you little ragamuffin. I know it's cold, but you asked to go out." Picking him up, she headed for the kitchen to let him out the back door. It was four in the morning, and Red was exhausted. She'd gotten home just after two and then spent an hour tossing in bed as she wrestled with the sense that bad things were happening in the county, and she was helpless to stop them.

Blue shivered in her arms. "Don't try to wring sympathy out of me. You're going out."

What was it about the dream?

"I wish you had a bigger bladder, old boy." She pushed him out the door and quickly pulled it shut. In this weather, Blue would not be long. As she turned from the door, she caught a faint swooshing sound, like boots sinking into the snow. The image of the shadowed man wearing a hunting cap and carrying a rifle with a skull floated through her head.

Her mouth was dry and tacky from sleep. "You need to drink more." Scotty was always after her to "hydrate." Eight glasses of water a day, she'd pronounce.

She filled a glass from the tap. As she brought it to her mouth, she was sure she heard another faint noise. She squinted at the closed kitchen door. The switch for the outside light was up, but no light shone in through the kitchen door. The bulb probably burned out. She couldn't remember the last time she'd changed it. Poor Blue. It was bad enough that she'd thrown the poor creature out in the sub-zero cold. She couldn't make the shivering dog pee in the dark, too.

Chuckling at her weakness for the dog's comfort, she hurried back to the door and pushed it open. If the outdoor bulb was out, at least Blue could pee by the light of the kitchen.

She couldn't see him in the winter night shadows.

"Blue?"

Silence. She listened hard but heard nothing, not even the sound of wind whisking through the treetops. A shiver crept down the back of her neck.

"Blue? Come on, you little rag mop. I'm cold standing here."

Silence.

"Come on, Blue. Don't tell me you've sunk into a snow pile."

A rustling noise by the side of the house caught her attention. She stepped out, and a shard of glass pierced the thin sole of her slipper.

Leaning against the door, Red pulled the shard out. It was a piece of light bulb. As her eyes adjusted to the shadowy dark, she saw the broken bulb.

"Blue? Where are you?" Bulbs didn't spontaneously combust.

Several boot prints led to and from her back door, but she'd been in and out a couple of times since the snow stopped. She assumed they were hers.

She commanded, "Blue, come here!" The cold seeped up her legs. The green pajamas wouldn't keep her warm long in this cold. Why would Blue wander so far? He was hardly a curious poodle. His goal in life was to find warmth.

"Where are you?" The sheriff calm she used to handle crises melted away. Panic choked her.

After doing a quick visual sweep and seeing no evidence of the dog, she stepped inside and pulled on her boots, oblivious to the blood seeping from the puncture wound in her foot. Grabbing a flashlight, she ran outside wearing only her green Santa Claus pajamas.

"Blue?"

Following the path to the driveway, she swept the beam of her flashlight back and forth, looking for little dog prints.

"Blue, come here!" The cold penetrated the pajamas, numbing her legs. Her hands ached, and her fingers stiffened.

As she rounded the corner to the driveway, she heard another noise—the sound of boots pressing through the crust of the windblown snow. She flashed the light in the direction of the noise. A dark shadow slipped away from the house, into the woods.

"Hey!"

Something scraped at her leg. She looked down. Blue stood on his back legs, his front paws scratching at her leg. In one motion, Red swept the dog up into her arms.

"You little troublemaker. You had me worried. What are you doing wandering so far from the door in this weather?"

The dog wriggled his butt and licked her face. For a moment, Red forgot the figure in the snow. When she looked again, the woods were quiet.

"Was someone out there, old pup?"

Ten minutes later, a snowmobile, its engine muffled, careened away across Lykkins Lake.

30

SHERIFF RED
THE ROSARY

In the morning, weak sunlight sparkled off the newly fallen snow as Red surveyed the area around her house. Near where the walk to the house and the driveway met, she saw something brownish in the snow. Picking it up in her gloved hand, she studied it. It appeared to be a frozen piece of raw hamburger.

She stared at it. Her first thought was that she'd dropped it when she brought in groceries. That thought vanished quickly because Red never bought hamburger, at least not since Scotty had harangued her about high-fat foods. Where did it come from? Had someone tried to poison Blue? She allowed a wan smile. Unlike normal dogs, Blue had no interest in hamburger.

Scrub bushes in the woods between her house and the lake whispered in the frigid breeze. Red's breath fogged in front of her. Half-filled-in boot prints led toward the lake. Because of the drifting, she couldn't tell the size of the boot or the type. She followed them until she came to a disturbance in the snow.

"Looks like a snowmobile turned around here," Red muttered. "What the hell?"

She was so intent on following the snowmobile tracks that she almost missed the shiny object in the snow. It was pressed into the track as if someone had dropped it and then ran over it. She picked up a silver rosary with black beads. The beads looked to be coral, not plastic. "Whoever you are, it looks like you lost something."

The tracks disappeared as soon as she reached the frozen lake. Wind had swept the snow away in patches, and it was impossible to see where the snowmobile had gone.

Red shaded her eyes against the early morning glare and looked out over the lake. All appeared to be calm. Puzzled, she walked back to the house. Who would snowmobile over the lake to drop a rosary in her woods?

Inside the kitchen, she popped the piece of meat into a baggie and shoved it in the freezer. She'd think about having it tested later. Right now, her stomach was grumbling, and her larder was bare. Breakfast at the Town Talk, even with Scotty's bad coffee, sounded good to her.

After sweeping up the shattered bulb, she let Blue out one last time before leaving. He walked only as far as he needed before he squatted. What had caused him to go further last night? And what had caused the outdoor bulb to break? Once he was safely inside, she patted him quickly on the head and said, "Stay out of trouble. Your sheriff is too tired, too hungry, and too worried to deal with you."

Blue licked her hand before she set him down on the recliner. *Ah,* she thought. *A sheriff and her dog.*

On the way to the café, she passed the Catholic church. Car exhaust fogged the air in the bitter cold. The Sunday faithful scurried inside, women clutching the arms of men as they slid in their dress shoes. She caught a glimpse of Bobbi and Tiffy Norgren linked arm in arm, but Hitch wasn't with them. Instead, Beldon Rafferty held the church door for them.

Both the rosary and the orange hunting cap from the RV dealership lay on the seat beside her. She was tempted to stop into the church and ask if anyone had lost either one of them.

She shrugged and drove on.

The Town Talk was Sunday-morning still. Red and Georgia were Scotty's only customers.

"I hate the cold. Should have opted for a place down in Arizona." Georgia blew on her mug of coffee. "What was I thinking?"

Scotty brought over two plates heaped with scrambled eggs and hash browns. "You two should be eating oatmeal and fresh fruit."

Georgia nodded. "I'll start tomorrow."

Red dug into the eggs, mentally checking off all the duties for the day. She told them about the shattered light bulb and the trampled snow. She did not mention rescuing Trevor Farnsworth.

"I followed tracks down to the lake. Whoever it was had a snowmobile." Red shifted in her seat, pulling the rosary out of her back pocket. "He left me this." She held it out. The crucifix gleamed in the artificial light of the café.

Georgia examined the rosary. "The cross is sterling silver. Take a look at how fine the features are on Christ's face."

"My God, you can see the agony." Scotty brushed her index finger across the crucifix. "I remember somebody used to come into the restaurant with a rosary. She'd finger those beads and mumble to herself while she waited for her soup and sandwich."

"It's a form of meditation for some people," Georgia commented.

Scotty shrugged. "Or penance."

"Do you remember who it was?" Red took the beads back from Georgia.

"Not offhand. But it will come to me eventually."

The oven timer dinged in the kitchen. Scotty hurried back to it.

"Burning her muffins again?" Georgia added more cream and sugar to her coffee. "Lord, she makes bad coffee."

Red nodded. "Small town. What can I say? People are used to coffee that tastes like dishwater."

Outside, the city plow lurched by, creating a bank around Red's Subaru. She should have parked at the courthouse and walked.

"I found something in the box that had some of the old Hammergren papers. I wonder if it's relevant." She pulled the fragile note out of the file she had with her. This morning she'd placed it in a protective plastic sheet.

Georgia squinted as she read the faded pencil scratching. "Hmmm."

Red filled her in on her conversation with Mrs. Jenkens, the old school nurse.

"Are you speculating that Rolf was sent away because of something he did to one of the neighbor kids?"

Red shrugged. "I hate to jump to conclusions, but from what she said, it sounded like something was done to Rolf, not the other way around. The tackle box also had what looked like commitment papers, but I didn't read them."

"Read what?" Scotty slid into the booth next to Red. "What's this?"

After she read the note, she paused, looking up at the Georgia O'Keeffe print behind Georgia.

"Didn't the Hammergrens live on Second Avenue in that two-story gray house?"

Red nodded. "I think so. It was before my time, but Will pointed it out to me a few years back. The house had fallen on hard times. It's gone now."

"I think the Weavers lived next door. Big Catholic family. This county used to be full of Weavers, but the family has scattered."

Red's cell vibrated in her pocket. She'd forgotten to turn the ringer back on. Excusing herself, she walked to a table in the corner and answered.

It was Billie, the dispatcher, checking in.

"Anything of note last night?" she asked.

"Yeah, my car wouldn't start. I had to walk to work." He paused as if he expected Red to acknowledge his sacrifice.

Billie lived all of five blocks away. Red refrained from commenting.

He reported, "Couple of cars in the ditch, a fender-bender down on Oak Street, and a report of snowmobile noise on Lykkins Lake."

"What time did the snowmobile report come in?"

Papers rustled on the other end of the line. "Looks like around four in the morning."

"Who called it in?"

"It doesn't say."

"Anything from the hospital on Trevor Farnsworth?"

More paper shuffling. "Nope."

Red sat back down with Georgia. From the kitchen, they heard Scotty swear.

"Burned the muffins, just like I said." Georgia set down her fork and looked at Red with a serious expression. "I hear that you found Trevor Farnsworth at the RV place lethally intoxicated."

Red took another forkful of eggs. "What? Do you have a hotline to all the news?"

"Small town."

"What news?" Scotty stood over them, pulling off an oven mitt.

Georgia looked up at her. "Trevor Farnsworth."

"Bad scene. Why would he do it?"

Red scratched her head. "How come everybody knows about Trevor?"

"Do you really want to know?" Scotty sat down.

"No, as long as it wasn't someone from my staff."

The buzzer in the kitchen went off again, and Scotty hurried away. Red watched her leave, hoping not to see smoke coming from the kitchen.

They ate in silence for a few moments. Then Georgia asked, "What's on your agenda today?"

"Missing teenagers, drunk teenagers, old murders. You know, the usual."

"Old murders?"

Red realized she'd said too much. "Never mind."

Scotty stood over her, holding a pot of coffee. "What are you talking about now? Damn muffins are keeping me from all the gossip."

Red paused and considered telling them about Missy Klein's letter to her mother. They might know some town talk that she didn't.

She decided to change the subject. Looking up at Scotty, she asked, "Do you know anything about land speculation up on Hammer Lake that probably happened twenty or thirty years ago?"

Scotty sat down next to her. "Tell me more."

Red told them what Mrs. Jenkens had said about a group showing interest in the Hammergren property. "She thought it had something to do with oil."

Georgia shook her head. "That would have been before I bought my savings-draining Ye Olde Antique Store."

"What about you, Scotty? You grew up here."

Scotty furrowed her brow. "Yeah, I remember some excited talk that lasted about five minutes."

Red waited. Scotty's lips moved as if she were counting to herself. "Yes, I was working at the hospital. That's about the time I met Alex." She turned to Georgia, explaining, "My drug-addicted ex-husband. Conveniently, he had just been hired as the new hospital pharmacist."

"Oh."

"And the land speculation?" Red prompted.

"Ah yes, some out-of-town group with big plans. They'd hired a geologist, who told them there was oil, or natural gas, or copper or something to be had."

"What happened?"

Scotty shook her head. "Flash in the pan, I guess."

"Is there something valuable beneath the Hammergren woods?" Georgia nibbled on a piece of toast.

Red shrugged. "Will never mentioned it. I'm not even sure we own the mineral rights. The railroads bought up a lot of them." She made a note to talk with the county engineer next week and find out more.

Scotty slid out of the booth as a timer went off again in the kitchen. As she walked away, she turned back and called, "Talk with Beldon Rafferty. His family was involved somehow."

Red was not about to discuss oil exploration with Beldon Rafferty. "When hell freezes over," she said under her breath.

The door to the café opened, and two locals walked in, stomping snow off their boots.

"You shoulda seen them guys in their new duds driving that big ole Escalade."

"I hear they were headed for Eddie's. Said they were going to get some ice fishing in."

"Hell, ice fishing! I'd say Mac Morris's got some girls going..." His voice slipped to a whisper when he noticed Red at the back booth.

Red pictured Walt LaFrance and his new clothes. What was the thing about ice fishing on Hammer Lake?

"Maybe the guys with the Escalade are with Walt LaFrance." Georgia pushed her plate away and sipped thoughtfully on her coffee. "There's a connection here, somewhere."

Connections, Red thought. That was what Will had said in her dream. "What do you mean?"

"I remember something a few years ago, a photo of Walt LaFrance with

Hitch Norgren. Back when Hitch was trying to make it in Hollywood, a la Jesse Ventura and Hulk Hogan? Didn't he have a bit part in a movie with Walt?"

Scotty returned with the coffeepot. "Yes, I do remember—but it wasn't about Hitch. Walt LaFrance got into trouble with drugs. I read about it somewhere."

"Using or dealing?" What Hollywood star hadn't gotten into drug trouble?

Scotty shrugged. "Sorry. Can't conjure it up. The brain doesn't work the way it used to."

Red stood up, stretching. "Well, enough of Hollywood gossip. I have crimes to solve. Let's hope we don't get another blizzard. I hate it when we have a one-two punch."

"Planning on delivering any more babies?" Scotty asked.

"I checked. We don't have any more pregnant women in the county. At least not that pregnant."

"Nice work," Georgia added. "We'll make a nurse out of you whether you like it or not."

Red shook her head. "No, thanks. You keep working at the Church to keep girls from getting pregnant, and I'll work on making sure the roads are open when we have someone in her ninth month."

The bell over the door jingled as a couple of people dressed in church clothes walked in. Cold air from outside swept in with them. Scotty looked at her new customers and then back at Red.

"Now I remember. The woman with the rosary had something to do with Hitch. Mother? Mother-in-law?" She shrugged. "Used to come in around the time Hitch moved back to town. I thought she was praying for him."

Red zipped up her coat. "Does she drive a snowmobile on Lykkins Lake in the middle of the night?"

"Too old for that. I'm guessing she's either long gone or in a nursing home by now."

Georgia called out as Red opened the door. "Have a nice day."

Sure, thought Red. *I'll have a fine day if I can find the connections and the missing Missy.*

It took some maneuvering before Red was able to get the Subaru through the snowbank created by the plow. All-wheel drive was essential in Minnesota winters. Fortunately, Ed had been in early to snowblow the courthouse parking lot.

As the sky lightened with the morning sun, Red felt a subtle ache in her jaw. *Damn*, she thought, *could another storm be working its way in?* Weather.com predicted more snow. She guessed the low-pressure system would start moving in tonight. Meanwhile, she wanted to organize a search party for Missy. She would start with the hunting shack near where Junior Klein had been found. Would Missy be holed up there? She was last seen on Friday morning, and it was now Sunday. Could she have survived the sub-zero temperatures that long?

"I hate winter," she grumbled, walking up the steps to the courthouse.

As her boots crunched on the snow, she thought through how to get to the hunting shack. She would need a snowmobile and a guide. Her first act, though, was to call the Ramsey County Coroner's office to find out when they'd have the autopsy results ready. Next, she needed to stop by the hospital in town to check on Trevor.

The door to the courthouse squeaked and groaned as she pulled it open. As it closed behind her, she was sure it whispered, *Stay in your warm office. Don't go out today.*

31

SHERIFF RED
TREVOR'S FLIGHT

The maintenance man had shoveled the sidewalk to the front entrance of Lykkins Lake Memorial Hospital down to the cement and spread a mixture of sand and salt to keep the walk from getting too slippery. Broken hips and arms were common in Pearsal County after a snowfall. Worse, though, the county usually lost at least one citizen a year to snow-shoveling heart attacks.

The reception desk was empty with a sign that directed visitors to check in at the nurse's station. The clock said nine, a good time to catch the doctor and the nurse.

Carmen Cruzan sat at the nurse's station, muttering as she punched information into a computer. She looked up at Red. "Damn thing was down most of the night shift. Had to revert to old-fashioned paper, so now I'm trying to catch up."

Red thought for a moment about the dancing sheriff on the web page and smiled. "Ah, the computer age."

"Electronic medical records were going to save our health care system. Instead, we created a monster that needs constant care and feeding." Carmen scowled.

"I know what you're saying," Red sympathized. "Is Trevor Farnsworth awake yet? I need to talk with him."

Carmen's eyes widened in surprise. "Didn't they tell you?"

Red leaned on the counter. "Tell me what?"

"Damn." Carmen flipped through a spiral notebook. "Says his mother took him AMA sometime early this morning."

"What? I asked the night nurse to let me know if anything happened to him."

Carmen rubbed her temples and looked at her with lines of weariness etched around her mouth. "With the storm, we've been working doubles and doubling back. Sheila, my night nurse, was on her seventh shift in a row. We were down an aide, and the damn computer wouldn't work. I'm sorry."

She squinted as she read the notes. "Report says that he was sleeping and vital signs were stable at four. At six when she rounded, they were leaving."

"Did she say where they were going?"

Carmen checked the computer notes again. "Here's what Sheila wrote. 'Mom states she is taking patient somewhere safe. Refused to sign the AMA paperwork.'"

Red's shoulders tensed. "Do you have any idea what she meant by 'somewhere safe'?"

Carmen tugged at her short dark hair and pressed her lips together as she thought. "I know Wendy Farnsworth a little from church. I seem to recall that her husband has family over in Fargo. Maybe that's where she went."

"I need to talk with Sheila. Can I get her number?"

"She'll be asleep by now."

Red nodded. "I'll have to wake her up. Trevor has some information I need."

Carmen flipped through an old-fashioned Rolodex and wrote the number down for her. She pointed to a little office the doctors used for dictation. "There's a phone you can use."

The phone rang five times before a sleepy voice answered, "Hullo?"

"Is this Sheila?"

"Um...who's calling?"

"Sheila, this is Sheriff Hammergren. I'm at the hospital to see Trevor Farnsworth, and I understand his mother signed him out AMA."

Sheila cleared her throat. "I was busy in the emergency room with a broken hip when I saw Wendy Farnsworth with her jacket on. She was half pushing, half dragging Trevor out the door. He could hardly walk."

She paused and cleared her throat again. "I tried to stop her, but I didn't have the time to spend with her. You know, the hip in the emergency room and all."

"Do you know if anything might have triggered her to take him?"

"Can't think of anything. But it was busy—only two of us on because of the storm."

Red thanked her and put the phone on the cradle. Why would Wendy suddenly decide to leave?

She tried calling the Farnsworth house. After six rings, it went to voicemail. "Wendy, this is Sheriff Hammergren. It's urgent. Can you call me as soon as you get this message?" She didn't add that she thought Trevor could be in danger. She wanted to scare Wendy enough to get her to call, but not enough so she'd panic.

Back at the desk, she asked Carmen to look at the notes again. "Did anyone else come to the hospital last night? I know about the broken hip, but anyone else in the emergency room? Unusual visitors?"

Carmen paged through the notes shaking her head. "I don't see anything, and I didn't hear anything in the report."

A light went on in a room down the hall, and a tremulous voice called out, "Nurse! Nurse!"

Carmen pushed herself out of her chair and hurried down the hallway. She was a big woman with strong arms. Red admired the work Carmen and all the nurses did. She hadn't known how hard it was physically to care for sick people until she became Will's caregiver.

There's a special place in heaven for nurses, she thought. Both Scotty and Lou had talked about the challenges of working in a rural area. "Think about being the only nurse in the building when an emergency comes in that you have to handle plus care for all the other patients." Scotty confessed, "I couldn't do it for more than a couple of years. It got to the point where I dreaded going to work so much, I'd throw up before my shift."

The phone at the desk rang. Red looked around to see if anyone would answer it. Carmen was still in with a patient, and she didn't see anyone else on the floor. She reached over and picked it up.

"Hospital, can I help you?"

A strange, low voice, one that sounded like someone was talking through a pillow, replied, "I'm checking on Trevor Farnsworth."

Red paused, knowing that she shouldn't have picked up the phone in the first place, but now she was curious. "May I ask who's calling?"

The sound was muffled, so low that Red couldn't hear it. "Pardon me. Can you repeat that?"

The caller hung up.

Red went back to the little dictation office and called Sheila back. "I'm sorry to keep interrupting your sleep, but do you remember if anyone called last night to ask about Trevor?"

Silence followed by rustling noises. "Um, come to think of it, someone did call. It was a woman who said she was his aunt."

"What did you tell her?"

"I told her she would have to talk with the mother because I wasn't authorized to give out any information."

In the background, Red heard the voice of a little girl. "Momma, are you up now?"

"Shhh...Momma still has to sleep a bit. You go watch your programs."

Red waited until Sheila could talk again. "Did she talk with Wendy?"

"I don't know. That's about the time the EMTs said they were bringing in a hip. I popped into the room and told Wendy that Trevor's aunt had called. He was sleeping and looked good."

"Was it after the phone call that Wendy decided to leave?"

"Yeah, that seems right. I was busy in the emergency room with the broken hip when I saw Wendy with her jacket on."

After Red finished talking with Sheila, Carmen returned looking harried. "Busy morning. I hope our ward clerk can get in this afternoon."

Red smiled. "Well, while you were tending to your patient, I took a phone call. Someone wanted to know how Trevor was doing."

Carmen looked surprised. "You answered the phone?"

"Sorry, I couldn't help myself."

Carmen waved a finger at Red, but she had a smile on her face.

"Anyway, please let me know if you get any more calls on him."

As if on cue, the phone rang. Red waited, hoping it was the anonymous caller. Instead, it was the lab tech to let Carmen know she'd be late because her driveway hadn't been plowed yet.

Once she hung up the phone, Carmen pointed down the hall. "Stop in and say hello to Sammy. I'm sure she'd like to show off her little girl."

On her way down the hall, Red peeked in on Albert Larsen. He sat in a chair with a blanket over his lap, dozing. An evangelist in a white suit with slick, shiny hair on the television anchored to the wall preached to the former undertaker. Red didn't stop to hear the message. She knew the evangelist was doling out forgiveness and requesting donations to continue building his temple to the Almighty. Or maybe he was the one who needed more money to buy another private jet to do God's work. Red wasn't a faithful church person, but she suspected that God had other things to worry about than whether a sleazy preacher got his jet.

"I'd rather give my money to the other Church," she mumbled under her breath.

Sammy sat in bed with her baby swaddled in a pink blanket. A smile spread across her face when Red knocked at the door.

"Oh, my God, it's you!" Her eyes sparkled. The baby made little grunting and sucking noises.

Red blushed, embarrassed by Sammy's enthusiasm. If she were the dancing sheriff with the buckskin skirt and the cowboy hat, she'd probably answer, "Aw shucks." She stepped over to the bed and leaned in to admire the baby.

"She's beautiful, Sammy."

A tear rolled down Sammy's cheek. "I wanted to name her Red after you, but Joe wouldn't let me."

"He's got good instincts." Red touched the soft black fur on the baby's head. "What is her name?"

"Emily Jo. Emily for my grandmother and Jo for...well, Joe."

The baby moved her clenched fist toward her mouth and started sucking. In a moment, she started to cry. The sound was loud and healthy.

Red smiled. "She'll keep you busy for years."

Outside the room, she thought she heard a whisper of footsteps. When she looked through the door, a hooded figure hurried by.

"Excuse me." Red hastened to the hallway, but it was empty. She called back to Sammy, "Sorry, I have to run. Take care of that little one for me. I'll need a new deputy in about twenty-five years."

Sammy laughed. "I will, Sheriff. I will."

Red took long strides down the hall, peeking in rooms as she walked. Only five others were occupied, including Albert Larsen. None had a visitor.

The nurse's station was empty. A machine beeped in the room closest to the station. Carmen's voice quietly murmured to someone in the room. At the very end of the corridor, the fire door between the hospital rooms and the main entrance eased shut. Red hurried to the door, opened it, and saw the main entrance door slide shut. She ran to it and arrived in time to see a dark SUV pull onto the street, gunning its engine in a squeal of tires.

Red was sure she'd seen one of the apelike Kazurinskis pass by Sammy's room. As she left the building, Red took a deep breath. "Am I seeing things?"

Kazurinskis and the wrestling team. Connections?

32

MISSY

Missy woke up cramped and achy from her cheekbones all the way to her ankles. Gray light filtered in from the skylight. The fish house no longer rattled from the snow blowing up against it. The storm was over, and she allowed herself a little hope as she stretched her weary arms. Her stomach told her she should eat, yet her head felt thick, like someone had stuck a sock between her ears.

Drink. Grampa Jack said to always drink. Dehydration was the enemy. Missy slid out from under the covers on the cot and squatted by the fish hole. The ice was at least two feet thick around the bored hole. How could she reach that far for water?

Think. If you don't think, they'll find you. The *Followers* aren't stupid. But you are.

The voice circulated behind her eyes in the frigid air of the fish house.

You took the money. They'll get you.

Suddenly the hope of a moment ago disappeared. Missy gulped back the panic. Count, she whispered aloud. Count to ten. Then think.

How long have I been here? One night? Two? The drugs, the storm. Her brain was fuzzy. Would the *Followers* find her here? Think.

Later, after she'd lit the little propane stove and melted a pan full of fresh, clean snow, she decided her plan.

Get to Grampa Jack. Leave the lake. Walk to the road and find somebody who would call Grampa Jack. But she was tired, so tired. Even sipping
the salty bouillon couldn't keep her eyelids from drooping.

Don't sleep. Think about what you have discovered. Think about how
you hid in the school janitor's closet with the door cracked. Think about
how you used your cell phone to make a video of the *Killer and the Followers*.
It was sloppy and out of focus, but it was there for Grampa Jack. And now
the cell phone was safely hidden.

Don't sleep. Get out before the *Followers* find you. Dream about how,
when it's all over, everything would be good. Spring will come with the
little violet flowers and the trillium that grow on the floor of the forest. You
will pick them and take them to the rock memorial you and Grampa Jack
made for Dad. And you will talk with Dad and say, It's okay now, you can be
with Mom.

Don't sleep. Find help. Go to the road and someone would help. Or go
to Eddie's and someone would help. Missy's eyes drooped as the heat from
the watery soup bathed her face.

33

SHERIFF RED
THE HARRINGTON LAND

Red and Jason studied the large county map in her office. She pointed to the area where the cabin had burned.

"Cal," she called to the outer office. "Can you come in here and show us something?"

Cal brushed crumbs from a muffin off his sweater as he walked in. His headset was draped around his neck.

Red pointed to the map. "Do you recall where Junior Klein was found?"

Cal squinted up at the map and said, "Let's see. The property belongs to someone from St. Paul now. They bought it two years ago. Here." He poked his finger at a spot about two miles west of the Henderson cabin. "That's the old Harrington land. My dad used to hunt deer there."

That was the area she had also identified. Red looked at Jason. "Is it possible that Missy would have gone in that direction?"

Jason shrugged. "People tend to go where it's familiar."

"How difficult would it be to get from the cabin to that part of the woods if you were on foot?"

Jason stepped back to get a larger view of the map, and Cal stood still as if calculating in his head.

"No roads nearby and pretty thick woods with undergrowth." Jason shrugged. "But possible, I guess, depending on the depth of the snow."

"If I remember right," Cal added, "we had a hard time getting in when Jack Klein found Junior. There's an old logging road within a half mile, but you have to walk from there."

"I can get in with a snowmobile." Jason's eyes lit up. Red saw the "oh boy" excitement on his face. "Do you want me to head out that way?"

As much as she wanted to go with him, she had other things she needed to look into. Plus, she wasn't fond of driving snowmobiles. She disliked the noise and the way they could destroy the fragile forest ecology. This was something she'd never tell her constituents, however. Snowmobiling added much needed tourist money to the economy.

"I want you to look for any signs that the girl might have been there."

Jason grinned. He loved trekking around the county on a snowmobile.

"Wait, before you go, do either of you know where Jack Klein's fish house is on Hammer Lake?"

"I think it's pretty isolated in that cove." Cal pointed to a spot across the lake and well north of the burned cabin. "I doubt anyone could have gone on foot from the cabin to the fish house. There's open water here." He pointed to the lake near the south shore. "You can't get by it easily."

Red remembered the Matt Carlson drowning last year and nodded grimly.

She sent Cal to work on arranging for the snowmobile for Jason. The sheriff's office didn't own one but had a rental agreement with the local dealer.

Beckoning Jason to sit down, she quickly filled him in on Trevor Farnsworth. "I think the phone call from the 'aunt' spooked Wendy. I left a message on her home phone, but I don't have a cell."

"Maybe Cal can find her husband. What is his name? Jess?"

Red nodded. "He's an over-the-road trucker and might be out on a run."

Jason turned to leave, but she stopped him. "One more thing. Have you heard anything about the Kazurinski brothers? Something about them doesn't sit well with me."

"I've seen them around. Big, lunky guys. But I haven't heard that they've been in trouble." He hesitated. "Oh, that reminds me, I checked with my sister, Betsy, about Missy Klein. She said she didn't know much except that she was surprised when Missy started hanging out with Jared. She mentioned seeing Jared with the Kazurinskis, but she didn't know anything about them other than that she thought they were weird and too old to be in school."

"Hmmm. It's time to check them out." Red studied the map once more. "Stay safe on that snowmobile."

"Aye, aye, Captain." Jason saluted before he walked out.

She called the Ramsey County Coroner's office to find out when they'd do the autopsy on Jared. After fifteen minutes on hold, a harried clerk answered.

"Do you know when the autopsy on Jared Peterson will be done? They brought him in yesterday."

"We're pretty busy here. A big shooting last night. Killed a couple of people."

"I'm sorry to hear it. Any estimate? We're working on a case here."

The woman on the other end of the line sighed. "The note here says they'll get to it on Tuesday or maybe Wednesday. Sorry."

Red hung up the phone thinking that despite the television programs, a coroner's job must be a dismal one, especially now with the wild proliferation of guns. Too many young people dying.

After she dropped her NRA membership, she'd talked with Georgia about the organization.

"They're nothing more than a lobby for the gun manufacturers. Imagine selling the public on the absolute constitutional right to have assault weapons. We're creating our own homegrown terrorists."

"Red, I didn't know you had such left-leaning politics." Georgia had chuckled.

"Not left leaning, just practical. Those crazies with guns are killing kids."

"Not only mass killings but domestic violence and a whole lot of other bad stuff. Gun deaths and violence are a significant health problem. The NRA should join hands with public health to stop it."

Scotty was less diplomatic. "The NRA president should be shot."

Red chuckled, thinking about that conversation. While she could express her opinions to her poker club, she was careful when she talked with anyone else in the county about guns. Another drawback of being in an elective office.

She set aside the notes she'd taken on Jared and concentrated on Trevor. Why would he be at the RV dealership? She stepped out to Cal's cubicle.

"What do you know about the RV dealership? I know that Earl Floyd manages it, but I don't think he's the owner."

"You mean where you found that kid last night? Belnor RV. It's a limited liability partnership between the Raffertys and the Norgrens. It was formed three years ago. Taxes are up to date."

On the off chance that he might know about someone named Coke, she asked him, "Does the name Coke mean anything to you?"

He wrinkled his brow and rubbed his neck. "Not offhand."

"What about a woman who took in foster kids about twenty years ago?"

He nodded. "Oh, you must mean Connie and Lyle Strand. They used to take in kids. Lyle died about ten years ago, but Connie is still around. Lives in the senior housing."

With Cal around, who needed a computer?

34

SHERIFF RED
COKE

As the sun climbed higher in the deep winter sky, a slight haze formed. With the sun reflecting off the newly fallen snow, Red's eyes ached from the brightness. The parking lot for the senior apartments had been plowed, but most of the cars were still piled with snow. The building had a security system, but as soon as Red reached the door, an elderly man using a walker let her in.

He asked the typical Minnesota winter question. "Hello, Sheriff. Cold enough for you?"

"How are you, Hjalmer?"

"Fit," he said with a laugh.

"I'm looking for Connie Strand. Do you know which apartment she's in?"

He pointed down the hallway. "One-oh-five. Hope she isn't in trouble. One of the nicest people on this earth."

When Red knocked, the door was opened by a tall, thin woman with short, curly gray hair. She blinked in confusion, "Oh my. I thought you were the boy who brings me the paper."

Red smiled. "Sorry I don't have a paper, just a few questions."

Connie invited Red in and pointed to the kitchen table. "I'm just having my morning coffee. Would you like a cup?"

Over the years, Red had learned that people were more apt to open up if you accepted their hospitality. "If it isn't too much bother."

The coffee was tepid and weak, like Scotty's. Even a teaspoon of sugar couldn't breathe life into it. The two chatted for a few minutes about the weather before Red brought up what she'd heard from Lou. "I'm looking for information on a person named Coke. Does that ring a bell with you?"

Connie's hand trembled as she raised the coffee cup to her lips. "Oh my. I hope nothing has happened to her."

Red set down her cup. "Do you know where I can find her?"

A smile crossed Connie's lips as she gazed beyond Red. She made a clucking sound. "That poor girl. Her parents were young and addicted. She would live with them for a while, and then she'd be taken out of the home. In and out. By the time she came to me, she must have been about sixteen."

Red pressed. "Do you know where she is now?"

Connie rubbed her chin. "Just a minute. Let me look it up."

As Connie made her way slowly into the living room, Red had a moment of excitement. Maybe she was finally getting somewhere. Maybe this Coke was sheltering Missy.

Connie came back to the kitchen table carrying a large photo album. "I tried to keep track of all my kids—even the ones I only had for a few days." She looked at Red with a brightness in her eyes. "I liked to think that some of the loving they got from us helped."

She paged through the album almost to the end. "Here she is. I remember she was so smart and could sing like one of those stars on television."

The photo was faded and little out of focus. Coke had long, straight black hair and a narrow face. She wore jeans and a T-shirt that emphasized her thinness. In the photo she had a laughing smile.

Red pointed to the photo. "She looks happy."

"I think she was for those short weeks we had her. Then they came and took her back to her parents." Her voice softened. "Lyle and I lost track of her until about ten years ago. Out of the blue she sent a Christmas card." Connie pulled a card from the sleeve of the album. "She got married and had two little girls. Calls herself Coco now. As far as I know, she still lives out west in Oregon."

Red felt the disappointment seep through her. She doubted this was the person Missy might escape to.

Connie slipped the card back in the album. "I hope she's not in some kind of trouble."

"No. It's part of an investigation."

To Red's surprise, Connie asked, "Does this have something to do with that boy who died?"

"I can't comment, of course."

"We were talking about it at the coffee club yesterday. We heard you were looking for someone who might have been named Coke or Cole. I didn't tell the ladies here about Coke. It's really none of their business, and it was a long time ago." She paused. "But it did remind me of something odd that Coke said when she was with me."

Red glanced at her watch. She needed to get over to the jail to talk with one of her prisoners. "Oh?" She hoped Connie wouldn't go into a long, drawn-out story.

"She tried out for the school musical. This was when we thought we'd have her longer than a few weeks. She would have been good in it. Like I said, the girl could sing. But she came back from the tryouts and said she didn't want to be in it because of one of the students that she thought was kind of scary."

"Scary? How so?"

"Well, that's where my head gets a little fuzzy. I think she said she found this person in a corner chanting 'Not me! Not me!' or something like that. Coke was wise beyond her years, and she told me she thought whoever it was might be crazy and she'd had enough craziness in her life."

"Do you know who she was talking about?"

Connie sighed. "One of the others trying out for the play, I guess."

Red wrote down the contact information Connie had for Coco before leaving. As she walked out into the bright, frigid air, names scrolled through her brain. Who was involved in the play besides Lou? Hitch, Bobbi, Mayme, and Junior. And now half of them were dead.

Connections?

35

SHERIFF RED
TITUS

Sonia Richards buzzed Red through the locked front door of the county jail. It was a low, one-story brick building constructed twenty years ago to house ten prisoners. On this blustery, arctic Sunday morning, the jail was only five over capacity.

She sat down at the desk where Sonia monitored the cells on television screens with remote cameras. Back in grade school, Red had taken a field trip to the courthouse. She remembered the jail from those days—one cell next to the sheriff's office in the basement of the courthouse. Bare, concrete, with a toilet and a sink. Will Hammergren, the newly elected sheriff and her future husband, had told her class that prisoners rarely stayed more than a day.

"We don't have too much business down here."

Times had certainly changed. With Reagan's war on drugs in the 1980s, jails and prisons began to fill with victimless criminals. Over the years, as they became overcrowded, a whole industry of private prisons sprang up— some of them in Minnesota. The average taxpayer now spent about $600 a year keeping the prison system going.

"They're behaving pretty well, considering that blizzards tend to stir them up," Sonia said. "I guess they're afraid if they cause trouble, I'll throw them out on the street."

The jail had two common cells that could house five each and one isolation cell. Currently, fourteen prisoners sat or lounged on cots watching television sets bolted to the wall.

In the isolation cell, a man with a grizzled beard and a sunken mouth slept.

Red pointed to the screen and said, "I need to talk with Titus."

Sonia sighed. "We just got him settled down. He was pacing up a storm an hour ago. You sure you want to disturb him?"

Titus was a bipolar, low-intelligence substance abuser who needed mental health and drug treatment, not jail. Since the public did not want to support a decent mental health system, jails and prisons had become the de facto warehouses for people like Titus Hixson. When he stayed sober and on his meds, he was like a friendly puppy. When he stopped his meds, drank, and snorted, he was a wild man. The two worker's comp files on her desk from injured jailers attested to his strength.

"Sorry, Sonia, I've got to find out if he knows who might be making a lot of cash right now."

"Well, it might be okay. We got a good dose of Thorazine into him a while ago."

Red didn't ask if he volunteered to take it. Best not to know.

Donnie, the day jailer, sat outside the locked cells reading a comic book. "*Spiderman?*"

He quickly snapped it shut but not before Red saw the bare breasts. "Uh, sure."

"Keep a close eye on the monitor, okay? If Titus gets set off, I don't want my nose broken."

The windowless cell smelled of Pine-Sol disinfectant and body odor. Titus, whether sober and sane or drugged and psychotic, smelled bad. Daily showers couldn't wash away the odors that seeped from his pores. Red noticed that this was a problem for many of her prisoners and wondered if anyone had ever studied crime and body odor.

She stood in the doorway and called out in a neutral, nonthreatening voice, "Titus? Are you awake?"

One eye opened, then the other. "Yump."

"I need to talk with you for a few minutes."

Titus blinked, his eyes bleary from the medication. "Wha?"

Red stepped closer to the cot. "It's Sheriff Hammergren, Titus. I need to talk with you."

Slowly Titus propped himself up, blinked again, and finally looked at her. "Yump."

Red approached the cot, arms calmly at her side. "I need to know if drug money is missing. Have you heard anything?"

Titus pulled himself up and stared at Red with a lethargic expression. "Wha?"

"Missing drug money, Titus. What do you know about it?"

He scratched at a scab on his face. Methamphetamine caused the willies—a creepy-crawly feeling in the skin. Meth heads sometimes scratched their skin raw trying to get at the itch. The half-dazed look in Titus's eyes turned sly. "What have you got for me?"

"Chocolate. Dark chocolate Dove bars." Red held a foil-wrapped bar in her hand.

The sly look disappeared, and Titus smiled, showing rotting front teeth. Another chunk of money to the dentist. Red made sure she wasn't close enough to have to smell his breath.

"Yump. Heard something about it."

"What did you hear?"

Red continued to show the candy—like she was tempting a puppy.

"Can't tell you. Big trouble for me."

Red sighed. "Titus, you are already in big trouble. Destruction of property, assault, felony possession. You could end up in Stillwater—or worse." Worse was Oak Park Heights, the top security prison. It was filled with not nice people.

Titus licked his lips, staring at the chocolate. "Kids. Something to do with the high school. The kids were supposed to turn it over."

"What kids?"

"Don't know."

"Who's behind this?"

"Kids on buses." Titus began to sag on the cot. The medication took over as his eyelids drooped. "Yump," he said in a slurred voice. "Kids on buses."

His eyes closed, and he began to snore.

Red took the foil off the Dove bar and left the chocolate on the cot next to Titus. He would tell her no more.

Kids on buses. What the hell did that mean?

36

SHERIFF RED
CHICO VINCENTE

Kids on buses. Could the drug dealing happen on school buses? Possible, but not likely. What about kids on buses going to sporting events? Will, or at least Will's ghost, had advised her to look for connections. Hitch Norgren and the wrestling team popped up too many times.

Red sat in the car, letting the air from the heater blow away the smell of the jail. It was time to talk to someone on the team. She remembered the friendly poker game among the wrestlers yesterday, put the Subaru in drive, and headed to her old house in town.

After her mother died, she'd sold the house to Julio Vincente. Maybe young Chico had some information that would be helpful. Maybe Chico knew who the Coke Jared was talking about might be.

The road in front of the Vincente house had been recently plowed and the driveway shoveled. The Vincentes had put a lot of work and sweat equity into her old family home. It looked much the same from the outside —a two-story clapboard with a steep pitched roof and dormers. But, by the time Red had sold it, the house had acquired a tired feel and appearance. The Vincentes added decorative shutters to the downstairs windows and painted the peeling gray outside a dazzling white.

She tried the doorbell, and when there was no answer, she knocked. Tracks in the driveway told her that someone had driven away. Probably no one was home. It was Sunday morning, and she knew the Vincentes attended the Catholic church. As she turned to walk away, the door opened and Chico stood there, disheveled in a pair of jogging pants and a sweatshirt.

"Yes?" He appeared to have just woken up.

"Hi, Chico. Can I come in? I have some questions for you."

"My parents are at church." His voice, with a slight accent, had a wary tone to it.

"That's okay. I want to talk to you."

He opened the door, and she stepped inside. The interior of the house had been radically remodeled. They had taken down the wall between the living room in the front of the house and the kitchen in the back, opening it up to an airy living-dining-kitchen complete with a center island.

"Wow, does this place look great!"

Chico smiled with uncertainty. "My parents worked hard on it."

To the right, a staircase led up to the bedrooms. It had a new soft blue carpet. She remembered climbing the stairs with its threadbare runner once to find her brother Lad's room locked. Inside, he paced as the voices of his mental illness said vile things to him. A much younger Sheriff Will had broken down the door and escorted him to a waiting ambulance. It was one of several trips to hospitals for treatment that never seemed to work.

She blinked the image away and smiled at Chico. "Can we sit down? This won't take long."

"Um, maybe I should call my dad?"

Red held out her hands in a gentle gesture of surrender. "Chico, you aren't in any trouble. I need to know if you can help me figure out what happened to Jared Peterson." She didn't add, *And Trevor Farnsworth.*

They sat on stools at the island in the kitchen. All the appliances were shiny gray metal and new. In her day, they'd had an old stove, refrigerator, and a microwave that sat on the chipped countertop. The Vincentes had a built-in oven and microwave and, more importantly, a dishwasher.

Times have changed, she thought, slipping out of her jacket.

"Several people have said that Jared was dealing drugs. Do you know anything about it?"

Red realized that she was putting Chico in a hard position. If his friends were doing this, he wouldn't want to be a rat. And if he was involved, he wouldn't want to admit it.

The vehemence of his answer surprised her, though. "Jared was stupid to get involved with the dealing. I didn't want nothing to do with him. He could ruin it for all of us!" He pressed his lips together into a straight line.

"What do you mean?"

"I have a scholarship to the University for next fall. I don't want to lose it." Color rose on his neck. "Anything to do with drugs and people immediately think it's us—the spics."

Red thought about what a former president said about the criminals coming across the border and how it fed into the phobias of people like some of her county commissioners. She felt a lot of sympathy for Chico.

"Chico, I don't think you have anything to do with the dealing. But I wonder if you know who does."

The boy stared down at the floor and said nothing. The refrigerator hummed quietly behind him. "I don't ask. If I don't ask, then I don't know."

Red nodded. "Does the name Coke mean anything to you? Do you know anyone called Coke?"

"Coke?" His expression turned puzzled. "Like a kid, maybe? No. We call Mr. Norgren 'Coach' but not Coke." He thought a little bit more. "Well... there's Mr. Rafferty. He always brings a six-pack of Coke to the meets. But no one calls him Coke."

Find Coke. Find her.

She leaned closer to Chico and said quietly, "Do you think Mr. Norgren has anything to do with drugs?"

Chico's eyes widened in surprise. "Oh no, not him. He kicks kids off the team if he even thinks they might be doing something."

Outside, she heard the familiar scrape of a shovel clearing the sidewalk. Otherwise, the street was quiet. The clock said 11:30. The second service at the church would be out soon. Red preferred not to be here when Chico's parents got home. Her presence might spell trouble for him.

"Do you know anything about kids on buses and possible drugs?"

Chico shrugged. "I always sit up front near Mr. and Mrs. Norgren. I don't pay no attention to the back."

"But something might be happening back there?" Would drugs be dealt on the bus under the nose of their anti-drug coach?

"Those Kazurinskis sit back there. Sometimes I hear rumors…"

"What kind of rumors?"

Suddenly Chico slipped off the stool and stood up. "I gotta put the roast in for Ma. They'll be home soon." He hurried around the island to the refrigerator. It was clear that the mention of the Kazurinskis upset him. Red decided not to push him any more.

She pulled on her jacket. "Thanks, Chico. You've been helpful."

"You won't say nothing to my parents?"

"Not a word."

Before she reached the door, she turned back to him. "Have you heard anything about missing money?"

"No." He was a little too quick to answer.

"Okay, thanks." Did Chico know more than he was willing to say? She felt like she was dealing with a lot of teenagers who weren't giving her the full story—for whatever reason.

As she walked out the door, she had her cell phone in hand. "Cal? Can you get me the address for the Kazurinskis? I need to pay them a visit."

Overhead, a few clouds rolled in, obscuring the sparkle of the sunlight against the snow.

37

SHERIFF RED

KAZURINSKIS

"It took some doing, but I found out where those Kazurinski boys live." Cal's voice was staticky on the cell phone.

Red sat in the car with the heater on full blast in front of Trevor's house. The house was quiet, and she saw no evidence that anyone had come or gone. One thing about the day after a snowstorm, you could see any fresh tracks in the snow.

"I had to call a couple of people. They're in that duplex on Grove Street —the one that Beldon Rafferty rents out now—used to have a hair salon downstairs."

The plow had been down Grove Street and left a large bank in front of the house. The house itself still had old aluminum siding from the 1960s and looked like it hadn't been updated since then. The walk was shoveled haphazardly, as if someone had taken a quick swipe with the shovel, just enough to get in and out but hadn't bothered to cut through the snow at the curb.

The downstairs used to be Lillian's Beauty Shoppe, the hairdresser that Red's mother used to go to. Lillian lived upstairs with her three cats. The salon always smelled of perfumed hairspray and ammonia. What the upstairs smelled of, Red didn't want to speculate. Her mother had complained that Lillian always had cat fur on her smock.

The sign for Lillian's was long gone, and the downstairs had been converted back to living space. Dark drapes were pulled shut against the outside cold.

Red waded through the snowbank and knocked on the door to the Kazurinskis. She heard the faint sound of a television set, but it came from upstairs. Could it be that Lillian still lived there? She knocked again but heard nothing. The door was locked.

"Hello," she called. "It's the sheriff. Is anybody home?"

Silence greeted her. Either the Kazurinskis were sound sleepers or they weren't there.

Moving over, she rang the bell for the upstairs apartment. After the second ring, a trembly voice called down, "It's open. Come on up."

The steep stairs creaked beneath her feet. Judging by the dust and the dirt on the bare wood, the steps hadn't been swept in a long time. The stairway smelled of a combination of stale cigarette smoke, mold, and cat pee. Or perhaps it was just left-over ammonia from all the permanents Lillian had given to the women of Pearsal County. The smell reminded her that she needed to get her haircut before the next county board meeting. Right now, though, that was hardly a priority.

A wizened old lady in a pink housedress and fluffy slippers stood at the top of the stairs. "Come in. Come in." Her voice was gravelly and raspy from years of cigarette smoking.

"Lillian?" Red held out her hand. The woman had not only aged but shriveled up since her days of hairdressing. Red remembered her as a blonde with tight curls. Her hair, what little she had of it, was white and flyaway like it hadn't been tended to in quite some time.

"Why, it's Delores, isn't it?"

Red smiled at her. "No, it's Red. Delores was my mother."

"Oh yes, of course."

Lillian's eyes were too bright and yet had a puzzled look as she let Red in. It reminded her of how her mother had looked in her mid-stages of dementia. Inside, the apartment was overheated and smelled of an overflowing garbage can. The living room was jam-packed with unopened boxes, and the television set in the corner announced the hourly bargain from the shopping network.

As far as Red could recall, Lillian had no family in the area. She made a mental note to talk with social services on Monday. Lillian might need adult protection to look in on her.

Lillian pointed to the kitchen table and an empty chair. "Did you want me to do your hair? It looks like you could use a cut, and maybe we should give it a perm?"

The table was filled with Styrofoam containers from the Meals on Wheels program. At least someone was checking on her.

"Not today, thank you. I'm wondering if you can tell me anything about the Kazurinskis who live downstairs."

"Who?"

"The people who live downstairs."

"Why, that's my shop downstairs. No one lives there." For a moment, a look of suspicion crossed Lillian's face. "Who are you?"

"I'm Red Hammergren, the sheriff." She used a slow, gentle voice.

"Oh, you look so much like Delores. How is she? I haven't done her hair in a while. You should tell her to make an appointment."

"I'm sorry. Delores died a few years ago."

"Oh, that's too bad. I wonder what happened to her daughter? Big gal with the funny name. What was it?" Lillian squinted up at the ceiling. "I remember now, she named her Red. Silly name for a girl with such dark hair."

Yes, Red thought. Silly name—a mistake, really. Her mother was trying to name her after Loretta Lynn, the country singer. Except she thought the name was spelled *Loredda*. From the time she was a baby, everyone called her Red.

Red waited a few moments and tried asking about the Kazurinski brothers again. "Do you know the boys who live downstairs now that you've retired from your shop?" She hoped the prompting might help.

"Oh yes, I closed up in 1999. My feet couldn't take it anymore." She looked down at her fluffy slippers.

"And the boys downstairs? Can you tell me anything about them?"

"Those boys are sweet. Sometimes they bring the packages up for me." She pointed to a stack of unopened boxes. "I get such nice stuff from those lovely girls on the television set."

Red wondered how much of Lillian's retirement went into buying from "those lovely girls."

"What can you tell me about the boys?"

She closed her eyes for a moment, as if she were thinking hard. "Oh, they come and go a lot." She pointed out her back window to the alley. "They have such a nice car."

The alley was empty, but a path had been shoveled to the parking spot. It looked like deep tire tracks led out through the unplowed snow, which would indicate either an SUV or a truck.

"Do you ever see them with anybody else?"

Lillian moved around to the other side of the table and gazed out the window. "It's so snowy out there. I do wish summer would come, don't you?" She turned to Red. "Is it Christmas time already? I'll need to get my shopping done."

The aged hairdresser was clearly an unreliable witness. Still, Red tried again. "Do you see the boys downstairs with anybody else?"

Lillian's voice had a vagueness to it when she finally spoke. It was as if she were trying to remember a name. "Norgren?"

"Hitch Norgren? Has he been here?" Were the dots connecting, or had she just managed to go down a rabbit hole?

Lillian turned to her with clouded eyes. "Who did you say you were? I'm afraid I don't have any more appointments today. You will have to come back tomorrow. I'm pretty busy right now."

Red had learned with her mother that dealing with dementia sometimes meant playing along. "I'll set up an appointment next week. Will that work?"

"Thank you, Delores. You know I could do a little frosting on the tips. I'll put you down in my book for an appointment."

By the time Red left, Lillian had settled in the living room listening to those "nice girls" on the television.

Back in her car, Red thought about who else might know something about boys in buses. Mitch Rafferty came to mind almost immediately. She pictured him with his haze of cologne sitting with the girls in the gym yesterday. She felt a moment of disgust as she remembered the familiar way he had acted around the girls.

"Cal, can you connect me to Mitch Rafferty? I think we still have his cell phone on file."

Last she'd heard, Mitch lived in the trailer court his mother owned. Red was disinclined to knock on his door and have to look at his smirking face. She waited for Cal, wishing all the pieces would suddenly fall in place and she wouldn't have to ask Mitch for help. Or ask him about Coke.

When the phone was finally answered, it sounded like Mitch was half-asleep. "'Lo?"

"Mitch, this is Sheriff Hammergren. I'm wondering if you could help me?"

"What?" Eighties rock played in the background, and the connection was poor.

Red decided to keep it simple and direct. "Do you know anything about drug dealing associated with the wrestling team?"

Mitch whispered at someone to turn the music down. She hoped it wasn't one of the high school girls. When he came back, he sounded clearer. "What? Why would I know anything about drug dealing?" She recognized the same condescending tone he'd taken during the political campaign. Red almost hung up.

"Mitch, I'm working on the Jared Peterson case. I'm asking because you help Hitch with the wrestling team. I've heard rumors that Jared Peterson had something to do with the team and drug dealing."

"Go to hell." The line went dead.

So much for the law sticking up for each other. If Mitch knew something, she was sure he'd share it in a way that would make her look bad.

38

SHERIFF RED
QUILT SHOP

Red sat at her desk and stared at the layer of frost that formed on the bottom of her office window. When the courthouse was refurbished in the 1990s, they hadn't replaced the windows with triple panes for better insulation. Probably they didn't want to spend the money even though they would have gotten it back within five years in lower heating costs. Ah, budgets.

Outside, the top layer of sugary snow eddied in the frigid breeze.

The visit with Chico in her old house brought back memories of her brother, Lad. Every time she saw a mentally ill burnout, she wondered if that was what Lad looked like now. Was he one of the scruffy street people living in a tent somewhere? Or was he dead and buried in a pauper's grave? Shortly after he'd disappeared, her parents received a postcard from Denver with nothing on it. They'd followed up with the Denver police but didn't find any trace of him. Red's efforts over the years had yielded nothing.

"I wonder where he is now? Or if he's still alive." Red was convinced that her father's early death from a heart attack was related to despair over not being able to fix or find his son. "My heart hopes he'll come back someday. My gut says it'll be in a box of ashes."

Cal called to her through the open door. "Jason's on his way up north.

They'll meet him with the snowmobile on County Road Six. Plows just got it opened."

"Thanks, Cal." She felt another tinge of regret that she hadn't assigned herself to look for the old hunting shack. Will once told her, "You can't do it all on your own. That's why you have deputies." And she knew she had some good ones. Still, it was hard to not be in the middle of the action.

She stretched her arms over her head and blinked away the fatigue that suddenly poured over her.

After checking through a couple of reports and pacing by the map, waiting for Jason to call, she realized she needed a little break from the missing Missy and all the loose threads around her. She asked Cal into her office. "Do you remember who used to live next door to Rollie Hammergren before he moved to the house on the lake?"

Cal scratched his head. "Let's see, that would be Second Avenue. Hammergrens lived on the corner. To the west was the old Catholic parish house. The church rented it to their custodian, Elton Weaver. Elton was married to Mary Homberg. They had seven children, three boys and four girls." He closed his eyes as if to read the census pages catalogued in his head. "The oldest boy was named Norman, and he became a priest—"

She stopped him, not wanting a complete list. "Did they have a daughter named Margaret?"

Margaret Weaver was listed as the mother on the birth certificate the lawyer had sent to her.

Cal shook his head. "Mary, Kathy, Beth, and Barbara."

Red thanked him and waved him away. She was grateful that Cal never asked questions.

She pulled herself from her musings and checked her watch—almost one. She needed another talk with Hitch Norgren. Could she connect any dots between the wrestling team, Trevor Farnsworth, Jared Peterson, the Kazurinskis, and the missing Missy? What about Belnor RV dealership? Beldon Rafferty? Mitch Rafferty? Or the possibly nonexistent Coke?

"This is making my brain ache." She needed a face-to-face with Hitch. Bobbi had said something about him going out of town, but maybe with the storm he was still home.

Before she left her office, she pulled out the old cold case file on the skull that had been found by a hunter and put it in her bag. For some reason, it haunted her today—maybe because she'd attached the Post-it note on it and put it away without following up. If she had a break, she'd look at it again.

The Norgren driveway was plowed with precision, and several sets of tires tracked the new snow. *Please*, she thought. *Be home, Hitch.* She really didn't want to talk with Bobbi again.

One set of tire tracks led to Bobbi's pole building. A battered Ford pickup was parked near the door. The back of the pickup was loaded with firewood to keep it weighted. City slickers didn't know that pickup trucks were useless in the snow unless you weighted down the back.

No one answered her knock at the house, so Red walked across the driveway to the shop.

A low hip-hop beat emanated from behind the shop door. Red knocked and tried the latch. The door was unlocked.

"Hello?"

Elena Vincente, Chico's aunt, looked at her with a startled expression. She sat at one of the industrial sewing machines. Her dark hair was pulled back into a tight ponytail, and she wore a down vest over a thick black turtleneck and fingerless gloves. It couldn't have been more than fifty degrees in the shop.

"I'm looking for Hitch. Have you seen him?"

She shook her head and stared at Red. Her eyes were wide.

"Are you all right?"

Elena blinked. "I...I was not expecting anybody." She pulled up the foot lever of the machine and slid her chair back. She was working on a small, braided pattern quilt—crib-sized. "Bobbi lets me do my own work on Sundays. She keeps the door open for me."

Red walked over to the machine. The quilt was multicolored with a star pattern working out from the center. "It's beautiful."

"For my sister in California when her baby comes."

On one end of the room, finished quilts hung on racks. Red studied one that at first appeared to be a random pattern of small squares. As she looked at it, a pattern emerged through the blending of the colors of the squares.

"It's a tree, isn't it?"

"*Muy bonita.* It will go in an art gallery."

She studied another one with larger squares done in yellows and ambers. The background was a plain brown. It looked primitive until she moved closer to the quilt to see that each six-inch square was actually made up of smaller squares, and inside those smaller squares were pictures. One was a farmhouse with a porch and a swing. Another, a living room.

"Looks like someone is telling a story with this."

Elena nodded. "It's beautifully crafted." She hesitated, and her voice dropped to a whisper. "But I don't like that one."

"Oh."

Elena was silent.

Red looked closely at another square—this time a church with a steeple and a cross on top. The third square stopped her. It showed woods in the fall with tiny brown and yellow scraps cut out in leaf patterns. Red blinked and looked again. Was that a skull by the tree? When she looked again, she wasn't sure.

"Where did this one come from?"

Elena shrugged. "It's been here since I started last year. Maybe the owner hasn't picked it up yet."

Behind Elena's machine was a door with a mirrored window. It was located in such a way that someone on the other side could see who walked into the shop. Red pointed to it.

"What's behind the door?"

Elena shook her head. "Bobbi doesn't let anyone back there. It's her office. She keeps it locked."

"But she keeps the finished quilts out here? I'd think she'd be worried about them."

Elena shrugged with a half smile. "I don't ask questions."

Red walked over and peered through the mirror but saw nothing but her own reflection.

Geez, I look like hell. Her hair was matted down on top from wearing a stocking cap, her eyes were puffy from lack of sleep, and the skin under her eyes looked like she'd smudged them with brown eyeshadow. No wonder Lillian wanted to fix her hair.

No sense waiting around here.

"Elena, does Hitch come around the shop much?"

"Sometimes."

"Have you noticed a lot of people coming in and out? High school kids or strangers?"

Again she shook her head. "Only the delivery people and those cousins."

"Cousins?"

"Kazurinski, I think."

"They bring the quilts?"

"No. They bring all the other supplies. Bobbi picks up the quilts from a place in Canada. She drives up to Winnipeg once a month to get them. She says she'd rather get them herself than trust the shipping people."

"I guess this is pretty valuable merchandise."

Elena settled back in the chair, flipped the lever on the foot feed, and positioned herself to begin stitching again.

"Take care," Red said, walking out the door. She shivered, wondering how Elena could stand it. The shop was so cold her fingers ached until she put her gloves back on.

As she stepped out of the office, a silver Lexus GS pulled into the driveway. To Red's disappointment, Bobbi was behind the wheel. She waved at Bobbi and walked over to the driver's side of the SUV.

"Hi," she said. "I'm looking for Hitch. No one answered at the house."

Bobbi eyes had a startled look. "Oh, he's out of town today. He'll be back on Tuesday. Would you like to come in?"

"No, thanks. When he gets home, would you have him call me?"

"I should put the car in the garage. It's cold, you know. Sometimes it won't start in the cold."

Tiffy interrupted. "Mom. It's okay."

Red stepped away from the car and waved. "Take care." She wondered how Tiffy ended up being such a normal teenager with a mother who startled when a pin dropped and a father who might have been dropped on his head one too many times.

She called Cal.

"No word from Jason. Pretty quiet except that the electricity is out down south of town. I keep getting 911 calls from Sadie Harwood. She thinks someone stole all her lights. I've called the utility company. They say they're working on it and should have it fixed in an hour or two."

"Thanks, Cal. Call me ASAP when Jason checks in."

At home, Blue danced at the door when Red walked in. "Listen, pal. I'm letting you out, but I'm going to watch you in case we have any more lurkers."

While Blue sniffed around outside, Red stood at the doorway, paging through the old cold case file. It was like reading the same chapter over and over. No matter how many times she read the file and looked at the photos of the skull, Doe stayed Doe.

The case had haunted Will in those last months while the cancer ate away at his lungs. "I'd like to go out with a clean slate," he'd said one day after finishing up some paperwork. By then he couldn't walk further than the bathroom without wheezing and breaking out in a cold sweat. "Who is this person, and why did someone put a bullet through his head?"

"I don't know," Red said out loud to the file in her hands. "I wish I could solve it for you, Will."

She tried drinking a cup of tea but couldn't shake the restlessness she felt.

"You know what? I'm banging my head against the wall." She picked up Blue as he trotted into the house. "Maybe I need a little relief. I think I'll see what our ice-fishing Eddie Bauer boys are up to before we get another storm. Maybe they've seen Missy." Or maybe they *have* Missy.

Outside in the brightness of the early afternoon light, a sun dog in pinks and blues shone across the lake. She took it as a good omen.

39

SHERIFF RED

LUXURY ON THE LAKE

Red called Eddie's Resort. Blue was settled contentedly on her lap and looked annoyed when she shifted positions to punch in the numbers.

After the tenth ring, Mac Morris picked up.

"Eddie's," he said with little enthusiasm.

"Hi, Mac, Sheriff Hammergren here."

Silence. She and Mac were not on the best of terms. He ran an illegal high-stakes poker game out of his back room. She also suspected he took bets on high school games and that those bets added to the pressures on the young athletes. A raid on his room was on her to-do list, but she kept putting it off because two of her county commissioners were regulars at Mac's. If she wanted funding for another deputy, she had to compromise some of her principles. As she once told Scotty, "Eighty percent of my job is pure politics. I could walk down the halls of Congress and feel right at home."

"I'm wondering, Mac, if you've rented your fish house to some big guys in North Face jackets lately."

"What makes you think it was me?"

Red stroked Blue's forehead and scratched him under the chin. Blue yawned, and his eyes drooped shut.

"Well, let's see. Number one, they came into Scotty's and asked how to find your place. Number two, you have the only fish house rental on Hammer Lake. And number three, you've got that luxury setup in the colony."

Mac hauled a trailer out on the lake every year and rented it to people coming up from Minneapolis who wanted a winter outdoor experience without really getting outdoors. It came complete with plush carpeting, a kitchen, two bedrooms and a fireplace. Rumor had it that Mac even sawed a hole in the floor so his renters could drop a fishing line from time to time.

"Okay, okay. Those guys rented it for a long weekend."

"Who exactly?"

"I promised them privacy."

"Since when have you kept anything private?"

"They paid a premium for me to rent to John Smith. Cash up front."

"John Smith? Really? Is the road plowed?"

Mac mumbled something and abruptly hung up.

Red looked at the phone. "I guess I can't count on your vote in three years."

She set Blue down in his favorite spot on the recliner and pulled on her boots and parka. "I'm off to see if those Hollywood guys caught any trout. I'll be sure to get you an autograph."

Blue refused to look at her. Abandoned again.

The clear sky and the low angle of the sun along with the sparkling snow created an achingly white glare as Red drove up to Eddie's. Fortunately, the highway was clear and the cold air had freeze-dried most of the pavement.

When she reached Eddie's, she gingerly drove out onto the lake and followed the roughly plowed road to the fishing colony. Smoke from the fish houses rose straight up, and the snow crunched with the brittle sound of sub-zero temperatures beneath the tires of the car.

Except for a distant buzz of a snowmobile, the fishing colony was quiet. Walt LaFrance's Escalade was parked next to a second Escalade in front of the fish house/trailer. They were both as close to the door as possible. It didn't look as if the snowmobiles had been taken off the trailer hitched to Walt's SUV. Snow had drifted in around the tires and up the wooden step that led to the door.

"Not much activity here," Red noted as she stepped out of her vehicle into the bone-chilling cold.

A sign over the door of the fish house/trailer said, "Walleye Heaven."

Red doubted the inside of that place had seen a walleye in a good number of years. She'd heard rumors that Mac brought in girls for "parties" in the fish house, but since she'd gotten no complaints, she'd had no reason to investigate. As Will used to say, "If it ain't broke, don't fix it."

Red pushed through the drifted snow to the front door. She heard music that sounded like a hair band from the eighties. After the third knock, the door opened, and warm, humid air brushed her face along with a lingering aroma of marijuana smoke. A good-looking man in his late twenties opened the door with a confused expression. "Yes?"

"I'm Sheriff Hammergren. I wonder if I could come in for a few minutes and ask you some questions."

The man's hair was wet and tousled, as if he'd just stepped out of the shower. He blinked at her with a slow, confused expression.

"Could I come in?" she asked again.

He rubbed his eyes, then glanced back at the living room. "I don't know. It's...it's kind of messy right now."

Red smiled in a benign way and said, "Mess doesn't bother me."

"Oh?" He didn't move.

Red pushed the door open farther and slipped past him. "Thanks. It's cold standing in the doorway."

The living room of the trailer was strewn with clothes, jackets, opened bags of potato chips, and beer cans. A laptop sitting on the coffee table in front of the sofa blinked the reds and greens of a screen saver. The beige shag carpet was cut out in the middle of the room to reveal a trapdoor. So, the rumors were true. Mac did keep a fishing hole for his renters.

"What is your name?" Something about his face seemed familiar, but she couldn't place it.

"Rex Waldon."

It took a few moments before it came to her. She'd seen him on the front page of one of the tabloids at the grocery store checkout. "You're King Rex, the wrestler?"

He nodded. She was surprised that in jeans and a T-shirt, he didn't look like the muscle-boy on television.

"Anyone else here?"

"Sleeping. Everyone is sleeping."

A bed squeaked as if to confirm his statement. Except that the bed kept squeaking in the age-old human-coupling rhythm.

Red stood near the door, taking in the chaos that looked like a long night of partying.

"We're looking for a missing girl—high school age, dark brown hair and blue eyes. She was wearing a pink jacket."

He shrugged. "I haven't seen her." He slipped a magazine over one of the ashtrays.

She smiled at him. "I'm not after drugs—unless you are dealing."

Color rose up his neck to his cheeks.

"Who else is here?"

"Just a couple of guys."

"Catching any fish?"

"What?"

She held back a chuckle at the startled expression on his face.

"Walleyes. This is Walleye Heaven."

The magazine he had grabbed to cover the ashtray had a slick cover of a man with shining bronze skin, posing so the ripple of his chest muscles showed. The room had a locker-room smell to it—sweaty bodies mixed with aftershave and marijuana. There was something familiar about the aftershave odor, but she couldn't put her finger on it.

She looked at King Rex in his ordinary clothes and suddenly wanted to ask if the wrestling matches were staged ahead of time. Her mother, for reasons she never understood, had been an avid wrestling fan. In her later years when Hitch was such a local star, she talked about him as if he were family. "Oh, Red, did you see that Hitch had a match with Mike the Menace. I was so afraid he'd get hurt."

However, the theatrics of sweaty men was not why she'd come. She saw no evidence of a clandestine meth lab or anything other than a boys' weekend of football and beer.

"If you see a girl in a pink jacket, be sure to call." She handed him her business card.

He nodded politely, still hovering near the ashtray.

As Red turned to leave, she noticed a jacket thrown into the corner by the door. It was a high school letterman's jacket similar to the ones she'd seen on the Kazurinskis in the gym. She pointed to it.

"Your jacket?"

He shook his head. "I don't know who it belongs to. It was probably here when we came."

Red's cell phone rang as she stepped out into the fresh, icy air.

"Sheriff, it's Cal. Jason radioed in. Said the shack was empty, but it looked like someone had been in it." The signal cut out for a moment. When it came back, Cal was in mid-sentence: "...energy bar wrapper on the floor but nothing else."

"I'll talk to him when I get back." Red slipped into her car. Could the girl have been in the shack and then gone somewhere else?

It wasn't until she was halfway back to Lykkins Lake that she placed the aftershave. Both Hitch Norgren and Mitch Rafferty smelled of it yesterday. Either it was a popular brand, or Hitch's "meeting" was on the lake. Did he have a girl on the side?

40

SHERIFF RED

FATHER PAUL

Jason was waiting when Red returned to the courthouse. His cheeks were ruddy and chapped from the cold.

"She might have been there," he said. "I found ashes in that rusted old stove in the shack, and the snow was tramped down by the door."

"Did you find any tracks?"

Jason shrugged. "With the storm and all, it was hard to tell. I took the snowmobile as far as the lake, but I didn't see anything."

Red studied the map. "I guess that doesn't tell us much."

He held out a plastic baggie with the energy bar wrapper in it. "Maybe we can test it for DNA."

Red laughed. "Sure. We'll pull all her phone records and bank records, too. Just give me a minute."

She logged in the baggie as evidence and told Jason to go home and take a hot bath. "I don't need you to get sick right now."

～

Red, Scotty, and Georgia sat around the table in the back of the antiques store. The late-afternoon sky darkened as clouds from the next front moved in. A headache from either tension or lack of sleep simmered behind Red's eyes.

"Any word on the money?" Scotty asked.

Red held her hands up in a gesture of surrender. What little she'd gotten from Titus was not enough to go public.

At least Cal had been able to track Wendy Farnsworth's husband down to see if they could locate Wendy. It turned out that he and Wendy had separated three months ago and she'd gotten a new cell phone. He didn't have the number. When he needed to talk, he either called the house or called Trevor.

Red tried Trevor's number several times, but it went to voicemail. The husband didn't know where Wendy might have gone.

"Since Trevor's troubles, she hasn't been herself." It was all he could offer. He said he'd contact the sheriff's office if he heard anything.

She stirred a teaspoon of sugar into the coffee. Georgia used a French press and made the coffee strong. Red needed the extra boost because weariness was overtaking her.

"We've been doing some research on your little problem." Georgia pointed to the letter from the lawyer.

"Tell me you found out it's a hoax."

Georgia shrugged. "The birth certificate seems genuine. But Scotty has dug up a little more information on Louise Weaver, the child."

"Googling after you closed the café?" Many law enforcement agencies now had a cadre of internet-savvy people who searched law enforcement databases. She had a phone book, Google, and of course the website that promised that the Pearsal *Country* sheriff would *project* and serve.

She sipped her coffee with a half smile.

"That's the thing." Scotty beamed. "You can Google all you want, but around here, if you need information, you use the magic of..." She pulled out her cell phone. Leaning closer to Red and still smiling, she pointed to the screen. "You take this thingy here and you use it to call people. Who knew?"

Red laughed. Really, who knew?

"So, first I called my former next-door neighbor. Old Chet knows the gossip going back to the fifties. He told me that Margaret Weaver was really

Mary Margaret Weaver and that she did live next door to the Hammergrens. In the late sixties, the Weavers 'adopted' a baby named Louise.
Everyone wondered if she really belonged to Mary Margaret because the
Weavers sent her off for the summer when she was a teenager to live with
an 'aunt.' She came back with the baby, who was a 'distant cousin.'"

"Typical in the fifties and sixties to send a pregnant teen to 'visit the
relatives.' They actually went to a home for unwed mothers." Georgia
paused for a moment. "Usually those babies were given up for adoption."

Scotty nodded. "That's what I thought, too. But Old Chet said the baby
wasn't 'right.' I couldn't get any more than that out of him."

A car rumbled by, going too fast for the icy roads. Even above the sound
of the furnace fan, they heard the noise of tires skidding on the road. Red
braced herself for the metallic crash, but nothing more happened.

"People need to slow down," she muttered. "Bad driving makes more
work for the Pearsal Country sheriff."

Scotty nodded in agreement. "The poor country sheriff needs a little
respite...and maybe a longer buckskin skirt."

"From all that projecting," Georgia added.

Red cupped her hand around the coffee mug, savoring the heat it
brought to her fingers. "Where is Louise now? I don't recall hearing much
about the Weaver clan."

"That's the thing." Scotty set the phone down on the table and leaned
back. "Chet wasn't sure, but he thought maybe DeeAnn, the housekeeper
for Father Paul, might know."

Georgia walked to the kitchen and brought back the coffee. "Refills?"

Red pointed to her mug and watched the steaming liquid pour out of
the carafe. "And?"

Scotty's eyes sparkled. "I called DeeAnn, and we had a nice chat. In fact,
she likes my idea of using local produce for the school lunches. She has a
huge garden and would be delighted to sell her vegetables to the school."

Red drummed her fingers on the table. She was thinking about Titus
and boys on buses. Did Hitch know more than he claimed to know? What
about Mitch Rafferty? Was he connected? What about the Hollywood
wrestlers? Was their visit simply a coincidence? Or was there a connection
between Hollywood and drugs?

Scotty raised her voice enough to pull Red out of her reverie. "Mary Margaret's sister Barbara still lives around here."

Red looked at her in surprise. "You talked with the sister?"

"Well, not exactly. The sister is in the Lakeside Nursing Home and not well. I tried to call her there, but the aide said she wasn't able to talk."

"Oh."

Georgia sat down. "We still have a plan, though. I know Barbara. She used to come into the shop from time to time. She also collected wooden decoys."

"Ah, your passion."

Georgia nodded. "She was quite knowledgeable." She sipped her coffee and set the mug down. "I have a new one I found at an auction before Christmas. I might just show it to her."

Red finished her coffee and leaned toward Georgia. "Thanks for your work, but this is my battle, ladies. I think you should retire from 'investigating' before I get complaints about nosy nurses." She stood up and stretched. "Back to the trenches."

Outside, the air was crisp and still. Red took a deep breath of it, savoring the smell of the fresh snow. She wished she could enjoy it more. She and Will used to love breaking trail with their cross-country skis after a snowfall. The peace of the woods and the rhythmic sound of the skis sliding over the snow was like a meditation to her. For a moment, she let the ache of loss wash over her.

"Enough relaxing. You have work to do," she mumbled.

Before going home, Red stopped in the office. Everything was calm, electricity had been restored in the south part of the county, and no disturbances had been reported.

She looked online at the weather forecast. "We're in for more snow."

"Yup." Cal sat at his station, poring over a map of the county. "Just trying to figure out if that girl was here," he pointed to the place where the hunting shack was, "where would she go?"

"Jack Klein thought she might go to his fish house." Red pointed to where she thought it was on the map.

Cal shook his head. "I can't see her getting there—especially in a storm. You know there's open water."

"Well, he had Joe check it out, and it was empty."

The golden window for finding someone alive was about forty-eight hours, and her time was up. "I hope the snow holds off a bit."

On her way home, she drove by the Catholic church. A light was on in the office in the back of the church. Maybe Father Paul knew someone named Coke or could tell her about the rosary. She pulled into the parking lot.

When she knocked at his office door inside the church, he turned to her with a startled expression. He was sitting at a large mahogany desk with an open ledger. Instead of priestly robes and a white collar, he wore black slacks and a thick black turtleneck sweater.

"Sheriff, you spooked me. I thought the Holy Ghost was coming to visit." He smiled broadly, his dentures too white for his face.

Red had an uneasy relationship with the priest. Two of her commissioners were members of his parish. She suspected that their opposition to funding the Church family planning clinic came from Father Paul. The Father and his congregation were traditional conservative Catholics, even though many of his female parishioners frequented the clinic.

Despite his opposition to birth control, Red gave him high marks for integrity. As Will once said, "Father Paul came in during a time of crisis for the church. The former priest had been embezzling from the church donations for several years. He cleaned up the bookkeeping and kept his parish afloat."

"Father Paul, I need your help. I'm looking for someone who might be called Coke. Does the name ring a bell?"

Father Paul chuckled. "The only Coke I know is the kind that comes in a can. My housekeeper scolds me anytime I buy it." He studied her. "Is this related to the Peterson boy?"

Red shrugged. "Not sure. Not sure that's even the right name."

He slowly shook his head. "Bad news with that kid. How do you comfort parents who just lost a child?"

Red raised her eyebrows. "I guess that's where you come in. My job is to find out what happened and why."

The furnace fan rattled as it blew warm air into the room. Red fingered the rosary in her pocket before taking it out. "On a different topic, I found this in my yard. It looks like someone dropped it, and I was wondering if it looked familiar to you." She handed him the rosary.

He studied it under the light of his desk lamp. "Hmmm. It's quite distinctive."

"I was hoping to find the owner. I know these can be important to people." *And I think someone was after me or after my dog.* She kept her thoughts to herself.

Father Paul squinted, looking up at the ceiling as if trying to retrieve a memory. After some thought, he said, "There was a time around 2000 when the church gave rather expensive rosaries to people who graduated from their lay-priest program. I remember seeing them at a conference. This looks like it could be one of them."

"Do you know any lay priests in the area?"

Father Paul shook his head. "The program only lasted a year or two." He studied the rosary again. "It was fraught with problems, but as I recall, we had one here in this parish."

The expression on his face said that he was wrestling with something. A clock behind him ticked in a comforting rhythm. "I guess this isn't confidential information." He rummaged in the desk for a key ring and sorted through several keys of various sizes until he found the right one.

"Maybe this will tell us something."

Red sat holding the rosary in her hand, resisting the urge to finger the beads, while Father Paul unlocked a file cabinet and pulled out a manila folder. The tab on the folder was bent as if it had been looked at many times.

He opened the folder. "This is the information we have on the lay priest. It was before I arrived at the parish, so I can't tell you much. The program was out of Boston and meant to relieve some of the priest shortages. Two or three lay priests were assigned to churches in Minnesota for training. One of them came here to study under Father Bernard." His voice dropped off as he cleared his throat.

Father Paul's crusade to clear up Father Bernard's financial mess had taken him several years. He lost parishioners during that time because

Father Bernard had been a very popular priest who unfortunately had a gambling and drinking problem. As far as Red knew, Father Bernard's sins were of a financial nature and not the sexual scandal that continued to plague the church.

"What happened with the lay priest?"

Father Paul shrugged. "I don't know. But that rosary certainly resembles the ones that the dioceses gave to the participants. See?"

He handed Red the file. On top was a black-and-white photo of a man with a crew cut and a serious expression. He held the rosary in one hand. His eyes, even with the matte of the photo, looked over-bright.

Father Paul took out a magnifying glass from the top drawer of his desk. "It looks just like the one you are holding."

Red scrutinized the photo and nodded in agreement.

"This might belong to him?"

Father Paul shrugged again. "Hard to tell."

The file consisted of an official-looking application with information on the lay priest including name, birth date, education, and a one-page essay from the applicant on why he wanted to devote his life to the church.

"Henry Holt." She said the name out loud. "Doesn't mean anything to me."

"A few years after I arrived here, I received an inquiry from a private investigator about Henry Holt. I checked the file and also asked my council and the bishop, but no one knew what happened to him."

"He doesn't live around here?"

Red wrote down the name and birth date. When she had time, she'd see if she could find more information on him. First, of course, she'd ask Cal.

The file also contained three sheets of lined notebook paper held together with a paperclip. The sheets contained writing in blue ballpoint pen, and the cramped cursive had faded as the paper had deteriorated. It was dated over twenty years ago—about the time Red was in college.

The notes were evaluation entries. The first stated that Henry was excited to be at the church and be part of the Catholic community.

"Do you think Father Bernard wrote these?"

"That would be my guess, but he didn't sign them."

She continued to read through them. The first notes indicated Henry was adapting well, knew his catechism, and the children in the parish liked him as a Sunday school teacher. Then no notes for several months, followed by several lines stating that Henry had become very friendly with a parishioner. It didn't state who the parishioner was other than to say the woman was a single parent and Henry took great interest in guiding her child in the ways of the church.

A clock behind Father Paul chimed a delicate five times. He cleared his throat. "I will need to leave soon. My housekeeper likes to serve supper on time, and she can get, uh, quite ornery when I'm not there."

Red nodded and quickly scanned the rest of the sheets. The last entry was a brief and abrupt note that "after consultation with superiors and much prayer, I have decided Henry is not the right person for our parish. He has been asked to leave."

One more entry had a date and only a few sentences: *He calls himself Jubal now. Living with...* The name was erased. *Worried for the child.*

Red pointed to it. "Do you know what that means?"

"No, I'm afraid I don't." He stood up. "But if I find out anything about a lost rosary, I will let you know."

"Do you know how I could reach Father Bernard if I have more questions?"

Father Paul studied her. "You are taking this lost rosary quite seriously, aren't you?"

"It's a nice piece, and I'd like to get it back to its owner." She wasn't planning to tell him about her suspicions that the owner might have been trying to hurt her or her dog.

"I'm afraid that Father Bernard died a couple of years ago. Liver failure." He sighed. "He'd left the church by then and fallen on hard times."

Defrocked? Red didn't ask. She handed the file back to him and slipped the beads back in her pocket. This was a mystery for another day. Right now, she needed to get some groceries and go home to a glass of wine.

41

SHERIFF RED

WEESEY

After talking with Father Paul, she drove to the grocery store. The rosary and the mysterious lay priest intrigued her. But she was hungry and tired and in desperate need of a glass of wine.

One thing that Red liked about the aftermath of a snowstorm was the cleanliness of the landscape with everything blanketed in a clean white sheet. As she drove into the parking lot of the grocery store, she noted that the snow piles that had been pushed by the plow to the edges of the lot were still pristine. In a couple of days, they would acquire a patina of grime she called "winter grease."

At five fifteen, the sun was down, and the nearly empty parking lot had a sickly yellow glow from the outdoor lights. Judging from the bare spots on the shelves, the citizens of Pearsal County had done a run on the store before the snow fell yesterday. *Good idea*, she thought as she added orange juice, eggs, and yogurt to her cart.

A small, thin woman wearing baggy pants and a long overcoat dropped a couple of cans of cat food as she tried to reach for the top shelf. Red stepped over to her.

"Can I help you?" Red recognized her immediately. Weesey Brandt, Lykkins Lake's unofficial bag lady. Weesey lived in the trailer court a couple blocks from the grocery store. In the summer, she pushed a battered stroller around town, picking up odds and ends from garbage cans. Red got at least one call a month about her. The consensus was that she was slow and harmless and would someday end up at the Lakeside Nursing Home.

She remembered the anonymous caller last fall who could hardly contain herself. "Someone should do something about her. It's embarrassing to the town to have her out in public."

Red was surprised that Beldon Rafferty hadn't been one of the complainers. He often brought complaints to her about things he thought she should handle. "Sheriff, you should..." She thought of it as a fill-in-the-blank game. Most of his "shoulds" were either too minor to deal with or out of her jurisdiction. That didn't stop him from complaining about her to the county commissioners.

Weesey nearly jumped at the sound of Red's voice. She was bundled up in a woolen scarf wrapped around her head and neck. Most of her back teeth were gone, and her mouth rotated in a chewing motion as she stared at Red. Red recognized the motion as the involuntary tics and spasms related to long-term use of anti-psychotics.

Red picked up the cans and handed them to her.

A clerk in a blue smock hurried over to her. "Weesey, you know you can't buy cat food with your food stamps."

The clerk turned to Red. "She tries to sneak these in. We catch her at it all the time."

"Can't I have these?" Weesey asked in a high, thin tone. "They're for my babies."

The clerk shook her head and said, "You know you can't. Your babies can find their own food."

As she reshelved the cans, the clerk said to Red, "Her babies are a couple of squirrels that she likes to feed."

"Mona says I'll have some money pretty soon and that I can buy all the food I want."

The clerk patted her on the shoulder. "That's nice. But right now, you need to put everything back."

Her cart was heaped with bags of dog food and cat food.

The clerk replaced the bags and steered her out of the aisle. "I'll call Mona to come and get you."

Red raised an eyebrow, and the clerk explained, "Mona Rafferty looks after her."

Mona? Really? Beldon's wife owned the trailer park, at least on paper. Puzzled, Red went back to shopping. Mona wasn't known for her charity. Last summer, she'd evicted an elderly couple who'd lived in the park for thirty years because they'd gotten behind on the rent due to medical bills. If Mona was involved with Weesey, someone must be paying her. She put that thought into the back of her brain and continued shopping. Weesey Brandt was not her problem today.

By the time Red checked out, Weesey was pacing by the front door of the store. Every time she walked by the automatic door, it would open. Exasperated, the clerk called to her.

"Weesey, please sit down. I haven't reached Mona yet."

Several people stood in line to check out as the clerk called Mona once again.

"I can drop her off at home," Red offered.

The clerk smiled at her with relief. "That would be nice."

Red tapped Weesey on the shoulder. "Would you like a ride home?"

Weesey grinned and marched out the door. "Gotta get home to my babies."

Red waved at the clerk as she hurried to catch up.

Weesey sat in the front seat of Red's car, clutching her bag of groceries. "Mona said to wait until tomorrow, but I couldn't wait."

"That's okay. I'll get you home."

The car filled with an odor of unwashed clothes and greasy hair.

"Does Mona look after you?"

"Uh-huh. She gives me money to buy groceries. Sometimes she brings me cookies." She smiled. Several of her top teeth were gray. They'd have to come out soon. "I like cookies."

"Me, too." Red made a note to talk with the county social worker about Weesey. Maybe they could get a home health aide to come out and help her with a bath. Also, someone needed to take her to a dentist. Would Mona Rafferty do this?

The lanes inside the trailer park had been plowed, but the walk to

Weesey's trailer was drifted in. One set of footprints led to the road. Red assumed those belonged to Weesey.

"Let me help you in." Red wanted to get a look at the inside of the trailer. On more than one occasion she'd had to call the county social worker for vulnerable people living in squalid conditions. The last time she'd encountered a mess, the old guy had been going around the neighborhood on garbage collection day collecting the plastic bags of garbage and hauling them home. The house was filled floor to ceiling with garbage bags. Social services found a nice adult family home to take him. The house, however, was uninhabitable and had to be demolished.

Red took a breath of fresh, clean air before stepping into the trailer. To her surprise, the little kitchen and living room were immaculate. The trailer smelled of lemon-scented cleanser, which contrasted with Weesey's unwashed smell.

Setting the groceries down on the counter, Red said, "It's very nice in here."

Weesey nodded with enthusiasm. "Barbara always said I had to keep it clean, or I'd have to go someplace bad."

"Barbara?"

Weesey's smile faded. "She's sick now, so Mona takes care of things."

Lights of a car shone through the drawn blinds of the living room window. The car stopped in front of Weesey's trailer, and the car door slammed.

"Weesey, are you all right?" A breathless Mona Rafferty whisked through the door and stopped dead, staring at Red.

Red smiled at Mona as her cheeks drained of color. The woman was tall and stringy with the pale complexion of one who doesn't get outside much. Now she looked ashen.

"I...I had a message from the grocery store. They said someone had taken Weesey."

Red continued to smile, puzzled by Mona's reaction. "Are you all right, Mona?"

"Well." Mona turned quickly to the door. "Well, I'd better get going."

"Stay warm," Red called after her. What was that all about?

. . .

Later, as Red sat in her kitchen with a glass of red wine, waiting for the frozen pizza in the oven to cook, she thought about Weesey. She was still puzzled by Mona but grateful that Weesey had someone to look after her. If she didn't have a local community that cared, she guessed that Weesey would be one of the people living on the street like her brother, Lad—if he was still alive.

The oven dinged, and Red pulled out a somewhat soggy Canadian bacon and pineapple pizza. The oven no longer heated beyond about 325 degrees, and one of these days she needed to get it fixed. On the other hand, she could count on her ten fingers the number of times she'd used it this year. Learning to cook for one was not on the top of her priority list. Too often, eating alone in the kitchen brought back memories of all the times she and Will sat together discussing work over a glass of wine or a beer.

"Blue," she looked at the dog on her lap, "you aren't much of a conversationalist, are you?"

The pizza had its usual cardboard-and-salt flavor, but the wine was full-bodied and tasty. She relaxed with a legal pad in front of her and made notes of all the activities since Friday afternoon. Perhaps if she saw things in writing, she could make some connections. She created a column for Missy, one for Jared, one for Trevor, and one for miscellaneous.

Under Missy, she created a sub-category for Junior and Mayme. She stared at it a long time, trying to remember more about Mayme. What had Missy written in her letter? Mayme was using drugs and getting them from someone local.

As she stared at the paper, she recalled another contact with Mayme. It had been about five years ago when she was on night duty and a call came in about a car in the ditch on County Road Eight near the Kleins' property. By the time she reached the area, the road and ditch were clear. Red pulled into Jack Klein's place to see if they had seen the car. When she knocked on the door, Mayme opened it. Her dark hair was disheveled, as if it hadn't been combed in days, and her gaunt face had scratch marks, like she had been picking at the skin.

Before she could ask any questions, Junior Klein came to the door and steered Mayme behind him. No, they hadn't seen or heard anything. He thanked Red for stopping by and politely closed the door. Red's impression was that he was protecting Mayme, but nothing more came of it.

Her wineglass was empty by the time she pulled out her cell phone and called Lou.

Lou answered almost immediately.

"Wow," Red said. "You must have had the phone in your hand."

"When I'm on call, I keep the phone pretty much Velcroed to my hip."

They chatted for a few moments about the weather before Lou asked if there was any news on Missy.

"I don't have anything I can share. I did follow up on the person you told me about—Coke. Sounds like she's living in Oregon and doing okay. But she told her foster mother something that made me wonder. Maybe you can shed a light on it." Red went on to tell her about Coke's encounter with someone she thought was crazy. "Does that mean anything to you?"

Lou was quiet for a moment. "I'm trying to think about all the people who tried out that day. Nothing comes to mind. In case you feel bad about missing the play, Mayme was too big to play Annie, and as I've said, Bobbi was awful."

"Thanks for the critique. What I really wanted to know is if you had any more information on Mayme."

"Remember, I was in seventh grade when she was a senior."

"Do you remember much about her?"

"Sure. She was good. She had something about her—a real gift for comedy, and she could sing. Junior Klein played Daddy Warbucks. He even shaved his head. All us little seventh graders were in awe of the two of them. We were sure they'd both go on to be big Hollywood stars. Ironically, it was Hitch and Bobbi who ended up in Hollywood. Who knew?"

Red thought about the gaunt woman with the messy hair and scratched face and had a hard time putting it together with the musical *Annie*.

"What happened?"

"Pregnant right out of high school, married Junior Klein." Her voice drifted off as if she were thinking more about it.

"What else can you tell me?"

Lou paused before she spoke. "She was a little eccentric and had an entourage—you know, a group that followed her around. You might want to talk with Bobbi Norgren. If I recall right, she was one of the followers."

Red silently shook her head, thinking about her conversation with Bobbi. No, thank you, she mouthed to Blue.

"Anyway, I heard much later that Mayme had a drug problem. I know that she would disappear for periods of time. Junior always took her back."

Red heard a clicking sound on the line.

"Sorry, Red. Gotta go, the nursing home is calling."

Red studied her list again. Somehow Hitch Norgren was tied in with this, but she needed something solid to pursue it. Maybe Trevor could tell her—if only she could find him. Or the Kazurinskis.

Blue whined and looked at the kitchen door. She opened it for him and smelled the crisp air. The ache in her jaw had subsided, and she hoped that meant there wouldn't be another storm. Overhead, the stars twinkled in pristine clarity. Not a cloud in the sky, and the temperature was steady at ten below zero.

Her thoughts turned back to Weesey Brandt. Why would Mona Rafferty care about the poor soul?

Her phone rang as Blue trotted back in the door.

"Sheriff, it's Cal. I wanted you to know that Jennie will take over at eleven."

"Good. Anything to report?"

"Quiet evening so far."

"Quick question, Cal. What do you know about Weesey Brandt? She was causing a little disturbance at the grocery store this evening."

"Didn't get a call on her."

"I know. The clerk handled it. I was there. But what do you know about her family? I hear that Mona Rafferty is looking after her now."

She pictured Cal doing some calculating in his head before he replied. "Lives in the trailer court with her sister. Been there since the last census." He paused. "No, her sister is in the home now. She lives alone. Weesey's real name is Louise."

She heard the beep of the phone system in the background. "Thanks, Cal. You'd better get that."

She ended the call. Picking up one more piece of the soggy pizza, she looked at Blue and said, "One more bit of information to chew on."

After she crawled under the covers that night with Blue comfortably settled next to her, she prayed in her own way. "Please, God, let us find Missy. Let this be a search and rescue, not a search and recover." As she closed her eyes, she pictured the young girl with her dark hair and her one dimple. She wondered if sleep would come, and then her eyes drifted shut.

42

MISSY
DARK NIGHT PLANS

Missy awakened to the crystal darkness. Even under the sleeping bag and with her pink jacket on, she was bone cold.

Shivering, she sat up not wanting to stretch, not wanting to uncurl because the cold would seep in deeper. Her breath smoked in front of her. Must get the little heater going again. How long had she slept? Was Grampa Jack coming? She lit the lantern, wishing she had a watch. What day was it? How long had she been away?

Must go. If Grampa Jack still hadn't come, then it was time to cross to the shore and get help. She squeezed her eyes shut, trying to wake up. Later, after she'd peed in the snow and covered it up and after she'd eaten a can of pork and beans, she would make a plan.

The pork and beans boiling on the little camp stove warmed her. She could think again. She would cross over by the cove and find the road. Someone must be living on that road. She'd go to them for help. Grampa Jack would come, and everything would be okay.

But outside it was night and dark. She stood at the door peeking out and felt something like a weight fall inside her. She didn't know the direction to the cove. She couldn't see anything even with the stars twinkling overhead. Grampa Jack and Dad once took her outside on a warm summer night with the cicadas singing and the moths flying at the light of the porch to teach her about stars and navigation. They took her into a clearing and pointed up to the sky.

Back in the olden days, the explorers used the stars to navigate, they said. Imagine that. But she wasn't interested, and now she was sorry. The stars were out, and she didn't know how to use them. She knew if she went out in the dark, she would get lost and be one of those people found frozen on the lake. Or worse, she would fall into the icy waters of the lake. She closed the door and crawled under the sleeping bag. What if no one finds me? Then it was all for nothing.

The only thing she wanted right now was to be a little girl and have Dad and Gramma Serena and Grampa Jack and even Mom tuck her in to bed. The only thing she wanted was a tender voice saying, It will be okay, honey.

In the morning, when the sky was light, she'd leave. She fell asleep dreaming about swinging with Dad and Mom pushing her high into the sky.

43

SHERIFF RED

BREAK-IN AT KLEINS'

The clouds rolled in during the night while Red slept. Dark, pregnant clouds filled with more snow. And wind. The second storm was brewing in the west.

Her cell phone rang at seven on Monday morning. Red woke up with a start. Not only had she slept so soundly that she didn't wake up to let Blue out, but she'd slept without dreaming. No ghosts of Will, no tossing and turning.

"Sheriff, it's Jack Klein. Someone just buzzed by my house on a snowmobile. I think they were after something."

Forty-five minutes later, Red and Jason pulled up to Jack Klein's house. Snow was falling in large fluffy flakes, and Red's jaw ached again. Despite what she had hoped last night, another snowstorm was moving in. At least it was a little warmer.

Jack met them at the front door, his mouth pulled tight with worry and anger. "Two of them on snowmobiles about an hour ago. I was sound asleep until they started circling the house. Then my phone rang. Heavy breathing and a whisper."

"What did he say?"

"'We're gonna get Missy.'" He shuddered. "The voice was so cruel. By the time I got my rifle, they were gone."

Snowmobile tracks circled the house and the workshop. Jack started to talk, then stopped, distracted by something in the direction of the workshop. "That's not right." He hobbled toward the shop.

Red and Jason followed him until he reached the door of the workshop. Footprints in the snow led up to it, and the door was pushed in.

"My God." Jack limped into the shop. "Look what they did!"

A desk stood near the door. The top of it was completely cleaned off, with papers and pencils scattered on the floor around it.

"Looks like they swept everything off the desk."

The rest of the shop was undisturbed.

Red squatted down in front of the desk and surveyed the mess on the floor. "Did you have anything valuable in here?"

"All my business papers, my tax stuff, my checkbook..." He pored through the papers. "Damn it! What did Missy get messed up with?"

Red placed a hand lightly on Jack's shoulder. "Take a deep breath, and tell me what's missing."

Jack dug through the papers with his cane, muttering, "If I wasn't so lame, I'd be after those guys in a second."

Red turned to Jason. "See if you can get John Briggs out here with a couple of snowmobiles. Maybe we can track them if the snow doesn't get too heavy."

Jason headed for the radio in the Forester.

Red studied the mess on the floor, looking for some pattern. It wasn't typical vandalism. Nothing else in the shop had been disturbed. "I wonder if the phone call and the snowmobiles buzzing around the house were meant as a distraction while someone broke in."

Jack picked up his checkbook.

"Look at the checks in the back. Sometimes they'll leave the top checks so you won't cancel the account."

He paged through the blank checks and shook his head. "Nothing's missing that I can see."

"They must not have found what they were looking for."

"Or I scared them off."

Again, Red studied the papers and desk debris. Something wasn't right. As Jack put things back on the desk, she compared it to her desk at work.

What did she usually have? Files, papers, trays for the inbox and outbox, a few little knickknacks, the photo of her with Will…

"Jack, did you have any photos on your desk?"

Jack looked at Red, then the floor. "I don't see it here."

"What's missing?"

"Oh hell." Jack's voice rose in agitation as he stooped down and dug through the papers on the floor.

The tightening in her chest that Red experienced when something was terribly wrong caused her to catch her breath for a moment. "It's a photo, isn't it?"

Jack continued to shuffle papers, his breathing coming harder and harder. "It's not here." He looked at her with deep grief in his eyes. "It's my last photo of all of us together."

"Who?"

"Me and Junior and Missy. Why would they take it?"

Red squatted beside Jack. "Tell me about the photo."

"Missy made it for me. One side is a picture of the fish house on Hammer Lake. The other is a map of how to get there." Jack's face tightened. "We took the picture the winter before Junior died. We used to go there on weekends. Missy loved to ice fish with us."

"And this is a picture of you in the fish house?"

"Outside. By the sign I put up."

Red closed her eyes and visualized the map of Hammer Lake in her head.

"Jack, is it possible that Missy could have gotten across the lake from the Henderson cabin to the fish house?"

Jack shook his head. "I had Joe check it out on Saturday, remember?"

How could she forget? Red pictured Sammy stuck in the pickup truck.

"Let's call Joe." Red touched Jack's arm and nudged him toward the house.

It took several rings before Joe answered. He was on his way to bring his new daughter home.

"I didn't see anything out of the ordinary."

"What time were you there?"

"I got there about noon on Saturday. I didn't stay long, though, because the wind was whipping up like crazy. With Sammy pregnant and all, I thought I should get back home."

"Maybe she wasn't there yet," Jack said softly. "I should have had you check yesterday."

No, Red thought. *I should have known to check when I was out talking with the Hollywood boys. Damn.* Maybe Mitch Rafferty was right. Maybe she wasn't competent to be sheriff.

She touched Jack lightly on his arm. "Who knew you had that photo in your office?"

Jack shrugged. "Lots of people. I think Missy showed it to her friends once when they were here."

The pieces still weren't connecting for Red. Right now, she needed to focus on getting to the fish house.

"We'll find her, Jack."

She ran to the Forester. "Call John back and pray that you can get hold of him," she yelled at Jason. "We need to get to Hammer Lake as soon as possible."

The snow fell harder.

44

MISSY

She dreamed that her dad and mom were outside knocking on the door. She tried to stand up, to open the door for them, but the weight of the room held her down. I'm coming, she shouted, but she had no voice. They faded away, but the knocking continued.

Don't leave, she pleaded inside her head.

And suddenly the door was ripped open, the doorframe shattered. Not Dad, not Mom, and not Grampa Jack. Someone in a black ski mask leapt toward her across the plywood floor of the fish house.

She smelled him—a *Follower*.

Before she could react and fight him off, the other *Follower* slammed through the door. One pinned her down while the other pulled a ski mask over her head backward so she had no eye and mouth holes. Then they tied her hands. The fish house went dark, and she felt like she couldn't breathe.

One dragged her out. Inside, she heard the sounds of pots being thrown around and the cot overturned.

Where is it? Where is it? the *Follower* shouted.

They wouldn't find it, though. Missy was proud of herself for hiding the money and the cell phone at the Church. She wouldn't tell them, and she wouldn't tell their boss.

The *Follower* half carried her across the snow. She kicked at him, but her feet only touched air.

Help me, one of them grunted as she dragged her feet through the snow. The other *Follower* grabbed her legs, and she was thrown onto a snowmobile. One *Follower* sat down behind her and held her around her waist so tight she thought he might break a rib. The machine roared beneath her.

Bumping, jarring, frigid wind whipped through her as the machine sped across the lake. Maybe I could throw him off, she thought. Pressing, she pushed back against the black thing steering the snowmobile.

Stop, he roared, cuffing the side of her head so hard that pain shot down her face and through her jaw. For a moment, everything went dark, then she was filled with dizziness and nausea.

Silence, Grampa Jack once said. In the woods, when you are stalking the bear—keep quiet, and it won't sense you.

Missy closed her eyes and clamped her mouth shut against the rage that boiled up inside her. I would be silent. Crazy. I know about crazy. Mom warned me. Watch out, Missy. Too much craziness here.

The *Follower* whispered in her ear, If you try to jump, I'll run you over and kill you. She knew that voice. It was hard and stupid like the man himself. The snowmobile vibrated beneath her. The blow to the head made her woozy. And the two days of huddling inside the fish house made her weak. The backward ski mask the *Follower* pulled over her head blinded her. It smelled of greasy hair. She needed to take some sips of air to stop from gagging. The wind, the roar of the machine created a cacophony of sounds within her head.

Hard to think. Keep calm. Keep calm. She knew what they didn't know. She knew where the evidence was hidden, and they wouldn't find it—ever.

45

SHERIFF RED

JACK'S FISH HOUSE

Connections, Red thought as they rushed back to town. Who would know that Jack held the clue to where Missy was hiding—if she was hiding? The fish house in its hidden cove. Missy must have told someone about the photo and the map.

Find Coke. Find her.

And the men from California suddenly showing up for ice fishing? Were they connected? If so, who was the glue? Hitch Norgren? What about Mitch Rafferty or Bobbi Norgren's apish cousins?

She turned to Jason. "Did you find out anything more about the Kazurinski brothers?"

"Not much. Believe it or not, their names are Ivan and Igor—sounds like they came out of one of those Russian novels. They showed up a few years ago—after Hitch moved back. They haven't caused any trouble—although my sister thought they were pretty creepy."

"Well, I guess 'creepy' isn't a crime. Hitch says they're related to Bobbi. Did you find anything about that?"

"Cousins of some sort. Came from Minneapolis. No one knows much about them."

Red's intuition told her the brothers were connected to this, but she had nothing concrete to go on other than Lillian the hairdresser saying she saw them with Norgren. Hitch?

She brought Jason back to the courthouse to arrange for snowmobiles. The snow stopped as soon as she pulled into the parking lot.

"Thank God something is going right."

After dropping Jason off, she sped north. The further she drove out of town, the more the snow fell from the sky. She would have to access the lake through Mac Morris's resort, and she was not looking forward to dealing with him.

Mac greeted her when she stepped out of her car. The light snow was coming down harder, and Mac's glasses beaded up from the moisture. He took them off and wiped them on the sleeve of his snowmobile suit.

"Mac, I need to get to Jack Klein's fish house. What's the best way?" If nothing else, Mac knew the lake and its residents better than anyone in the county.

"You can't get there right now. Too much drifting. Unless you've got a snowmobile."

Red looked behind her, hoping that Jason would pull up soon with the snowmobiles.

"Mac, have you got a machine I could use?"

She saw the glint in his eyes. "County can't get you one?"

Red felt her stomach muscles tighten in irritation.

"Mac," she said in a low voice. "If you don't have a snowmobile, tell me now. And if you have one, bring it to me."

"How much are you going to give me?"

"How much do you not want to be arrested for your backroom gambling operation?"

Mac's eyes narrowed as he threw her a look that said, "If I could stab you, I would."

In a tight voice with just a hint of tremble, he said, "This way."

Once she mounted, the snowmobile made a bone-jarring leap onto the lake. As soon as she reached the open expanse of snow, Red was hit with an icy wind that ripped through her parka. She was immediately sorry that she hadn't put on long underwear and heavier gloves. The helmet that Mac had given her was slightly big and smelled of bad breath and spit.

She would have been more attuned to her discomfort if it weren't for the words of the boy. She needed to find Missy before the unknown others did, and she was sure the girl was hiding in the fish house. As she raced across the lake, the snowmobile skidding along far faster than it should have, she noted fresh tracks leading in the same direction as Jack Klein's fish house.

"Let it be someone out to catch a few walleyes," she said out loud. Her voice shimmied with the vibration of the vehicle.

Ahead of her, she saw the luxury fish house. One of the Escalades was missing. By the freshness of the tracks, it hadn't been gone long.

She sped by, concentrating on getting to the other side of the colony. As if the heavens knew of her haste and her distress, heavier snow began to fall, dropping a gray veil over the lake. Soon, if the wind picked up, blizzard conditions would prevail once again.

In the few minutes it took her to reach the end of the ice-fishing colony, visibility had dropped. Many of the fish houses were drifted in, and as she peered through the snow, she saw little evidence of activity around them. The area appeared abandoned except for the fresh snowmobile tracks in front of her.

"Please be there." She was now beyond the cluster of houses and heading to the cove that hid Jack's place. The snowmobile jarred as it tracked through the rippling drifts. At one point she hit an icy pile of snow that caused the snowmobile to careen almost sideways.

Slow down or you won't get there in one piece. People died when these machines flipped and landed on top of them. A high school friend of Red's ended up a paraplegic from reckless snowmobiling.

For a few moments, the snow poured out of the sky like Mother Earth was dumping ashes from a bucket. Disoriented, Red lost sight of the cove and almost turned the wrong direction. As quickly as the snow came down, it suddenly stopped, and she saw that she was headed toward the south end of the lake, not toward Jack's fish house. She corrected sharply, and the snowmobile fishtailed into a skid.

Deep breath and slow down. Red's pulse raced.

As she neared the isolated house, her heart sank. Snowmobile tracks surrounded the house. It appeared to be two different snowmobiles. When she pulled up by the door, she could see a muddle of footprints. The door was open and swaying in the wind on a broken hinge.

Red leapt off the machine and ran to the door. "Missy! Missy! Are you there?"

She was met with only the sound of the wind as it swept the snow across the ice of the lake.

A dusting of icy snow had drifted through the open door and spread across the wooden floor of the house. The inside of the house had been trashed.

And it was empty.

Red stood at the door, surveying the mess. An empty can of Dinty Moore Beef Stew lay on its side. Spilled oatmeal covered a part of the floor, and the little propane cook stove lay in pieces next to the cot.

Gingerly, she stepped inside. The fish house was warm enough to indicate that it hadn't been abandoned long. In the dim light, she stooped to examine something wet and sticky on the floor.

"Goddamn it!" Little drops of blood led out the door.

Jason arrived as Red picked through the empty soup cans and litter in the house.

"She's not here. Someone tossed the place. They were looking for something besides Missy." The money? Were they looking for the money that had been left in the donation box at the Church?

Jason peered around the small space and finally pointed to the corner of the cot.

"What's that?"

Red stepped over and picked up a small piece of fabric with her gloved hand. In the light that filtered through the small skylight, she studied it. It was a pink fragment from a jacket.

"She was here, and they have her."

46

SHERIFF RED

CONNECTING THE DOTS

Red closed her eyes and visualized the sheet of paper she'd written out last night. She kept coming back to Hitch Norgren. Too many notes under his name. Could he be the head of a local drug operation? He didn't really have a day job, and he had easy access to vulnerable teenagers. Titus had said, "Boys on buses." And Jared Peterson said, *Find Coke. Find her.* Did he mean find Coach and you will find Missy?

"Red?" Jason pulled her out of her thoughts. "Maybe I can catch them. It doesn't look like they have much of a head start." He pointed to the tracks. "They're not filled in yet."

Red noted how quickly the snow was coming down and drifting in and shook her head. "It's too dangerous. It looks like they're going toward the south part of the lake. With the snow coming down and all the open water over there..." She stopped to think. "Go back to town and see if you can find the Kazurinski boys. I have a gut feeling they are connected here."

She left Mac Morris's snowmobile in the front drive of the resort. Already her car was covered with an inch of snow. She needed to *find Coke*. As she sat in the car waiting for the windshield to defrost, she called the school in hopes that someone would be there. She knew they'd pulled the buses and closed the schools as soon as the snow front came in.

A harried secretary answered with, "Yes, all schools are closed."

Red cleared her throat. "This is Sheriff Hammergren. Can you tell me if Hitch Norgren is in the building? His wife said he'd be out of town, but I'm checking in case he came back."

The secretary hesitated and then apologized. "Sorry for answering the phone that way. I've been deluged with calls. You'd think now that we have this text and tweet system that people would know the schools are closed."

Red kept the anxiety out of her voice. "I need to reach Hitch. No one answers at his house."

"I've got a cell for him."

She took down the number and was about to dial it when she remembered something about her visit to the luxury fish house. The letterman's jacket, the one that King Rex said must have been left there by a previous renter, and the faint fragrance she associated with both Hitch and Mitch. Could Hitch be in that trailer with Missy? The snowmobile tracks at Jack's fish house had pointed across the lake...but...

Peering through the snow, she noted that the road on the lake to the trailer still looked passable. She radioed Billie, who was working the day shift, and told him where she was going.

"If you don't hear from me in forty-five minutes, find Jason and tell him where I've gone. He'll know what to do."

"Oh boy!" Billie's excitement crackled through the radio.

It took less than five minutes to get to Walleye Heaven. Again only one Escalade was parked in front of the trailer, and no snowmobiles were evident.

She knocked hard on the door, raising her voice above the roar of the wind sweeping across the lake. "Sheriff Hammergren here. Please open up."

This time Walt LaFrance opened the door. He was dressed in a pair of khaki pants, a thick sweater, and a scarf around his neck. He looked tired, as if he'd been up all night.

"Yes?"

Red pushed her way in. "I'm looking for Hitch Norgren."

She surveyed the living room for any evidence that Missy had been here. The beer cans and food wrappers had been cleaned up. A closed suitcase stood near the entrance.

"Why would he be here?" Something in his voice rang false. Not only was Walt a bad actor, but he was also a bad liar.

The jacket was still on a chair near the door. Red pulled out her phone and called the cell number given to her by the school secretary. An Irish lilting tune rang from a cell phone on an end table.

"I believe that's his phone."

Walt stared at it as if he'd never heard a cell phone ring tone before.

Without asking and without thinking about search-and-seizure laws and search warrants and all the things that could screw up a court case, she marched past the kitchen to the doors of the bedrooms. The first one was locked from the inside. She pounded on it.

"Open up or I'll break it down!"

"Wait," a groggy voice replied.

Behind her she heard the hatch over the fishing hole being lifted and a clattering as something was dumped down into the water.

A very disheveled King Rex answered the door in boxer shorts. Someone was in bed with him.

"You have no right to come barging in here." Were these lines from a bad car-heist movie?

Red pushed past King Rex and flipped on the overhead light.

The person in the bed sat up, blinking at the sudden light.

"What?" Mitch Rafferty shaded his eyes.

She took a deep breath to disguise her total surprise. "Where's Hitch?"

"What?"

She didn't have time for this. She turned and tried the second bedroom. It was empty and the bed neatly made.

"Where is Hitch?" She stood near the hatch of the fishing hole, glowering at Walt LaFrance. She didn't care if the wrestling boys had a little love nest going. She cared that Missy Klein was in danger. "Why is his phone here?"

Walt finally answered. "He got a call early this morning." He patted the pockets of his khakis. "Damn it! He must have taken my phone instead of his."

"When is he coming back?"

"Soon, I hope. I need my phone back."

"Call him." She handed him her phone. "You know your number, I hope."

Walt punched in the numbers and listened. "Went to voicemail." Walt shrugged in a boyish way that did not amuse Red.

Red wanted to slap him. She grabbed her phone and left. Outside, the wind was picking up. Gusts whipped across the lake hard enough that sometimes it appeared the snow was coming sideways.

Back in her car, Red slapped the steering wheel before she started the car. She should have asked if Hitch took a snowmobile when he left, but at this point she had no interest in talking with Walt LaFrance, King Rex, or Mitch Rafferty. If they were involved with the missing Missy, she wouldn't have been able to storm out of the trailer the way she did. Three strong, trained men against a female sheriff who had lost her temper?

The back of her Subaru fishtailed as she gunned the engine and headed off the lake. Bobbi Norgren might know where her husband was. She radioed Billie and told him she was on her way to see the Norgrens.

47

MISSY

They hit a drift of hard, icy snow and she'd bounced almost out of her seat. The *Follower* squeezed harder around her waist to keep her in the seat. She grunted, fighting for her breath. Ahead, she heard the other snowmobile slide across the lake into a thick fog of snow.

She knew now where they were going, and she knew the lake. The open water lay between here and the south shore. If they crashed through the ice into the water, if the snowmobile went down and she drowned in the icy depths of Hammer Lake, she would die knowing the truth.

She prayed Grampa Jack and the nurses at the Church would find what she'd left for them. Not just the money, but the phone. It had the video showing the *Followers* handing money to their boss, the one who appeared so safe and yet had the crazy eyes.

Beneath her, she felt a change. The sound of the snowmobile was hollow, as if it skated over brittle ice. She wanted to warn him, to tell him the ice wasn't safe, but her cries were swallowed by the wind, and when she cried out again, the *Follower*'s grip around her waist tightened as he yelled, Shut up! The snowmobile moved deeper and deeper into the dangerous part of the lake.

Then she heard a crack. The lake was angry, angry with the snowmobiles and tired of their weight across its skin. Water ahead! But he didn't listen, didn't know the danger of the lake.

Open water, open water ahead! The *Follower* yelled again, Shut up, bitch!

Underneath her, the lake began to shake, like a dog shaking the water off after a swim. Ahead, suddenly a scream rang out above the sound of the snowmobile. A cry. Oh fuck! and the sound of open water.

They were on a course to follow the lead snowmobile, follow the *Follower* into the icy depths of the lake. The lake would take them.

With all her strength, she gathered herself as the snowmobile skidded forward. The *Follower* loosened his grip on her as he called out, Ivan!

Taking a deep breath, she jabbed her elbow as hard as she could into the *Follower*. Surprised, he let go, and when he did, in the second of relief from the crushing grasp around her waist, she hurled herself to the side away from the water just as the snowmobile crashed through the ice. Water so cold it was hot licked at her boots as she landed. The lake wanted to pull her in like it pulled in the *Followers*.

48

SHERIFF RED

A CRY ON THE LAKE

The Norgrens' driveway was carefully plowed just like it had been yesterday. Red saw no sign of vehicles, although tire tracks indicated someone had been in the drive recently.

She knocked on the door at the house.

"Bobbi, it's Sheriff Hammergren."

No answer.

Someone should be home because school was closed for the day. She was sure Bobbi wouldn't leave Tiffy alone.

She knocked again. Then she pulled out her cell phone and tapped in the phone number for the house. Inside, she heard a faint jangle as the phone rang. After four rings, Tiffy's teenage voice answered, "Hi, you've reached the Norgrens. We can't come to the phone right now. Please leave a message...or else." The message closed with a little giggle.

Red started toward her car and her radio. She wanted to get an update from Jason on whether he'd tracked down the Kazurinskis. She stopped as a noise from below the shop caught her attention. It sounded like the low roar of a snowmobile followed by a cracking sound, as if the ice was breaking. She strained to hear more. At first, she only heard the wind whistling through the trees. Then, as a gust died down, she heard something again. It was high pitched and faint, like a child's cry.

The shop was built at the top of the bank that led down to the lake. A swath of trees had been removed to provide a better view of the lake. As Red peered down, she thought it strange to create a view like this for a workshop. However, she wasn't the architect and didn't have the time to speculate on this.

The sound came again. She was sure it was a cry.

A track, barely visible through the drifting snow, led from the driveway to the back of the building. It had been used since Saturday's storm. She hurried down the track, her boots sinking and slipping in the snow. When she reached the back of the building, the wind died down for a moment and she could see to the lake. A boathouse and a shed stood on the shore. Now it made sense. Norgrens probably also kept their snowmobiles down there.

Beneath her feet, she felt the edges of wooden stairs. The cry came again. Red hurried down the steps.

"Help!" The voice was faint but clear. Someone was calling from the lake.

She was ten feet from the bottom when the heel of her boot caught the back of the wooden step. She pitched forward, twisting the ankle she'd once broken in a bicycle accident. She fought to control the fall.

A wrenching pain shot up her leg, sending black dots behind her eyes. "For God's sake, don't faint." She squatted down until the dizziness subsided.

Another cry—this time weaker. The wind gusted, and the snow created a veil between her and the lake. Cold sweat broke out on her forehead as the pain settled in her injured ankle.

"Help! Please help!" The voice sounded female and young. Missy?

Red stopped for a moment, gripping her ankle. *Think*, she told herself, willing the pain to go away. What did she know about this part of the lake? Natural springs fed into it from the Norgren property. It was one of the reasons the lake stayed clean and fresh throughout the hot, muggy summers, but also the reason the lake was so dangerous in the winter. The spring kept the water from freezing even after a long below-zero spell.

"Help!"

Red lunged forward, trying to keep as much weight as possible off her left ankle. Beside the boathouse, the door to the shed was open and empty. Multiple snowmobile and boot tracks covered the area. Most were nearly filled in, which told Red they were at least an hour old.

Red stepped out onto the lake, following one of the tracks that went in the direction of the cry.

"Keep calling," she yelled. "I'm coming."

With the snow swirling and the wind roaring, it was important that she keep her bearings. The track helped, but it probably didn't lead directly to the voice.

"I'm here!" The voice sounded choked. "Wet. Can't hold on much longer…" The words drifted off.

Red sped up, the pain in her ankle causing her to gasp as she ran.

"Can't hold on…"

Was the sound coming from the right or the left?

"Call out again," she yelled, panting as she ran.

"Here." The voice no more than a croak.

Stopping to catch her breath, Red peered through the wall of snow. It was like trying to see something through a white bedsheet. *Listen to the lake,* she told herself. *If there is open water, you will hear it.*

She closed her eyes and pictured the lake covered in ice and snow. Where was the open water?

To her left. She turned, feeling a burn all the way up her leg.

"Here." The voice was so faint, she wasn't sure she heard it. But she did hear the crackling of the shifting ice.

When she looked down, her boot print quickly filled with water. Carefully, she put her foot in front of her, feeling for the sag or the cracking of the ice. She inched forward, praying she would reach the voice before she reached open water. With the temperature and the wind, a person wouldn't last long in the icy depths of the lake. She knew that people could die within two minutes of falling into an icy lake. They died not from hypothermia but from cold shock that caused the heart to stop.

Go back, the voice of reason in her head counseled. *You will never reach the person on your own. You could be another victim of the lake. Get help.*

Her right foot sank a little farther into a puddle of water. Behind her, the lake was solid; ahead was someone in distress. Will used to say, "You like to skirt the edges, honey. One day you are going to fall in." She was on thin ice now.

"Can't hold on."

She was close enough to confirm it was a female voice. Red was sure this was her missing Missy.

"Missy?"

"Can't..."

"Missy, it's Sheriff Hammergren. You need to keep talking so I can get to you."

"Open water, sliding in. Can't hold on."

For a moment, the wind died down, and the sheet that was blinding her lifted. Ahead, to her right, she saw it—a pink coat.

"I see you, Missy." She moved with great care now toward the girl. The wind gusted again, and the coat faded. Beneath her, the lake groaned. Ahead, beyond the girl, the lake cracked like a large tree split by lightning. The lake was opening up to swallow the human intruders.

Red was now within five feet of the girl. She could see that a black ski mask had been pulled over her head. She was lying belly down on the snow-swept ice with her hands tied together, clawing at the snow and ice in front of her. Her lower legs were in water and sinking.

At one time in her life, Red had been a staff guide for the Outward Bound program. She led greenhorns into the Boundary Water Canoe Area and taught them how to survive in rough conditions. One of the lessons she taught was a shore-to-water rescue. Lie flat to distribute your weight and anchor yourself.

She threw herself forward onto her stomach and splayed out her legs, inching her way to the girl. Her ankle screamed at her to stop. Water seeped through her coat, and when it reached her skin, it stung and sent an ache like an abscessed tooth through her back and up her neck. The ice was sinking, and she and the girl were sinking with it.

"I'm slipping," Missy cried in a hoarse voice. She kicked her legs to push her up. The water poured over the ice.

"Stay still." Red kept her voice calm and tried to keep the shiver out of it. "I'm going to grab your hands. When I do, I want you to wiggle toward me like an inchworm."

"I can't see you." Her voice rose in panic.

"You don't need to see me. I'll pull, and you pretend you are the worm. Okay?"

It took three times of thrusting her arm toward the girl before she was able to catch her wrist.

"Now, slowly come toward me. Feel the pull? Move toward the pull."

As Missy inched forward, Red inched back. The ice water now soaked through her pants.

They moved so slowly that it was hard to know if they'd made any progress at all.

"I can't anymore. Too tired. Need to sleep now."

"No!" Red bellowed. "Move it, Missy. You can be tired later."

Above her, the wind howled, and the snow came down in icy shards.

They inched along. Red fought off the voice that said, *You aren't going to make it. You aren't going to make it.* For a split second, she thought, *Fine. Then I can join Will under the old oak tree. Our bodies will nurture the woods.* Then she remembered the birth certificate and the stranger claiming Will's land. *No, I need to fight for Will's woods.*

Looking up, she saw that behind Missy, the water was pouring in. With the toes of her boots, she kicked at the ice, sending a blinding pain up her leg from her injured ankle. For a moment she felt the nausea rise in her throat. *No,* she told herself. *I will not give in to this.*

Beneath her, the ice felt solid for the first time in at least ten feet.

"Missy, I'm going to pull as hard as I can on the count of three. I want you to push off like you're diving into the lake." She pulled her knees up under her to give her more leverage.

Missy groaned and said nothing.

"One, two, three." Red yanked with all the upper body strength she had. Missy popped forward like a fish reeled out of the water.

They were both now on solid ice.

The first thing Red did was pull the ski mask off Missy's face. The girl looked at her with wide eyes.

"I thought I was going to die," she whispered as tears fell down her cheeks.

"We're not off the lake quite yet, but I think we'll make it."

Missy looked behind her as Red used her Swiss Army knife to cut the twine that bound Missy's hands.

"The Kazurinskis, the *Followers*, they went through the ice." A look of fear crossed her tear-stained face. "They could find us."

Red gathered her in her arms. "I'll keep you safe."

49

SHERIFF RED
NOT ME

It took twenty minutes of agony to half drag Missy off the lake and up the stairs. It took another fifteen minutes for the ambulance to get to them. They sat together wrapped in blankets in the back seat of the Subaru as the car pumped out heat.

In that time, Missy, through chattering teeth, told Red what she knew about the drugs, her father's death, and the connection with the wrestling team.

"I have them on a video—all of them on my cell phone." Missy wrapped the blanket tighter. "I hid it at the Church."

When the ambulance finally arrived, Red watched as they loaded Missy on. She said nothing to the EMTs about her own injured ankle or the wet cold that sent an ache through her bones. She had work to do.

At home, showered and in dry clothes, Red wrapped her ankle with an Ace bandage. It was already swollen. Slipping into her boots was painful enough for her to cry out loud. Blue licked her hand sympathetically.

Her phone rang as she was lacing up the boot on her injured ankle.

"Oh, Red, I'm so glad you answered."

"Lou?"

"I found something that I think you need to see at the Church. I'm here right now. Can you come?"

"Can you tell me what it is?"

"You need to see it. Please come."

Something in Lou's voice wasn't right. She was always calm, never rattled, yet she sounded nervous and pressured. Red had once witnessed her at a bloody car accident scene calmly triaging the injuries and keeping everyone from panicking. This was not the Lou from the accident.

"I'm on my way. It might take a few minutes because of the weather."

Before Lou ended the call, she said in a too cheerful tone, "Sorry I beat you at the last poker club."

Red hadn't been at the last poker club because of the fire and the missing Missy. Her stomach tightened into a knot. She needed to get hold of Jason right away and have him meet her at the Church. She tried calling Billie and got a recorded message telling her that all circuits were busy and to please try again. Since the county hadn't invested as much as it should have into the 911 system, if it was overloaded, callers would get the message to call back. Great service to a panicked caller.

As soon as she got into her car, she tried the radio. At first there was no response. Finally, when she was almost out of the driveway, her radio crackled to life.

"Sheriff, it's Billie...Norgren is here with...daughter. Needs to talk to you right away."

With so much static on the line, she wasn't sure she'd heard it right. "Billie, please repeat."

The radio faded and then came back: "...life and death."

"Repeat."

The radio crackled more, but no voice came through.

"Repeat, Billie." She shouted into the receiver this time.

Again, only noise.

She tried one more time. "I didn't get that message. Please find Jason. I'm going to the Church. Send him there." Hell of a time for the communications system to break down. She hoped she'd gotten through.

The roads were slippery, and the visibility was no more than half a block as Red hurried to the Church. The streets in Lykkins Lake were deserted as the snow swept across the roads and drifted in. Plows again had been pulled until the snow stopped and the wind died down.

Red kept the car at a steady twenty miles per hour and did not slow at intersections. She prayed no one else would be out. If she slowed or had to stop, she knew she would get stuck.

What was Lou doing at the Church at this time in this weather?

It seemed like it took hours to go the three miles from her house to the Church. Every so often, a gust of wind would cause the road ahead of her to disappear into a thick white curtain of snow.

A block from the Church, a red SUV pulled out from an alley in front of her. Red braked and swerved as the vehicle darted past her. Her Subaru spun around in a semicircle as Red steered counter to the spin to try to steady it. The car slammed into a drift of snow.

"Goddamn it!" Red tried to reverse, but the tires spun in the snow. She was stuck. Either radio for a tow or get to the Church on foot. She didn't have time to wait.

She tried raising Billie on the radio. Nothing came through but more static. Either the system was down or something was wrong with her receiver.

Red stepped out into the howl of the storm, careful to keep as much weight as possible off her ankle. It took a few moments to get her bearings. She would have to face the wind and the driving snow. She reached over to get her flashlight and her service weapon. When she unlocked the glove compartment for her gun, it was empty.

"Goddamn it!" She'd left the gun in its holster hanging by the door. In her haste, she'd forgotten it. "Red, you are an idiot!" For a moment she remembered what Will had said to her: "I'll handle the shooting, you handle the people."

She needed to either go back to retrieve it or wait for Jason. The voice in the back of her head, the one that Will said was spidey sense, told her she didn't have time. Grabbing the flashlight, she headed into the storm.

By the time she reached the Church, Red's face was numb from the icy onslaught of snow. She'd broken into a cold sweat from the pressure on her ankle. Only one car sat in the parking lot. Lou's car was covered in snow, and all tire tracks had been obliterated by the storm. She noted what she thought were faint snowmobile tracks leading back toward the cemetery. Lou was not alone in the clinic.

Before Red opened the door, she stopped for a moment to consider her options. She could announce herself, or she could try the element of surprise. Announcing herself would give the person who was with Lou—and she was sure someone was with her—a heads-up. Quietly letting herself in might give her a brief advantage—especially if she needed to overpower the person with Lou.

This wasn't Hollywood, she decided. She would leave the stealth approach to actors and stuntmen.

She opened the door and stood in the back of the church. The lights were off, and the pews were shadowed in the dimness that filtered through the stained-glass windows.

"Lou," she called out. "It's Red. Are you in the exam room?"

At first, she was met with silence.

"Lou?"

Above the rattling of the rafters from the wind outside, she heard some low thumps and voices.

The door to the exam room opened, and Lou walked out. She stood, stiff like a wooden nutcracker with her arms at her sides. Her face was in the shadows of the light from the open door.

"Come up, Red. I have something to show you that's even better than my winning hand."

"You really pulled the trigger on that one, didn't you?"

Lou kept her eyes on Red. "You know it."

Lou was not alone, and whoever was in the exam room had a gun.

Time to get reinforcements. Red reached in her pocket to discover her phone was missing. It must have fallen out of her pocket as she hurried to the Church. "Damn it!" she said under her breath. All she had was the flashlight and a couple of latex gloves. No time to berate herself for her stupidity.

She walked past the rows of pews. "The weather isn't letting up. We might have to get the plows out here to dig you out."

Lou nodded again. "And wouldn't you know, the back tire on the passenger side of my car is low. Fortunately, I have a quilt in the trunk if I get stuck here."

"Great." She now knew that the person in the room was to the right of the open door, and she knew who that person was.

When she was less than an arm's length from Lou, she stopped. "Listen, I know you have something to show me, but I also have something for you." She patted her right pocket. "I found this rosary in my driveway." She raised her voice. "Someone probably dropped it. I think it's sterling silver, and maybe the beads are black coral. I thought we could put it on eBay and raise some money for the clinic."

With those words, the door to the exam room swung wide open. A high, childlike voice cried out, "Give it to me!"

Red quickly stepped in front of Lou. "Bobbi, what are you doing here?" Red's voice held no surprise.

Bobbi stood gripping a hunting rifle. The childlike voice quickly turned adult. "I'm protecting you from Hitch. He heard that his drug money was given to the clinic here. He's coming for it."

"Put the rifle down or you might hurt someone." For a second, Red imagined the cartoon sheriff in the buckskin skirt uttering the trite phrase. She pressed her lips together. Not the time for humor.

A gust of wind rattled the wooden frame of the old building. For a moment, Bobbi shifted her weight as if uncertain. Red gauged the hesitation but knew she physically could not reach Bobbi and disarm her before the shotgun did to her what it had done to Junior Klein.

Bobbi held on to the rifle. "I can't do that. Hitch isn't right, you know."

Red thought for a moment about Lad and what she had needed to do to get through to him when he was ramping up in his room at home. Lad in his illness didn't think in linear ways.

Red kept her voice calm as she held tightly to the flashlight in her right hand. "You made that beautiful quilt that's in the shop, didn't you? The skeleton by the tree was done so delicately."

Bobbi didn't move, but the childlike voice came back. "Not Me. Not Me did it. Shot Jubal dead." She giggled. "Then it all stopped. Not Me did the penance with the beads." Her eyes were wide in the dim light. "Now it's all okay with the Virgin Mary."

Red switched again and said in a conversational tone, "The Kazurinski boys went through the ice this afternoon on their snowmobiles. They're your cousins, aren't they? We couldn't get them out." She paused to let it sink in. "I'm sorry for your loss."

The furnace clicked on. Its old fan belt squeaked as tepid air poured out of the heating ducts built into the floor of the altar area.

Adult Bobbi hissed. "Liar! You can't fool me!" She raised the barrel of the rifle.

"You won't get the rosary if you shoot. Father Paul says it's yours."

Bobbi hesitated. When she opened her mouth, the child voice cried out, "Give it to me! It's mine! It's mine! I earned it!"

Red thought of the lives lost—Junior Klein, Jared Peterson, and even Mayme Klein—and the lives ruined by Bobbi and her drug operation. Suddenly she was bone-tired. Her ankle throbbed, she had a roaring headache, and she was just plain weary to her core.

"Stop!" She put her hand up, palm out. "Just stop it, Bobbi! It's over."

Bobbi moved a little closer and chanted louder, "Not me! Not me!"

Red shook her head. "It is you, Bobbi. I guarantee it."

"I'll squeeze and pull and you'll all be red!" Bobbi had her lower lip pushed out like a child about to have a tantrum.

"And you'll be dead."

"No, not me!" Bobbi advanced. At this rate, a shot would be point-blank.

Red weighed her options. If she could distract Bobbi long enough, she might be able to grab the rifle and disarm her. Not exactly the protocol they taught at the police academy.

"We're over here!" she shouted, pointing to the main door of the church.

Bobbi turned in surprise to the door. In those few seconds of distraction, Red wound up and hurled the flashlight at Bobbi's head. It hit the side of her head with a bone-cracking thud. Bobbi fell backward, and the rifle tumbled to the floor. As Bobbi rolled and scrabbled for it, Red threw herself onto her, pinning her arms to the worn red carpet that covered the altar area. Searing-hot pain from Red's ankle shot up her leg.

Kicking and flailing, her teeth bared, Bobbi fought back. "Not me!" She growled like an animal.

Lou stood glued to the spot behind Red, her mouth open in shock and astonishment.

Red yelled to her, "I need tape or rope or something."

Lou ran into the exam room.

Then Red put her face as close to Bobbi as she dared, still pinning her shoulders down.

"Stop," she commanded. "You're Bobbi Norgren, not some wild animal."

Bobbi went limp, as if someone had turned a key and shut off her engine. Tears streamed down her cheeks.

Red relaxed but kept the pressure on Bobbi's shoulders. She looked at the woman under her, the woman she thought was simply a little addled, and thought how wrong she had been. Will claimed she could read people, but she'd missed all the clues.

Find Coke, find her didn't mean "find coach and you'll find Missy." It meant if you find the coach, you'll find Bobbi. Bobbi always traveled with the team to chaperone and keep Hitch company—and to ensure that the Kazurinskis were getting the drugs to the high school dealers in the other small towns.

As these thoughts roared through her head, it was Bobbi who read her and saw the moment of distraction. Bobbi suddenly kicked out, her foot striking Red's injured ankle straight on. The pain was so intense that for a few seconds, the world went dark. In that time, Bobbi struggled her way out from under Red and lunged for the rifle. She was the hunter now, and Red was her prey.

Dazed, Red looked up. In the glow of the light from the exam room, Bobbi was staring at her with wild eyes.

"Squeeze, pull. Squeeze, pull, and see the red. Oh, the red. It feels so good."

Bobbi took aim. Red felt the floorboards beneath her creak. *All this work for such a stupid ending,* she thought.

Instead of a gunshot, though, Red heard a whacking sound. The rifle fell out of Bobbi's arms as she pitched forward and collapsed to her knees.

Above her, Lou stood wielding a metal speculum. "I always knew it had more than one use."

A vision of the dancing cartoon sheriff from the web page popped into Red's head. She would have laughed out loud except that her ankle was killing her.

50

SHERIFF RED

THE AFTERMATH

Before Jason and the ambulance arrived at the Church, she and Lou sat with Bobbi Norgren. Though white-hot pain shot up Red's leg every time she moved, she managed to duct-tape Bobbi's hands behind her. Bobbi's eye was swelling where Red had hit her with the flashlight, and the back of her head was matted with blood from the speculum.

"We should put an ice pack on that," Lou commented, not moving. She still held the speculum.

Red shrugged. "She'll live."

Just as Red heard sirens in the distance, Bobbi started talking in a soft, singsong little girl's voice.

"Jubal made me! He made me!" Her eyes were unfocused, and she rocked like a child on the step leading to the altar. "Squeeze, pull, he said. Squeeze, pull, and you will be filled with God." She stopped and looked at Red with a sly smile. "I showed him. Bam! Right through his forehead. Bam! Bam! An explosion of red and the animals to eat his eyes out."

The church door banged open, and Bobbi said no more. She simply gazed out at the empty pews, her body rocking back and forth.

～

Two days later, the courthouse lawn sparkled in the sunlight with the newly fallen snow. The plows were out, and Lykkins Lake was waking up from a winter nap. Down the street, orange school buses dropped off the kids who'd had a two-day break from classes. The school had now used up its allotment of snow days. If another storm came through, the students would be taking classes into June.

Red cursed under her breath as she used the crutches to hobble up the courthouse steps. Thank God for Ed and his fastidious snow shoveling. The boot Dr. Vijay had given her at the hospital was unwieldy, and she had to search through the back of her dresser drawer to find a woolen sock without holes in the toes to wear under it. The pain in her ankle grew with each step.

"Cold enough for you?" he asked, staring at the Grinch-themed green sock that covered her toes.

"It's going to warm up," she replied. Ed hurried up the steps and held the door for her.

Cal greeted her. "Quiet night." Two nights ago had been a different story—the blizzard, the snowmobiles in the lake, and Bobbi Norgren at the Church.

On top of her desk was a cell phone in a pink case with a decal of a local rock band. Next to the phone was a thermos of coffee, a bran muffin, and a note written in Scotty's scrawl.

It was in a drawer in the exam table.

Missy had left it in the exam room when she dropped off the drug money. Scotty had put it away for safe keeping, assuming that whoever left it would come back for it.

Red planned to call Jack Klein later and have him bring Missy in to show her the video she said was on the phone. The video, according to Missy, featured Bobbi giving instructions to the Kazurinski brothers about collecting drug money. In it, Missy was sure Bobbi had said, "Don't screw up. You know I can kill."

Right now, Red felt cranky and not very competent. All this drug dealing had been going on under her watch and under Will's watch for six years, and she hadn't gotten more than a whiff of it. The image of the dancing sheriff in a buckskin skirt popped into her head. Maybe Mitch Rafferty was right to challenge her for sheriff.

Lou called her at ten o'clock.

"How are you doing?" Red asked. She worried that when the shock of her interaction with Bobbi wore off, Lou would have to deal with significant trauma.

She sounded normal on the phone. "I'm fine, but I'm still not happy that I let Bobbi lure me to the clinic."

"You aren't the only one she got to."

"I wanted to make sure that Scotty turned the phone over to you."

"It's on my desk."

Lou hesitated. "Did you find out anything about a Jubal?"

Red looked at the Doe file of eighteen years ago. "I'm working on it." Red suspected she had found the missing lay priest, Henry Holt.

After a few moments of silence, Lou's voice perked up. "Poker tonight at Georgia's. I'm bringing some treats."

"Jell-O shots?"

"You'll have to come to find out."

She shifted in her chair, biting back a groan as an aching pain crawled up her leg. On her computer, she opened the Word file labeled *Missing Missy* and reviewed it. The pieces were falling together. Walt LaFrance said that Hitch had gotten a call at Walleye Heaven the day Red went looking for him. What she didn't know at the time was that Hitch's call was from a nearly hysterical Tiffy saying that something was wrong with Bobbi. Tiffy had told her mother about the money the nurses found in the donation box and that she remembered Missy talking about the fish house. Tiffy wondered if Missy had gone there. That was the moment when Bobbi changed from caring, banana-bread-baking mom into another creature altogether.

Yesterday, when Red interviewed Tiffy, she'd said, "Mom started pacing and suddenly she had this funny voice and kept saying, 'Not me, not me'?" Her eyes filled with tears. "Is Mom crazy?"

Tiffany was yet another victim. A victim of her mother and of a Jubal from long ago.

A half hour later, Georgia came into the office with hot coffee and sandwiches.

"I know that Scotty sent something over earlier, but I'm guessing her muffins were hard and chewy and her coffee tasted like she'd reused the grounds."

"Pretty much."

"How's the ankle?"

Red shrugged. "I've got an appointment with the orthopedic doc on Monday when he makes his rural rounds at the clinic." She didn't add that Dr. Vijay had warned her that he thought she had significant ligament damage and might need surgery.

Georgia pulled off her coat and sat down across from Red. She had a sparkle in her eyes that caused Red to say, "What have you been up to?"

"Very interesting conversation with Barbara Weaver at the nursing home this morning. I brought the new decoy to show her."

"Oh? Is this part of your regular ministering to the old and feeble?" Red did not smile. "As I recall, I suggested that you leave the investigating to me."

Georgia ignored her remark. "The poor woman is down to skin and bones and not much more. But her mind is intact. I showed the certificate to her." She took the copy of the birth certificate for Louise Mary Weaver out of her bag.

Red groaned and elevated her leg onto a chair. Outside, a horn honked and another honked in reply. The citizens of Lykkins Lake were happy to be out and about again.

"Just as we thought, Barbara is Weesey's aunt. Her sister Mary Margaret Weaver had Weesey when she was sixteen. She told me that Mary Margaret did not want to keep her or have anything to do with her."

"Barbara took care of her, and the family said she was a cousin?"

"There's more to the story."

They were interrupted when Rick Berras, the county attorney, peeked into the office. "Can I talk with you?" His bow tie was crooked, and part of his white shirt was untucked.

"I can meet with you at eleven. Come back then."

Red did not add, *You are driving me crazy.* Poor Rick. This Bobbi situation was the biggest case he'd ever had, and he was a wreck. Red suspected that he'd already bought out the county supply of Pepto-Bismol.

"Sorry, you were saying?"

Georgia continued. "First off, Barbara said that as an adult, Weesey was very vulnerable. She married a guy named Brandt—God knows where she met him. He walked off with her disability check and all her paltry savings. That's when Barbara obtained guardianship."

Down the hall, she heard Ed greeting one of the county recorder clerks. "Cold enough for you?" For some reason, she found comfort in the predictability of those words.

Georgia smiled and went on. "As best as I can understand it, Mary Margaret had an incestuous relationship with her older brother." She looked at Red with a knowing expression. "Barbara used the words 'unnatural behavior.' When she became pregnant, Rolf Hammergren was a convenient scapegoat."

Red thought about the little boy in the photo with the Mona Lisa smile. He was sent away for something he didn't do. She wished she could turn back time for him.

"I got just a little bit more before the poor old lady nodded off to sleep. She said that Mary Margaret felt guilty about accusing Rolf and visited him a couple of times in the state hospital. After her last visit, she came back and told her sister that they were doing 'bad things' to him. Poor soul. I'm guessing they were doing shock treatments."

Red took a deep breath. "I'm glad at least that Will didn't know any of this."

Georgia nodded.

"Thanks for the information. At some point I'll have to respond to the law firm of Raymond and Raymond and threaten them with a request for DNA or something." She sighed. "And I'll have to get his death certificate. But not right now. I'll be tied up with Bobbi for months."

～

By mid-afternoon, Red's ankle throbbed and was so swollen she had to loosen the boot. It was too hard to keep it elevated and iced at the office. It seemed she was interrupted every few minutes either by a phone call or someone stopping in the office. She directed Jason and two other deputies to coordinate with the dive team that was coming from the Twin Cities to find the Kazurinski brothers. She asked her receptionist to handle any press inquiries with a statement that this was an ongoing investigation. She put the file on Junior Klein front and center on her desk and prepared to leave.

Closing her eyes, she envisioned her recliner at home, several pain pills, and a cup of hot tea. Maybe she could get an hour of uninterrupted sleep.

She had her jacket on and crutches in hand when Mitch Rafferty knocked.

The gnawing ache from her ankle inched up her leg. "Mitch." Her tone was flat.

"Uh, sorry to bother you." He stood in the doorway with an uncertain look on his face.

Red hobbled back to her chair. "Come in and sit down."

Mitch stood in front of the desk, not meeting her eyes.

"Yes?"

"The other day?" He stopped as if trying to find the words.

Red kept her eyes on him. "Is that what you're here about?"

"Yes and no." He pulled up the chair and sat down. He didn't look at Red.

Red checked her watch. She was due another pain pill in ten minutes. She wondered how she would make it that long.

Mitch finally met her gaze. "Um, I talked with my mother. She's Weesey Brandt's legal guardian now that her sister is sick. She's going to call the lawyers in Minneapolis and drop the claim."

Red kept the surprise out of her voice. "Why?"

Mitch's voice was a low rumble. "We think it's the right thing to do."

In her pain and her tiredness, she felt too cynical to think that any of the Raffertys were concerned about "the right thing to do." Mitch was afraid his secret life would get out.

Red clasped her hands together in a tight grip. "Mitch, whether your family pursues this or not, I have no interest in letting the world know about your sex life."

He winced at the directness of her words but said nothing.

Red studied his face and decided not to add what she was thinking—that it's the twenty-first century and who cares? In reality she knew that even with great human rights progress, Pearsal County was still stuck in last century—or the century before that.

With that, she waved him away. She needed her pills, her rest, and a night of poker.

51

SHERIFF RED
THE POKER CLUB

Scotty shuffled the cards with ease and dealt two down to each of them. Behind her, the heater labored to keep the back room in Georgia's Antiques warm.

Georgia studied her cards before glancing at Red. "I guess you can't comment on an open investigation, but we, your poker buddies, have put the puzzle together. And it isn't very pretty. Simply nod if we're correct."

Red smiled at her. "I don't provide any insider information."

"Yes, but our county attorney apparently hasn't trained his staff on privacy issues. One of his clerks has been talking to everyone who walks into my café. I heard the boys at the back table laughing as she told them how Lou walloped Bobbi with the speculum. I'm not sure any of them knew what a speculum was, but they found it very funny."

Lou smiled sweetly as she picked up her cards. "She probably didn't tell everyone about how Red nailed her with a flashlight. It was a perfect fastball."

Georgia turned to Red. "You did?"

Red preferred the world not know that she went crashing into the Church armed with only a flashlight and a pair of latex gloves. She shrugged, studying her cards.

Scotty continued. "She says they think Bobbi made contacts in California through Hitch's Hollywood crowd and decided that she would start a little drug import business here in Lykkins Lake."

"The money for that house and shop wasn't from quilting." Lou kept her eyes on her hand, but Red noticed a slight tremor when she picked up the cards. She hoped Lou would take her advice and get some counseling.

"According to one of my sources, she made some money with the quilting. Enough that Hitch didn't question the money she spent building the house and the shop."

"Hitch didn't know anything about this?" Georgia raised her eyebrows. "How could he not?"

"I think he was scared of Bobbi and scared that she'd let the cat out of the bag about his true love for male wrestlers." Scotty quickly picked up her cards.

Red stared at her. "What?" She'd said nothing to anyone about her visit to Walleye Heaven.

Scotty shrugged. "Mac Morris told a couple of his customers that he didn't see any girls at the place, and they left a bunch of 'muscle-boy' magazines."

"Two plus two sometimes makes four and sometimes makes five." Georgia smiled.

"Hmmm." Red repositioned the ice on her ankle, thinking about King Rex and Mitch.

"Anyway, another weird thing this morning. The boys were going over the drama again—between asking for more coffee and complaining about the scrambled eggs. Lester Thomas started blustering to Mitch Rafferty that if he'd been elected sheriff, none of this would have happened. All this drug dealing under the Hammergren nose, et cetera, et cetera."

She turned to Red and put a hand on her arm. "Suddenly"—she paused for the dramatic effect—"Mitch Rafferty stood up and said, 'Red Hammergren knows what she's doing. Let it go.'"

Georgia and Lou looked at Scotty in surprise. "He said that?"

Scotty nodded emphatically. "I know because I was about to pour hot coffee all over Lester's lap."

"Wow."

Red smiled, picturing Scotty with her carafe of coffee poised for battle.

"That's certainly an interesting turn of events. Are you sure you aren't holding something over Mitch?" Georgia peered at Red with a speculative smile.

Red tried to smile back, but in truth, her whole body ached, and her head felt crammed with cotton. "Could we start the game? If I don't get home soon, Blue will be peeing on my pillow." She didn't tell them that she was anxious to get home to another pain pill. She feared a lecture on opioid addiction.

Georgia raised an eyebrow. "Hurting?"

Red didn't answer.

"So?" Georgia directed her question to Scotty. "What else did the clerk say?"

Red sat back, remembering how it felt when Bobbi kicked her ankle. Inwardly, she winced. She hadn't slept well for the last couple of nights and was sure she wouldn't sleep well again tonight even with the painkiller.

"She said that they sent Bobbi to the locked psych unit in Duluth after she scratched her face up in her jail cell."

"Yuck," Lou tsked. Her expression, however, carried no sympathy.

Red nodded. This was public information, already reported in the paper. Bobbi went crazy—or Bobbi *cleverly* went crazy, screaming about Jubal and how he had raped her over and over and scratching—gently—at her cheeks. Red suspected that Bobbi would use that information when it came to bargaining for a sentence.

"Here's the kicker." Scotty leaned forward to pull the circle of friends in. "Bobbi was dealing drugs to Missy's mother. When Junior found out about it, he tried to stop her. Everyone thinks that Bobbi shot him. That's what Missy was onto."

"And the Kazurinski cousins?"

"Bobbi's couriers and muscle, according to the café boys. They're the ones who whacked Jared in the head and burned the cabin. Bobbi paid them well."

"I heard the divers found one of them but not the other. Rumors are flying that the second one survived and got away." Georgia rolled her eyes. "Now Pearsal County will have a boogeyman. The children will be told, 'If you don't behave, Igor will come and get you.'"

Red suspected Hammer Lake would give up Igor in the spring. Meanwhile, she wasn't putting any more resources into trying to find him—or his body.

"Wow." Lou studied her cards. "You never know."

Red stretched her arms over her head. "I think I'm going to fold. It's too hard trying to stay warm and ice my ankle at the same time. Send my ante to the Church, please."

She hobbled on her crutches out into the starry night. The temperatures had moderated, and it felt good to inhale the fresh, fifteen-degree air. Tomorrow, and for weeks to come, she would be piecing the Missy investigation together. Tonight, she needed to be alone with a mug of hot chocolate, a couple of pain pills, and a ratty little dog on her lap.

She looked up at the stars as a wisp of a cloud obscured the moon. In that moment she thought about Will resting beneath the sparkling snow that surrounded the oak tree. And she thought of Will's older brother, Rolf, in an unmarked grave somewhere on state hospital property. The brothers should be together. Maybe she'd look into that—someday.

52

SHERIFF RED
ROLF

On Valentine's Day, Red sat in her office with Father Paul. He turned the church's file on Henry Holt over to her with a shake of his head. "Who knew such evil could lurk in our own community?"

Red took it and added it to the growing evidence on Bobbi Norgren. Several people had come forward after the news broke about Bobbi to tell Red about their suspicions when Bobbi's mother took in the lay priest.

"Father Bernard should have put a stop to it," one of the old neighbors told her. "We knew something wasn't right."

Red had tracked down the old missing person report and found Henry Holt's cousin. The skull and dental records were being investigated, but she was sure she'd solved the case.

After Father Paul left, Red picked up the photo of Will and dusted the glass. "At least we're down to two cold cases now. Who knew the last ones would be related?"

Georgia interrupted her. "Talking to yourself, are you?"

Startled, Red nearly dropped the photo. "What? Did you tiptoe in?"

Georgia smiled. "Just stopped by after doing some errands to invite you to a special Valentine's edition of the poker club."

"Please don't tell me I have to bring roses."

"Nope, just your cheerful old self."

Red thought about the last couple of weeks and had to admit that "cheerful" was hardly the word to describe her mood. "I'm surprised you want me around."

"We felt a need to interrupt your twenty-hour days." She stopped at the door. "Oh yes, we'll feed you, too. I'm guessing you've been living on microwaveable food substitutes."

~

Red left the courthouse at 5:30 as the sun was setting. With the days growing longer, she found her mood lifting. Yesterday she'd gotten word from the orthopedic doctor that she wouldn't require surgery on her ankle. She could now walk with a stabilizer boot instead of crutches.

At home, Blue greeted her with his usual enthusiasm. "I'm so sorry, pup, that I've been busy. Maybe next week we can have a whole day to ourselves." She laughed, picturing the two of them on the couch with popcorn watching old movies. "I'll even let you choose the movie as long as it isn't either *Mary Poppins* or *Annie*."

On her way to take a quick shower, she peeked into the office with all the paperwork piled high. At least the lawyers were no longer after her. The Hammergren acres still weighed on her, and she resolved, once again, to attend to it. She felt Will's presence assuring her that all would be well.

As she turned away from the room, she thought she glimpsed him just out of the corner of her eye. She blinked and no one was there.

The back room of Georgia's Antiques filled with the earthy aroma of chicken soup. A cake in the shape of a heart sat in the middle of the table. When Red limped in, Scotty, Lou, and Georgia were already sitting. Even before she had her coat off, she sensed an excitement in the air. Scotty's cheeks were rosier than normal, and Lou wore a close-lipped smile.

"What?" Red slipped into a chair. "You guys look like someone is going to announce they won the lottery or found the love of their life."

Georgia spoke first. "We do have something to share, but maybe we should have a glass of sparkling wine first."

Red hadn't had any alcohol since her ankle injury because of the pain pills. She was down to taking a couple of ibuprofen a day, however, and sparkling wine sounded great. Scotty uncapped the bottle. The cork popped, and they all clapped.

"At least you didn't send the cork into my ceiling like last time," Georgia remarked as Scotty poured.

After they all had their glasses, Lou raised hers. "To the sheriff and her gang solving yet another mystery."

Confused, Red took a sip, feeling the effervescence of the wine in her mouth. "What mystery?"

"Well," Georgia began, "you know how you shared that birth certificate with me, and it started a discussion about Rolf Hammergren?"

Red stared at her. "Didn't I tell you that was mine to investigate?"

Scotty broke in, "Yes, but we ignored you." The three of them laughed.

Red sat up straighter, trying to look offended. "I could have you arrested for being public nuisances or something."

Georgia cleared her throat. "Hold that thought, because we put our heads together and looked at all our resources over the years and decided to find out where Rolf died and where he was buried."

Scotty raised her hand. "Turns out we have some good contacts in the state."

Now Red was interested. "And?"

Scotty slowly shook her head. "We didn't find where he was buried."

Red tried to keep the disappointment out of her voice. "But did you find a death certificate?"

Again, Scotty shook her head. "Nope."

Red wrinkled her brow. "I don't get it."

Georgia leaned forward. "We didn't find all of that because Rolf is still alive. We found him!"

"What? Will said he died years ago." She thought about the life insurance policy sitting in the tackle box unclaimed. "I mean, what?"

Over the next hour, they told her the tale of consulting old work acquaintances, cajoling people, and generally causing a nuisance until they'd tracked him down.

"He got lost in the system. Somewhere along the line, someone wrote down the wrong name for him. Instead of Rolf Hammergren, he became Rolf Ammer. He's alive and living in a nursing home in Minneapolis."

Scotty handed Red her phone. "I had a nurse at the home send me a photo."

Red studied it. Even in his old age, he had the innocent expression she'd seen in the family photo. She noted how much he looked like Will. "I don't know what to say."

"Ha," Scotty laughed. "We've flummoxed our sheriff."

After dinner and the cake and a few hands of poker, Red excused herself. "Sorry, but I have a deposition tomorrow and another staffing problem. I need to get home to my dog and my bed. But many thanks to all of you. If you ever need a parking ticket fixed, I owe you."

At home, she sat in the beat-up old recliner with Blue on her lap. As she explained to the dog about Rolf, she was sure she felt a gentle hand on her shoulder. Automatically, she reached up to touch it. "We found your brother, Will, and he's okay. I promise I will visit him soon."

The hand dissolved, and she was once again alone with Blue.

THE PINES WERE WATCHING
Book #2 in the Sheriff Red Mysteries

The pines are watching, the shadows are creeping closer, and no one—not even the sheriff—is safe from the secrets of the Northwoods.

When Joanie Crea is found strangled on the grounds of the crumbling Grandgeorge estate, Sheriff Red Hammergren faces a chilling mystery as dark as the dense forest surrounding the crime scene. All eyes turn to Derek Grandgeorge, the reclusive heir with a penchant for wearing a green jacket—even in the sweltering Minnesota summer.

But soon, a second body surfaces—a victim found with Joanie's house key shoved into their mouth.

The gruesome discovery sends a shiver of dread through the tight-knit community. The key isn't just evidence—it's a macabre message from a killer who's growing bolder and more brazen with each passing day. As the oppressive summer heat bears down and the shadows deepen, Red glimpses unsettling flashes of green at the edge of her vision. With a cunning murderer on the loose and the town spiraling into panic, Red must unravel the connection between the victims...before she becomes the final piece in the killer's twisted game.

ACKNOWLEDGMENTS

Many thanks to Severin River Publishing for believing in Sheriff Red. To my editor Kate Schomaker, to Julia Hastings and everyone involved in bringing this book to publication. To my agent, Cindy Bullard. To my writer's group, Jan Kerman, Carol Williams and Randy Kasten who were kind but firm in their comments. A special thanks to Tim Held of the Minnesota Department of Health for sharing his EMT experience delivering babies. Also, to the nameless people I met along the way who provided information and expertise. And, of course, to Jerome who was my first editor.

ABOUT THE AUTHOR

Linda Norlander is the author of *And the Lake Will Take Them* the first in the Sheriff Red Mystery series. She is also author of A Cabin by the Lake mysteries and the Liza and Mrs. Wilkens mysteries. Norlander has published award winning short stories, op-ed pieces and short humor featured in regional and national publications. Before taking up the pen to write novels, she worked in end-of-life care. Norlander resides in Tacoma, Washington with her spouse.

Sign up for Linda Norlander's reader list at
severnriverbooks.com

Printed in the United States
by Baker & Taylor Publisher Services